NATIONAL VELVET

ENID BAGNOLD

HERITAGE

EGMONT

HERITAGE

EGMONT

First published in Great Britain 1935 by William Heinemann Ltd
This edition published 2012 by Egmont UK Limited
The Yellow Building, 1 Nicholas Road, London W11 4AN
www.egmont.co.uk

Text copyright © 1935 The Estate of Enid Bagnold

The moral rights of the author have been asserted

ISBN 978 1 4052 6418 1

1 3 5 7 9 10 8 6 4 2

A CIP catalogue record for this title is available from the British Library

Printed and bound in Italy

51073/1

EGMONT LUCKY COIN

Our story began over a century ago, when seventeen-year-old Egmont Harald Petersen found a coin in the street.

He was on his way to buy a flyswatter, a small hand-operated printing machine that he then set up in his tiny apartment.

The coin brought him such good luck that today Egmont has offices in over 30 countries around the world. And that lucky coin is still kept at the company's head offices in Denmark.

FOREWORD

The tale of how Velvet Brown, the youngest and frailest daughter of a butcher, came to win the Grand National on a totally unknown horse, has been the stuff of dreams for many a pony-mad child. And yet this internationally famous story was never originally intended as a children's book.

It was Geoffrey Eastwood, a young clerk to the House of Lords, who first sowed the seed in writer Enid Bagnold's mind for the story that was to become *National Velvet*. Eastwood was a frequent guest at the family house in Rottingdean, Surrey, where Enid lived after her marriage to Sir Roderick Jones. "Do you still have that terrible piebald that jumps everything?" he asked. When Enid said that they did, he replied that she should, "stick it in her new book . . . and make it win the Grand National."[1]

From this simple throwaway line, Enid Bagnold created the story that has enchanted generations of readers since its first publication in April 1935. Enid herself thought the book was for adults, but its heart-warming subject matter has found a home in the hearts of young and old alike.

Family life is central to the book. Throughout, Enid's love for her children, and the purity and clarity of a child's decisions in particular, shine through. Velvet herself was a mixture of Enid's daughter Laurian, to whom the book is dedicated, and Enid's memories of herself as a child. The rest of the family were based on real people, including the four Asquith sisters, granddaughters of the prime minister, also guests at Rottingdean, and on the Hilders, a local butcher's family. Donald, the beloved youngest child, is based on Enid's son Dominick.

National Velvet is also the story of a wonderfully observed friendship. Velvet and Mi are a true partnership, a living echo of the earlier partnership between Velvet's mother and the coach that helped her swim the channel. They achieve their destiny through their shared passion for the horse whose potential only they believe in.

Enid Bagnold's wonderfully immersive story with its beautifully drawn characters continues to enchant generation after generation.

[1] Quoted in *Enid Bagnold* by Anne Sebba, Weidenfield and Nicholson, London 1986

CONTENTS

AUTHOR'S NOTE

With reference to Chapter Thirteen, the race in this book is run prior to the Clause which made it necessary for a horse to have distinguished itself

'by being placed first, second, or third (by the Judge) in a steeplechase of three miles and upwards value 200 sovs. to the winner' –

and for all I can find in the Rules a zebra could have entered, provided he was the proper age.

As regards the objection which was lodged after The Piebald passed the post, I don't think this objection would eventually have been sustained on the ground of 'dismounting before reaching the unsaddling enclosure' alone. The fact of the rider's sex of course disqualified her. But the contention that the objection would immediately have been lodged is based upon Rule 144 of the National Hunt Rules.

144. 'If a rider does not present himself to be weighed in, or dismount before reaching the place appointed for that purpose, or touch (except accidentally) any person or thing other than his own equipments before weighing in, his horse is disqualified, unless he can satisfy the Stewards that he was justified by extraordinary circumstances.'

CHAPTER I

Unearthly humps of land curved into the darkening sky like the backs of browsing pigs, like the rumps of elephants. At night when the stars rose over them they looked like a starlit herd of divine pigs. The villagers called them Hullocks.

The valleys were full of soft and windblown vegetation. The sea rolled at the foot of all as though God had brought his herd down to water.

The Hullocks were blackening as Velvet cantered down the chalk road to the village. She ran on her own slender legs, making horse-noises and chirrups and occasionally striking her thigh with a switch, holding at the same time something very small before her as she ran. The light on the chalk road was the last thing to gleam and die. The flints slipped and flashed under her feet. Her cotton dress and her cottony hair blew out, and her lips were parted for breath in a sweet metallic smile. She had the look of a sapling-Dante as she ran through the darkness downhill.

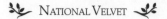

At the entrance to the village the sea was pounding up the sewer with a spring gale behind it. She passed to the third cottage, stopped at the door, opened it, let a gush of light on to the pavement, closed it and carried her tender object inside.

Edwina, Malvolia and Meredith sat in their father's Mr Brown's sitting-room just before supper time. It was dark outside and hot inside, and outside in the darkness the Hullocks went up in great hoops above the village. There was an oil stove in the corner of the sitting-room and lesson books on the table. The ceiling was low and sagged. An Albert lamp with a green glass shade lit the table. There was no electric light. Donald, the boy of four, was asleep upstairs.

Edwina, Malvolia and Meredith were all exactly alike, like golden greyhounds. Their golden hair was sleek, their fine faces like antelopes, their shoulders still and steady like Zulu women carrying water, and their bodies beneath the shoulders rippled when they moved. They were seventeen, sixteen and fifteen. Velvet was fourteen. Velvet had short pale hair, large, protruding teeth, a sweet smile and a mouthful of metal.

Mr Brown was swilling down the slaughter-house, as Mi Taylor was away for the day. The sound of the hose swished at the wooden partition which separated the slaughter-house from the sitting-room.

'He went beautifully!' said Velvet, and laying down a tiny paper horse on the table she wrenched at the gold band that bound her teeth back and laid it beside the horse.

'Father'll be in in a minute,' said Edwina warningly.

'It's going in again directly I hear a sound,' said Velvet and sitting down she swept the plate into her lap.

'Look at him,' she said lovingly, taking up the paper horse. 'I must unsaddle him and rub him down.' The heads were bent on the lesson books again and Velvet took a tiny bridle of cotton threads from the horse. Then going to a shell-box on the sideboard she brought it to the table.

'It's just supper,' said Mally. 'You'll have to clear.'

Velvet opened the box and took out a stable rubber two inches square, a portion of her handkerchief hemmed round. Laying the little horse flat on the table she rubbed him with delicacy in circular motions, after having taken a paper saddle from his back.

The horse was a racer cut from the Bystander. He stood three inches high and had a raking neck and a keen, veined face. By dint of much rubbing the paper had given off a kind of coat, and now as Velvet rubbed there came a suède-like sheen on the horse's paper body. He was dark, most carefully cut out, and pasted upon cardboard. The bridle was made by the fingers of a fairy, noseband, chinstrap and all, in black cotton.

'He has a high action,' said Velvet. 'A lovely show canter, but a difficult trot. I didn't jump him today as he needs to settle down.'

In the shell-box other horses lay.

'There's a marvellous picture of mares on the back of *The Times* today, but you can't cut a single one clear. They're all mixed up with the foals.'

'I saw it,' said Velvet. 'I called at the Post Office. But it was no good.'

'I called in too,' said Mally. 'They said in the Post Office that one of us looking at *The Times* was enough. We'd better take turns.'

'Yes,' said Velvet. 'You can't think how lovely it was galloping up there. It was nearly dark. He never put a foot wrong. Somehow you can trust a horse like that.'

'It's blood that counts,' said Mally darkly.

'I haven't got the racing saddle cut right,' went on Velvet. 'I wish I could find a picture of one. I ride short when I ride this horse and with this saddle the knees come right off on to his shoulder.'

'You need kneeflaps,' said Edwina.

'I suppose there's not time,' said Velvet, 'to take the chestnut down for a stand in the pond? His hocks are still puffy.'

'It's not you to lay tonight,' said Mally. 'You've got ten minutes.

Don't let father see . . . Mind your plate! It's fallen!'

Velvet dived under the table, picked it up, and examined it anxiously. Opening her mouth she worked it painfully in with both hands.

'S'bent a bit,' she gasped. 'It's a hell plate . . .'

'It's no good. Don't go on! Get on down to the pond.'

Velvet packed the racer in the shell-box and carefully abstracted a smaller horse, a coloured picture of a polo pony cut from *The Tatler*. Putting the box away she slipped through the door with the chestnut and was gone.

A door at the other end of the sitting-room opened and Mrs Brown came in. She stood and looked at the daughters for a moment – an enormous woman who had once swum the Channel. Now she had become muscle-bound.

Towering over the Albert lamp she threw her shadow across the books and up the wall.

She said: 'Lay supper.' And went out.

'Meredith,' said Edwina mechanically without looking up. Meredith got up and began to collect the books. When all the books were gone the two sisters sat tilting their chairs back so that Meredith could get the white cloth over the edge of the table past their knees. When this was done all their chairs came forward again. Kneeling by the Victorian sideboard Meredith pulled out plates, bread-knife, platter, sugar, knives and forks and salts and peppers.

The street door opened and Velvet stood on the mat. She had her shoes in her hand and her bare ankles were green with slime. Mrs Brown who had come in glanced at her and took a duster from the sideboard. 'Wipe them up,' she said and threw the duster on to the mat. Velvet mopped her slimy ankles, whispering to Mally, pointing with her finger towards the door – 'Stars like Christmas trees. Terrible stuff in the pond. Spawn. I stood five minutes.'

'We ought to get some,' said Mally. 'I'll get a bottle after supper.'

'Any spawn,' said Mrs Brown without looking up, 'goes on a tin tray.'

'Yes, mother.'

'Larder,' said Mrs Brown.

Velvet put her shoes in the corner and the horse in the shell-box and disappeared. The others sat in silence till she came back with the tray.

Cold ham, jam, butter were placed on the table, and a dish of radishes.

Mr Brown came in by the slaughter-house door, gumboots drawn to his thighs, his sleeves rolled up, his hands wet from the hose. He passed through the room on his way to wash for supper.

Velvet and the three golden greyhounds sat on in brooding silence. A smell of liver and bacon stole in from the kitchen.

The two doors, that on the street and that on the kitchen, opened suddenly together. Out of the black hole of the street came Mi Taylor, brushed up for supper. Mrs Brown came in from the kitchen carrying the liver and bacon.

The room filled with smells. Mr Brown came in putting on his coat. Everyone sat down, Mi last of all, pulling up his chair gingerly.

'Well . . .' said Mr Brown, and helped the liver round.

Meredith went out and fetched in the jugs of coffee and milk.

'Bin over to Worthing?' said Mr Brown.

'I have,' said Mi.

'Got that freezing-machine catalogue for me?'

'Shops shut again.'

'Good God!' said Mr Brown exasperated, 'Don't you ever learn the shut-shop day in Worthing? Whadyer do then?'

'Had three teeth out. Dentist was all there was open.'

'Oh Mi, where?' said Velvet.

Mi opened his jaw and pointed to a bloody wound.

'Oughter eat pap for it,' said Mr Brown. 'It's pulpy.'

'S'got to learn to harden,' said Mi.

'Donald asleep?' said Mally.

'This hour gone,' said Mrs Brown.

They ate, sleek girls' heads bent under the lamp, Mr Brown and Mrs Brown square and full and steady, Mi silent and dexterous with his red hair boiling up in curls on his skull.

Jacob went grinning round the table, from sister to sister.

'Nobody feeds him,' ordered Mi under his breath.

His red hair boiled up on his skull fiercer than ever at Jacob's presumption.

The yard spaniels remained in the street on the doorstep through meals. They lay and leant against the front door, grouped on the step, so that the door creaked and groaned under their pressed bodies. When the door was opened from the inside they fell in. When this happened Mi sent them out again with a roar.

Jacob had been allowed in all his life. His fox-terrier body, growing stout in middle age, still vibrated to a look. His lips curled and he grinned at the blink of a human eyelash. His tail ached with wagging, and even his hips waggled as he moved. But under cover of these virtues he was watchful for his benefit, watchful for human weakness, affected, a ready liar, disobedient, boastful, a sucker-up, and had a lifelong battle with Mi. Mi adored him and seldom said a kind word to him. Jacob adored Mi, and there was no one whom he would not sooner deceive. At meals Jacob wriggled and grinned from sister to sister, making a circle round

Mi, whose leg was scooping for him.

Just outside the slaughter-house was a black barking dog on the end of a string. This dog had a name but no character. It barked without ceasing day and night. Nobody heard it. The Browns slept and lived and ate beside its barking. The spaniels never opened their mouths. They pressed against doors and knee and furniture. They lived for love and never got it. They were herded indiscriminately together and none knew their characteristics but Mi. The sisters felt for them what they felt for the fowls in the fowlyard. Mi fed them.

But Jacob's weaknesses and affectations and dubious sincerities were thrust upon everyone's notice. When Velvet came in at the front door, and pressing back the leaning spaniels, closed it, Jacob would rise, wriggle his hips at her, bow and grin.

'How exquisite, how condescending, how flattering!' said he, bowing lower and lower, with his front legs slid out on the floor and his back legs stiff. But if asked to go for a walk, not a step would he come outside unless he had business of his own with the ashbin, or wanted to taunt the chained and raging dog with the spine of a herring dragged in the dust.

The chained dog chiefly barked. But sometimes he stopped rending the unheeding air and lay silent. Then he would whirl out on his chain like a fury and fall flat, half choked. And Jacob

would stand without flinching, banking on the strength of the chain, and think, 'You poor one-thoughted fool . . .'

The Browns loved Jacob as they loved each other, deeply, from the back of the soul, with intolerance in daily life.

As the girls ate, a private dream floated in Velvet's mind . . . It was a little horse, slender and perfect, rising divinely at a jump, fore-feet tucked up neatly, intelligence and delight in its eager eye, and on its back, glued lightly and easily to the saddle . . . she, Velvet . . . Gymkhana Velvet. As she took the visionary jump her living hand stole to her mouth. She pulled out the torturing plate and hid it in her lap. Mi's eyes were on her in a flash, he who never missed anything.

'Be windy for the Fair Thursday,' said Mrs Brown.

'It's coming in wild from the South West,' said Mr Brown.

'Always does when it comes in at all,' said Mrs Brown. 'Three-day gale.'

All the trees in the dark village outside attested this. They were blown like fans set on one side. The rooks shuffled and slept in them, waving up and down among the breaking twigs. The village street was white with rook-droppings.

'Put that in again, Velvet,' commanded Mrs Brown.

'She got it out again?' asked Mr Brown looking up sharply.

'It aches me an' aches when I eat,' said Velvet.

'Ache or no, argue or no, that plate cost me four pound ten and it's solid gold an' it goes in,' said Mr Brown. 'I'm not going to have a child like a rabbit if I can help it. You girls have got your faces for your fortunes and none other. I've told you often enough.'

The three golden greyhounds sat up straighter than ever and Velvet fumbled with her teeth.

'It's got hooked up.'

'Unhook it, then,' said Mr Brown. He sat back, satisfied, commanding and comfortable, and pulled the radishes towards him. Then he passed the dish round.

'Take a radish, Velvet.'

'Couldn't bite a *radish*!'

'Go without then,' said Mr Brown happily, and leant back to light his pipe.

All the Browns tilted their chairs. Nobody ever told them it would hurt the carpet. They ate, ruminated, and tilted. Only Mrs Brown sat solid and silent. She did not talk much, but managed the till down at the shop in the street. She knew all about courage and endurance, to the last ounce of strength, from the first swallow of overcome timidity. She valued and appraised each daughter, she knew what each daughter could do. She was glad too that her daughters were not boys because she could not understand the courage of men, but only the courage of women. Mr Brown was with dignity the head of the family. But Mrs Brown was the standard of the family. When Velvet had fallen off the pier at the age of six her mother went in thirty feet after her, sixteen stone, royal-blue afternoon dress. A straight dive, like the dive of an ageing mammoth. The reporter from the *West Worthing News* came to make a story of it and said to Edwina, 'Your mother swum the Channel, didn't she?' Edwina nodded towards her mother. 'Better ask *her*.' 'What's past's past, young man,' said Mrs Brown heavily and shut her mouth and her door.

Mi Taylor's father had trained Mrs Brown for her swim, trained her when she had been a great girl of nineteen, neckless, clumsy, and incredibly enduring. Mi himself had been a flyweight boxer, killed his man, because the wretched creature was in status lymphaticus, got exonerated and yet somehow disqualified, tramped the country, held horses, cleaned stables and drifted nearer and nearer to the racing world, till he knew all about it except the feel of a horse's back. Arriving somehow in the ebb of Lewes races he had been taken on by Mr Brown for the slaughter-house, for running errands, and lately even for negotiating for stock.

Mrs Brown stared at him when he came with a look of strange pleasure in her hooded eyes. Mi Taylor, the son of

Father Taylor! He knew all about her, Taylor did. The only one who ever did. He knew what she was made of. He'd had the last ounce out of her. He and the doctor at her five confinements, those men knew. Nobody else, ever. Mi was his son. Mi was welcome. He could stay. Henceforth he ate with the family and lodged in the extra loose-box. And Araminty Brown, embedded in fat, her keen, hooded eyes hardly lifting the rolls above them, cooked admirably, ran the accounts, watched the shop, looked after the till, spoke seldom, interfered hardly ever, sighed sometimes (because it would have taken a war on her home soil, the birth of a colony, or a great cataclysm to have dug from her what she was born for), moved about the house, brought up her four taut daughters under her heavy eye, and thought of death occasionally with a kind of sardonic shrug. Nobody could have said exactly whether she had a dull brain or no. Ed and Mally and Meredith behaved themselves at the wink of one of her heavy eyes. Velvet would have laid down her stringy life for her.

'Yer ma,' said Mi, "sworth a bellyful. Pity she weighs what she does.'

'Why?' said Mally.

'Binds her up,' said Mi. And it was not constipation he was thinking of.

'Mi,' said Mally to her mother, 'thinks you ought to be riding in Lewes races.'

Mrs Brown made a noise in her nose.

'What?' said Mally.

'That's all right,' said Mrs Brown.

'You can never tell what mother's thinking,' said Mally to Velvet.

'She doesn't think where we do,' said Velvet. 'She thinks at the back.'

In the sitting-room at the close of supper Mrs Brown stretched out an arm and turned the Albert lamp lower.

'Box,' said Mr Brown indicating the sideboard. Edwina rose and brought him his small cigar.

The shadows whirled.

'Monday,' said Mrs Brown.

'Driving night,' said Velvet.

'What I was thinking,' said Mrs Brown. 'Get on off!'

'First?' said Velvet.

'First,' said Mrs Brown.

Velvet hunched her shoulder-blades and sniffed. Was driving worth it? She never could make up her mind. Out of bed it didn't seem so, but in bed it was worth while.

'Hush!' she said suddenly and held up her hand. 'Cough . . .' she said, and went to the slaughter-house door.

'Gone to rub Miss Ada's chest,' said Mi grinning.

In the sitting-room the books for homework came out again.

'Gotta see a boy,' murmured Mi as he went out into the street.

Velvet lit the hurricane lamp standing in the corner of the empty slaughter-house and passed through to the shed where the old pony lived.

Miss Ada was an old pink roan gone grey with age, her ears permanently back, a look of irritation about her creased nostrils, backbone sagging, horny growths on her legs.

'Hullo,' said Velvet and opened the door. Miss Ada moved definitely round and turned her backside on Velvet.

Velvet put her hand on the quarters and the skin twitched irritably.

'You never do anything about being decent!' said Velvet. 'Have you got a cough?'

Miss Ada bent her head suddenly and rubbed the itch off her right nostril on to her leg, and as she did it she flashed a robust, contemptuous look at Velvet. 'Is there sugar?' said the look, 'or no sugar? I want no subtleties, no sentimentalities. I don't care about your state of heart, your wretched conscience-prickings, your ambitious desires. Is there sugar or no sugar? State your reasons for coming to see me and leave me to brood.'

Velvet produced a piece of sugar and the pony bent her head

round with a look of insolence, as though she still suspected the sugar to be an imitation lump. She took it with her lips, but she pressed her old teeth for a minute on the child's palm, and at this trick, as old as Velvet's childhood, Velvet thrust her arms over the sagging backbone and buried her face among the knobbles of the spine. The pony munched her lump stolidly, flirting her head up and down as though she were fishing for extra grains high up among her teeth.

'If we had another pony,' said Velvet, 'nobody would love you less. But we can't go on like this, it's awful. The gymkhanas all coming and nothing to ride. And you hate all that. It puts you in your worst mood.'

The door opened and Mally came in.

'Has she got a cough?'

'She hasn't coughed since I've been here,' said Velvet.

'Get over, you awful old thing!' said Mally, 'and let me pass.'

'Don't, Mally . . .'

'The only way is to be as horrid to her as she is to us.'

'I've left the lamp down there. Hang it up somewhere. I can't reach the hook.'

Mally hung the lamp carefully out of way of the straw. The two sat up on the manger together. The pony, utterly disgusted, drew her ears back almost flat with her head, hung out her twitching underlip and faced round at an angle from them, her tail tucked sourly in.

'Look at her!' said Mally. 'My God, what a mount!'

Velvet took out her plate and wrapped it in her handkerchief.

'Don't you leave it here,' said Mally. 'It won't help us any. It was your plate-fiddling that went wrong at supper.'

Mally got up on to the manger's rim, reached to a ledge of wood below the window and took down two sticks of dark gold paper.

'Crunchie?' said Velvet her face lighting.

'I got them this morning.'

'On tick still?'

'Yes. She was cross but I swore we'd pay by Saturday.'

In the gold paper was a chocolate stick. Beneath the chocolate was a sort of honeycomb, crisp and friable, something between biscuit and burnt sugar. Fry's chocolate crunchie. Not one of the sisters ate any other kind of sweet that year. It was their year's choice. The year before it had been Carmel Crispies.

'We must pay her. She's a wispy woman. She's pappy.'

'Aren't you queer about people? Always cutting 'em down to the bone.'

'I don't like people,' said Velvet, 'except us and mother and Mi. I like only horses.'

'Pity you weren't a boy.'

'I should a bin a poor thin boy. With muscles just on one arm. From meat chopping.'

'As it is,' said Mally, 'we're all going into tills. Into cages. To count out money.'

'I'm not,' said Velvet, examining her crunchie. 'Do you like the end best or the middle?'

'I like the ones that don't seem cooked. Sticky in the middle.'

'I wish I had a proper coat with checks,' said Velvet.

'You? Why Edwina's never had one.'

'Edwina isn't me. I'm not going to be a jersey-jumping child in a gymkhana any more.'

'I don't know how we're going to do anything in the gymkhanas at all. Miss Ada's turning sourer and sourer on us. She'll end by refusing to go into the ring.'

Miss Ada, seduced by the smell of the chocolate, turned slowly towards them, approaching by fractions.

'It's all right, Mally, I'll give her a bit of mine,' said Velvet. 'You bought 'em.'

'It doesn't matter who bought 'em,' said Mally. 'We're all owing together . . . She can have a crumb of mine too. Don't blow so, you idiot! She's sneezed her crumb off my hand!' Miss Ada stooped her head and began a vain search for one chocolate crumb in two inches of dingy straw.

The stable door opened and Mi put his head in.

'Meredith in here?'

'No . . . Whad'you want'er for?'

'*Canary Breeder's Annual*'s come. Come on last post.'

'Don' know where she is,' said Malvolia. 'She won't be fit to live with for weeks.'

'Mi . . . Mi . . . Mi!' called a voice from the dark.

'In here. He's got your *Canary Breeder*.'

'Mother said so! Oh . . . I'll come in. Give it to me!'

Meredith took the book from Mi. 'You've taken off the wrapper,' she said disappointedly, 'I like to take it off myself,' and leant back against Miss Ada, unconscious of the pony's body.

''Nother time you can fetch your own annual,' said Mi.

'Bet you don't remember next year,' said Mally.

'Listen to this! Listen to this! It's what I always thought!' said Meredith. 'Listen to Mr Lukie. He says (J. Lukie Esquire it's signed) he says, "Cod liver oil should be given to mating birds. My own birds did magnificently on Poon's Finchmixture Cod liver . . ."'
Miss Ada removed her support sharply and Meredith sat violently on the straw. 'Blast!' she said, without looking round at the pony, opened the annual and searched again for the page.

'Yes but his birds were already mating,' said Mally. 'You keep wanting to give them the cod liver oil to make them mate. It doesn't make them mate. Lukie doesn't say it does!'

'I don't see why . . .' said Meredith, still hunting for the page. 'You've got to be lively to mate. Vital or something. Cod liver oil gives vitality. I read it . . . it's here . . . "gives vitality to the mating bird".'

'Miss Ada'll step on your hand if you leave it there,' said Velvet.

Meredith got slowly up, reading as she rose. 'It doesn't say whether it's the cock bird or the hen. Which do you think it is, Mi?'

'Cock before, hen after,' said Mi.

'There you are!' said Meredith. 'I *wish* mother'd let me order it.'

'You got it all over the sofa last time.'

'But I've got a fountain pen filler now. I've trained the cock on drops of water. He's as good as gold. The hen makes a fuss. I could do her in the yard.'

'Bed,' said Edwina from the darkness outside.

They filed out without a word, Meredith reading to the last by the flare of the hurricane lamp. The spring gale had gone. The spring sky was indefinite and still, with a star in it. There was a new moon.

'Are you coming, Velvet?'

'You can't leave Miss Ada with nothing when we've used her

stable. I'll be a second.' She opened the corn bin and Miss Ada dropped ten years off her looks. She plunged her nose on the two hands that cupped the corn and ducked her head to sniff out the droppings before they sank too far in the straw. Velvet, alone, saw the new moon. She bowed three times, glanced round to see that no one saw, then standing in the shadow of the stable door she put her hands like thin white arrows together and prayed to the moon – 'Oh God, give me horses, give me horses! Let me be the best rider in England?'

CHAPTER II

The next morning Meredith had to take some suet and a shin of beef over to Pendean. School was at nine. It was the last day of term. She rose at six. Mi called her on his way downstairs. He heated the coffee left over from last night and gave her three sardines between two pieces of bread. Then Meredith went out to saddle Miss Ada.

Miss Ada had a crupper to her saddle, partly because the hills were so steep and partly because she had no shoulders. Meredith forgot the crupper and left it dangling. She put the girths on twisted, put the *Canary Breeder* in the basket with the suet, and started off. Miss Ada tapped smartly up the village street on the tarmac. The flints on the church shone like looking-glass. Meredith trotted east into the rising sun. Her toes were warm and the sardines and the bread and coffee digested comfortingly. Over the Hullocks and down into the valleys, sun and shadow, cup and saucer, through the tarred gate, the wired gate, the broken gate, and finally into the Pendean valley and to the house. She gave in the beef and suet, would have stopped to talk to Lucy the farm daughter (only Lucy had a temperature), started on the home journey, crupper still dangling, and Miss Ada restive now from the sore of the twisted girth.

'We'll go the Dead-Horse-Patch way,' said Meredith suddenly, aloud; and then disliked the sound of the spoken words in the lonely landscape. One of Miss Ada's ears came forward. They were above the village now, though still two miles away. There were two ways down to the sea level. One by the two steep fields and the chalk road whence she had come up, the other by two more steep fields, two gates, a broken reaping machine, a cabbage field, to a haystack – and a place where a horse had once dropped dead.

For thirteen years Miss Ada had said that place was haunted. She had told Mr Brown so plainly when Velvet was crawling. And he had never insisted with her, but let her come down the way she had planned for herself by the chalk road. Now to Meredith's mind came the desire to take Miss Ada the way she had never been taken by Edwina, Malvolia, Velvet or herself.

Even before the division of the ways the intention became communicated to the pony. A hardening took place, a clenching of spirit. A weight came into Miss Ada's head. She hung it provocatively upon her bit. Meredith sat uneasily and watchfully in her saddle.

Miss Ada's way was to the left. Meredith's was to the right. Miss Ada had two methods of getting her way. Either she didn't cede at all, or when Meredith pulled she ceded too fast and whipped round. This method she chose and the saddle slipped over on the too-slack girths. Meredith fell off. Miss Ada with a look of sudden youth flicked her heels, cantered to the wire fence, stooped her head and cropped. The basket with the *Canary Breeder* had fallen too and Meredith, getting up, picked up her annual, glanced at Miss Ada and after a minute sat down in the sun to read. She was now faced with a walk home. Nobody ever caught Miss Ada once she was loose. She would go home her own way and at her own time.

Meredith read comfortably what Mr Lukie had to say, then closed her book and trudged off.

'You'll look an idiot!' she said partingly to Miss Ada, 'Coming home with your saddle all upside down.' The whites of Miss Ada's eyes glinted as she cropped. Meredith went down towards the Dead-Horse-Patch. When she was out of sight Miss Ada moved off by the way she had intended to go.

Meredith ran down over a steep field that lay in shadow with its back to the rising sun, then up the opposite slope with the sun shining on her back. Over the rise she saw a rider in the distance nearing the haystack that stood at the edge of the cabbage field, the haystack where the legendary horse had laid down and died. The rider coming towards her – she could not see at first whether he was walking or trotting . . . Then came a flick of movement and he was off. The horse as usual had shied at the Dead-Horse-Patch.

When Meredith reached him he was on his feet dusting himself down, a tripper-rider, a great lad with loose flannel trousers and bicycle clips. The horse, like Miss Ada, was cropping feverishly as though it had never seen grass before.

'You got Mr Belton's Bumble Bee,' said Meredith.

'What's the matter with him? Seen a ghost?' said the young man.

'Yes, he did,' said Meredith.

'Eh? How? You had a fall too?' eyeing the green-grass stain on her hip.

Meredith looked round to see if Miss Ada was in sight. 'Bin sliding,' she said.

'Can we catch the horse?' said the tripper.

'Maybe,' said Meredith, 'but I shouldn't think so. I got to be in time for school.'

'Jumped his whole length sideways,' said the tripper.

'They always do, here,' said Meredith, edging gently towards the horse.

'Why here?'

'There's a ghost in the ground. A horse ghost. Steams up mornings and evenings. Specially early when there's a dew drying off.' Her hand was within a foot of the reins, extended soothingly. The young man saw her intention and ran round the other side. The horse, startled, removed itself another length away.

'You mucked it,' said Meredith. 'I must get on.'

Miss Ada got home first. Velvet was putting saltpetre on her girth-gall as she stood in the sunlight on the street by the front door. The saddle was pitched up on the railings. The front door was open and Mr Brown bare-headed, was enjoying his after breakfast pipe.

'My girl,' he said when he saw Meredith, 'Yer fifteen, annt you?'

Meredith nodded and stood still before him.

'Seven years you've saddled that pony and put her bits of leather on her, and to this day you onny hang 'em round her like blind cords. She's got a sore'll take a week to heal.'

Miss Ada looked at Meredith with smug reproach.

'If it was canaries . . .' muttered Velvet, dabbing with a rag.

Meredith glowered at Velvet as she passed her to go in for her school books.

Inside the sitting-room Mi was telling Donald to get on with his porridge. It was cold porridge, turned out of a cup. There was a hole in the top and treacle was poured inside. Donald was laying a sap from the side in to the centre.

'You aren't eating what you cut out,' said Mi, cleaning a rat-trap with emery paper and the rust covering the cloth in showers.

'I am,' said Donald. But he wasn't.

'Donald done yet?' called Mrs Brown, 'I'm washing the plates.'

'He's fiddling,' said Mi.

Mrs Brown came to the door. 'You get down and bring that porridge in here,' she said as she rubbed a plate.

The sweetness of Donald's face remained unchanged. He watched the treacle run out down the sap. 'I dooont . . .' he drawled.

Mrs Brown gave no second chances. It was her strength.

She took Donald in one great arm and the plate of porridge in the other and removed him. The sweetness of his face was still unchanged.

'He'll never eat that,' said Meredith. 'You're sitting on my atlas.'

Mi pulled it out from beneath him. 'He never eats anything

he's fiddled with,' said Mi, 'because it's turned into something else in his mind. Hark to them hammering . . .'

'You'd never think, to look at the Green, that there'd be a Fair in twenty-four hours. Just a lot of old sticks and men hitting them in.'

'It'll be ready. You won't be though.'

'I'm just going. Last day. Holidays tomorrow.'

'All four hanging round the house all day. Life'll be a joke.'

'This bit a millet, Mi,' said Meredith, dragging a length out of the sideboard drawer. 'Stick it in for the male, Mi, *please* . . .'

'Them birds . . .' Meredith blocked the light in the doorway and was gone.

'Blast and blast and hell . . .' said Mi softly. He had caught his finger in the rat-trap.

'Hell,' said Donald softly in the doorway. His silver hair hung in a lock over his forehead. His eyes were film-eyes and blue, with film lashes. His platinum-blond, Hollywood head was set on a green jersey. His bottom was bare and his pants hung down unbuttoned.

'You've got off your pot!' said Mi threateningly. 'Get on back.' Donald disappeared again into the inner room, his behind gleaming like the white polish of two peeled and hard boiled eggs.

Edwina went in to Worthing for a piano lesson. Mally, Meredith and Velvet waded through a last day of grammar and map reading behind the walls of the village school. The children's voices droned behind the windows and the hammering on the Village Green increased. At break the children watched the hammers from the corner of the asphalt yard. The greasy pole was up, the cokernut shies were up, there was a frail porch with 'Welcome' written on it.

Marks for the term were read out, and prizes given. Malvolia got *Hiawatha*.

At home it was steak and kidney pudding for dinner and Mr Brown poured in the boiling water through a hole in the suet. Velvet kept her plate in and swallowed whole. The kidneys went down like stones. Mr Brown finished his Meat Fancier as he ate. Donald ate his meat well and said gently some six or seven times, 'Is it castle puddings?' Nobody knew. His question was not insistent but soft. Sometimes he said it through his meat.

'Yer spitting, Donald,' said Mi.

'I *said*,' said Donald, dreamily . . .

Mrs Brown looked at him. 'It is,' she said.

'You never used to tell *us*!' said Velvet.

'Times,' said Mrs Brown, 'I don't do what I always did.'

Malvolia cleared the plates. Mrs Brown fetched in a city of

castle puddings and a jam-pot full of heated jam. She served Donald, the baby, first. Two castle puddings and a dab of jam on the plate. He looked at his two puddings and began to examine them. He drooped his Hollywood head like a smiling angel.

'Fiddling again,' said Mi ominously. 'You wanted 'em too much.'

'Yore putting it into his head,' said Mally.

Edwina walked in and put down her music roll and her hat. She pulled a chair up.

'Your bit's there,' said Mrs Brown, 'on the sideboard.'

'Guvner an' me we wash,' said Mi into his plate. 'Funny how men wash for girls an' girls don' wash for men.'

'Anybody knows boys are dirtier than girls,' said Mally.

'Maybe. But grown men wash freer than women.'

Edwina sat down, ignoring criticism.

'Get on, get on,' said Mrs Brown to Donald.

'I am gettin' on,' said Donald, and opened his mouth to show that it was full.

'Bin turning round and round,' said Mi. 'Give a swaller.'

'Can't swaller,' said Donald, ''tisn't slidy.'

'Isn't he lovely!' said Velvet, coming out of a dream quite suddenly and looking as though she had seen him for the first time. 'Shall I teach you to ride, Donald?'

'You've put him off proper,' said Mrs Brown.

Donald opened his eyes and struggled with his mouth. Then he leant over his plate and spat out the revolving mass. 'Yes,' he said, when he was empty, 'yes, when? Now?'

Mrs Brown rose slowly, took her own empty plate away to the sideboard, moved calmly and without anger round to Donald.

'You'll finish alone,' she said, and gathered him up. Donald and his plate sailed into the back kitchen.

'Well, really, Velvet,' said Edwina.

'He doesn't care,' said Velvet. 'Wouldn't he be lovely in the under-six?'

'On Miss Ada?' said Mally.

'She's too wide really.'

'You want a little narrow thing like Lucy's Rowanberry.'

'Lucy never can find anyone small enough to ride Rowanberry anyway.'

'Could we start him, father?' said Velvet.

'Eh?' said Mr Brown, struggling to leave his page.

'Teach Donald. So's he could be ready for the under-six?'

'Under what?' said Mr Brown. 'The under what?'

'Gymkhana,' said Velvet. 'The class for children under six. Six years.'

'Ask your mother,' said Mr Brown, and returned to his page.

'Then that's that,' said Velvet, rising happily. 'Can I get down?'

There was no answer.

'F'whatayave received thank God,' said Velvet to no one in particular, and disappeared into the kitchen.

'Did you give 'em that millet?' said Meredith suddenly.

'Forgot,' said Mi.

'F'whatayave received thank God,' said Meredith with a dark look at him, and shot from the room. Mr Brown pushed back his chair.

'You girls said your grace?' he said, getting up.

'F'whatayave received thank God,' said Edwina. And the meal was finished.

The candle in the scarlet-painted candlestick was burnt low and had a shroud. The bottle-candle was high and gave a good light.

Spring and evening sky showed between undrawn cotton curtains.

Mrs Brown sat on a stout mahogany chair before her dressing table, and Velvet knelt behind her unhooking her dress from neck to waist at the back. The dress was dark blue rep, built firm. It was like unhooking the strain on a shrunk sofa-covering. Hook after hook Velvet travelled down till at last she reached far below the waist. Then Mrs Brown stood up and the dark blue dress dropped to the floor, leaving her in a princess petticoat like a great cotton lily. The strings of this, untied at neck and waist by Velvet, disclosed her in bust-bodice, stays and dark-blue cloth knickers.

'The iodine's in the wall cupboard,' said mother.

Velvet went to the wall cupboard and extracted the iodine from an army of bottles and jars.

'N' the cotton wool,' said mother.

Velvet, behind her, undid the strings of the bust bodice. Got down to bedrock, she knelt and examined the wound.

'Mus' take your stays off, mother.'

Mrs Brown rose and drew breath. Working from the bottom up she unhooked the metal fencework within which she lived, and sat down again. 'Star out,' she said, staring through the window. The star was like a slip of silver tinfoil plumb between the hang of the curtains.

'M'm,' said Velvet, and she glanced at the star over her mother's shoulder. 'Metal's worked right through the top of the stays and cut you,' said Velvet.

'Ought to get whalebone,' said Mrs Brown, sniffing at her own economy.

'Yes,' said Velvet, 'you ought. S'made a nasty place.' She

dapped the iodine on the abrasion caused by the jutting shaft of the stays. 'Hurt?'

'Stings,' said Mrs Brown. The star winked and stuttered.

'Stick on a band-aid piece,' said Mrs Brown. 'Thur's a tin'n the cupboard.'

Velvet stuck the plaster on to the wide hard back.

Mrs Brown glared at the star.

'Pray to God y'don't get fat, child,' she said.

Velvet sat back on her heels aghast.

'You can't *be*,' said Mrs Brown, 'what you don't *look*.'

'You can, you can!' said Velvet. 'You *are*, mother!'

'Maybe,' said Mrs Brown . . . 'But you gotter dig. You gotter know. You gotter believe.'

Velvet put her thin arms on her mother's shoulders and kissed her on the enemy fat. She winced at a sign of regret or weakness in the beloved mountain.

'There's nothing, *nothing* you can't do, mother. You've got us all beat. Mi thinks you're Godalmighty. N'we all do.'

Mrs Brown smiled in the glass. 'Chut, child! Don't mount up in a torment. M'not grumbling. M'out of condition, but it came on me. I'm only saying . . . you poor thin, hairpin . . . KEEP thin! There's no song an' dance . . .' Mrs Brown was bolting herself back into the fence. She stood upright.

'S'awful to grow up,' said Velvet.

'Nope,' said Mrs Brown.

'Why isn't it?'

'Things come suitable to the time,' said Mrs Brown.

The thin slip, the quivering twig looked back at her mother.

'Lot o' nonsense,' said Mrs Brown, 'talked about growing up.' She stepped into her princess petticoat and drew it up. 'Tie me,' she said. The candle in the red candlestick drowned itself in fat and went out. 'Child-birth,' said the voice, gruff and soothing, talking to the star and to the child (and the child knelt at the strings of the petticoat), 'an' being in love. An' death. You can't know 'em till you come to 'em. No use guessing and dreading. You kin call it pain . . . But what's pain? Depends on who you are an' how you take it. Tie that bottom string looser. Don't you dread nothing, Velvet.'

'But you're so mighty. Like a tree,' said Velvet.

'Shivery to be your age. You don't know nuthin'. Later on you get coated over.' (Silence, and the hypnotic night.) 'S'a good thing to be coated over. You don't change nothin' underneath.'

'All the same it's awful to grow up,' said Velvet. 'All this changing and changing, an' got to be ready for something. I don't ever want children. Only horses.'

'Who can tell?' said Mrs Brown.

'I've got Me,' said Velvet, putting her thin hand across her breast. 'I can't ever be anything else but Me?'

'You're all safe,' said Mrs Brown carelessly, stooping with grunts to pull up her dress. 'You got both of us, you *an'* me. Say your prayers now an' get along.'

'Not yet, not yet.'

'Say your prayers, I say. Down on your knees an' say your prayers. You go plunging off this time o' night, don't you? Getting into your bed all of a daze an' a worry. Say your prayers, I say!'

Velvet went on her knees in the middle of the floor. Mrs Brown sat down, the dress in wreaths around her, and took a knife to her nails.

'Ah . . . v'Farver . . . ch . . . art'n'eaven,' mumbled the voice from the floor. The blue in the window had gone and the star had companions.

'. . . power n'a GloryamEN. Mother . . .'

'Yes.'

'You're all right, aren't you?'

'M'as good as living for ever. Get on off to bed. N'I'm not comin' to say good-night. Father is.'

Velvet kissed her. 'Come an' say good-night . . .'

'No, I'm not. Hook me up before you go.' Velvet nicked up the great line of steely hooks to the top.

'Now go.' Velvet went.

'Child gets all alight at night,' said Mrs Brown to herself.

Velvet's head came back round the door.

'Good-night, mother – where you going?'

'Down the village.'

'What for?'

'Will you GO!'

Mrs Brown went down the village with the key of the empty shop in her pocket. She had accounts to finish. The Hullocks rose above her in hoops into the sky. The stars floated in the olive glaze of the weedy pond. The boys and girls were hushed, black and still, against the doorways. Edwina stood like a statue at the cobbler's doorway as her mother passed, but her mother knew her.

'Growing,' muttered Mrs Brown as she went on. 'Poor lass has to hide it.'

The beautiful boy beside Edwina breathed again. He was golden-haired, and trying for the police. He felt he had no real chance for Mr Brown's Edwina, and he had no idea he was her first, her breathtaking first man.

'What'll Velvet . . .?' murmured Mrs Brown, looking a moment at the sky, and seeing Velvet's bony, fairy face. 'What'll men say about my Velvet?'

The sound of hoofs striking on metalled road came out of the darkness, and down the street, all alone, galloped a horse. Bodies shot out of the doorways and shouts sprang from shadows. Something black and white and furious raced down the street. Mrs Brown stopped and stepped off the pavement. With a striking of hoofs, sparks flying on the flints, a piebald horse, naked of leather, wild and alone, slid almost to his haunches and stood stock-still, shaking and panting. He lowered his head.

'A suitor for Velvet!'

A suitor for Velvet. The horse glared at Mrs Brown. It had strange eyes, a white wall eye and one of darkest blue. The light from the corner street lamp swam in its eyeballs. It trembled and glared; then at Mrs Brown's slowly extended hand, shook its neck with a shudder, half reared, and turning, galloped off up the street towards the Hullocks.

'That perishin' piebald from Ede's,' exclaimed a voice.

'That you, Mr Croom?'

'Give me a turn,' said Mr Croom. 'That's the third time this week that creature's got loose. Ede says he'll raffle him for the Fair. Wouldn't be a bad idea. Wonderful what you get for those raffles.'

While Malvolia and Meredith were undressing, Velvet was driving her big toes with long pieces of tape. She lay on her back in bed, her knees bent, talking in a monotonous voice like a sleepwalker.

'Careful through the gate now. Mind now. Get on, Satin!' and she gave the side of her thigh a switch with a light twig she held in her hand. The long tapes ran through her fingers which she held on her stomach, and both her knees pranced up and down – a restive pair of well-matched chestnuts in the shooting wagonette. With another switch and a spring forward the knees rose slightly in the air, were drawn back firmly by the reins, reined in, and stood still before the porch of the old castle . . .

The door opened and Mr Brown surveyed the spectacle of his youngest daughter, bare to the waist, her nightgown fallen on her chest, the bedclothes peeled to the floor, her eyes bright and her toes chained to her hands by tapes. Mally was cleaning her teeth in her drawers. Meredith was covering the bird cages.

'Mother says it's time,' he said, removing his pipe. 'Ah . . . yer daft, Velvet.'

'I'm only allowed on Mondays. I've two minutes more.'

'Where'd you get it from I want to know? D'you other girls go driving nights a week?'

'I used to,' said Mally. 'Now I'm bigger mother says I'll break the bed.'

'Where's the baize off the cages gone to?'

'Velvet's used it under Miss Ada's saddle. That time she got a sore back.'

'What's that you got on them?'

'It's Edwina's knickers she had for the party. They got burnt, drying.'

'Shame burnin your good knickers. Canaries wake early with that thin stuff. Thought I heard 'em yesterday morning. Where's Edwina?'

'Be up in a minute. Just gone down the street a second.'

'There . . . I've finished!' said Velvet, fishing for the bedclothes from her bed. 'The chestnuts hardly needed a rub down. They were cool. I've left the roan cob for tonight. He can stay out to grass.'

'Daft as a sparrow,' said Mr Brown at random. 'I doubt if a girl ought to be what you are.' Stooping, with his pipe in his mouth, he flung the bedclothes up on top of her, blew out the candle and made for the door.

'I'm not in bed!' said Mally.

'Then you ought to be,' said Mr Brown. 'Say your prayers.' And disappeared.

Velvet heard the cruelty and wild abandon of the iron feet and shuddered and sat up, excited. It was too late to move. The horse was gone. Gone into the sea? Was it a horse? The bed clung round her like protecting arms.

'Did you hear it?' (from the bed beside her).

In three beds three bodies were upright. Edwina's bed was empty. Then, after the pause, the iron feet plunged back again, and too late all three were at the window. The door opened and the curtains blew.

'Edwina!'

'Yes. Hush.' Edwina was panting. She had flown up the street and up the stairs.

'Father put the light out?'

'Yes. What horse . . .'

'Did he say 'bout me not being here?'

'I daresay he thought you'd gone with mother. What horse . . .'

'Piebald. Ede's piebald. Let me . . .'

'Didn't know Ede had a piebald. How d'you know what . . .?'

'Be quiet. Get back. I'm getting into bed.'

'Aren't you going to wash?'

'No.'

'TEETH?' said Mally, impressed.

'NO.'

'You bin with Teddy,' said Mally with satisfaction, getting back to bed.

'You shut up,' said Edwina. 'Won't tell you about the horse.'

'Thur's nothing to tell. Piebald horse. Farmer Ede's. Teddy's told you that.'

'Huh, an' near ran into mother!' snarled Edwina, naked, pulling her dressing gown over the clothes tumbled on the chair.

'Mother? What's it done to mother?' said Velvet sharply.

'Mother was in the street,' said Edwina in a wasp's voice, pulling on her pyjamas.

'Touched her? Knocked her?' said Velvet, flashing out of bed.

'Keep your hair on,' said Edwina.

'Bitch!' sobbed Velvet and flew out of the door and down the stairs.

'Now you bitched yerself!' said Mally calmly. 'Now they'll know you bin out with Teddy. You know well mother's not hurt.'

'Of course she isn't hurt. Should I be here?' hissed Edwina.

'Stringing Velvet off like a catapult! First you go off with boys. Second you upset Velvet. Third you'll be found out. Fourth Velvet'll be sick all night. *Sense*, haven't you?'

'Be . . . quiet . . .' said Edwina, in bed, in a dull strangled voice. 'Meredith . . . Merry . . . Get her back . . .'

'What did the horse do to mother, 'Dwina?'

'Sort a bowed to her. Slid to a full stop and hung its head and really sort a bowed to her. An' it reared and dashed back up the street home again. Get Velvet, Merry.'

Father was sitting looking at nothing in the living-room. He was just tipping his chair and swaying.

'Father!' said Velvet, scared, in the doorway, 'is mother all right?'

'Fine,' said father without moving. He turned his eyes slowly.

In the shadow behind the sideboard sat Mi mending Jacob's collar.

'There's bin a horse down the street . . .' said Velvet uncertainly.

'Gallopin',' assented father round the stem of his pipe.

There was a pause.

'I dreamt it hit mother,' mumbled Velvet.

'You did?'

'Yes. But it *was* a horse. That wasn't the dream.'

'I just come up the street,' said Mi. 'Yore ma's sitting with the blinds up, in the shop, totting up.'

'I'll go back,' said Velvet. 'It was a dream.' She turned and saw Meredith's face come round the doorway from the dark stairs.

'I had a dream, Meredith,' she said. 'I'm coming back.'

Mi put the collar down and crossing to Velvet bent down and felt her ankles. 'Cold as railings,' he said. 'I'll getchu a brick. Keep your stomach steady.' He disappeared into the kitchen and Velvet turned back to the stairs. Suddenly, at the stairhead something caught her jumping heart. She was back in the room again at her father's side, by his tipping, swaying chair.

'You all right, too, father?' she whispered. He put his arm round her and pulled her on his lap. 'You get them teeth straight!' he said to her, and rocked her meditatively while his pipe smoked up through her cotton hair.

CHAPTER III

The back window on the yard was blocked with cactus pots. In front of the window stood the fern-table with two big ferns in brass holders.

The street window had pots of blue and red and pied cineraria standing along its shelf, looking like a Union Jack. The eastern light of the morning burst through the cactus greenery on Mally laying the table with a darned and yellowing cloth. She clattered the crockery on from the sideboard, and the girls' voices called from the larder and kitchen.

'Mice bin at the bottom . . . It's all run out!'

'Mice where?'

'Porridge packet. They've made a hole.'

'Don't cut the rim off the toast, D'wina. I like 'em with the binding.'

Mi looked in with a packet in his hand. 'Whur's Velvet?'

'VelVET!'

'Coming down now.'

'Mi's got your pumice.'

'Mi?' said Velvet coming through the attic stair door. 'Oh, thank you, Mi.'

'Do it now,' said Mi.

'Clean my plate before breakfast!' said Velvet, outraged.

'Yer pa's sure to ask.'

'I do it AFTER breakfast! What's the good a doing it before!'

'Acids of the night,' said Mi and disappeared.

'Acids of what?'

'Get on an' do it,' said Mally.

'You'd think that plate was jewellery!' said Velvet and went into the scullery.

'Cost more than your mother's engagement ring,' said Mr Brown, passing through to the slaughter-house. 'She grumbling again?'

'Gone to clean it,' said Mally. 'Kedgeree!'

Mother brought in the soup basin of kedgeree. Donald stumped near her skirts. Edwina and Velvet came in and sitting down began to eat.

'I bin sick in the night,' said Donald.

'You haven't,' said Mrs Brown. 'Get on your chair.'

'Why haven't I?' demanded Donald.

'Don't let him start whying!' said Mally.

'Why haven't I, I say?' demanded Donald. 'Tell me why, I say?'

'Get on to your chair and don't let's hear any more about it,' said Mrs Brown.

'Why haven't I, I say?' Donald held on. 'You changed my sheets. The new ones was cold.'

'I changed your sheets for other reasons,' said Mrs Brown. 'Now get on.'

'The new ones was horrible,' muttered Donald subsiding. 'Is it kedgeree?'

'Did you wash your neck, Velvet?'

'Yes, mother.'

'Before your frock or after your frock?'

'After.'

'Then don't. Your frock's soaking. Where's Meredith?'

'Canary's loose.'

Mr Brown opened the door again and came in.

Donald brightened. 'I was sick in the night, daddy.'

'Donald!'

'I was sick all over . . .'

Mrs Brown removed Donald and the kedgeree to the kitchen.

'Lie. He wet his bed,' said Mally.

'Oh,' said Mr Brown and helped himself to kedgeree. 'I heard

your mother moving about. Why don't she leave him wet? He won't hurt. He's no more than damp.'

'Bad for his habits,' said Mrs Brown returning. She sat down and drew the marmalade towards her.

'I've caught her!' Meredith came in glowing.

'Take your kedgeree into the kitchen and let Donald tell you how sick he's been,' said Velvet.

'You'll do no such thing,' said Mrs Brown. 'That child gets on one idea like a railway track. It's you and your stomach, Velvet, that puts him on to it.'

'Can't help my stomach,' said Velvet. ''D' give anything in the world to change it.'

'You'll grow out of it.'

'Sixteen, you said.'

'Sixteen, I said.'

'Why sixteen?'

'You eat,' said Mrs Brown.

'Can I come back now?' Donald appeared in the doorway, holding his plate unsteadily in his fists.

'Yes, if you've finished.'

'I've finished.'

'All?'

'All except the bones. Jacob's eaten them.'

'Oh . . .' Velvet flew up and left the room. 'Mi!' she called into the yard from the kitchen. 'Jacob's eaten fish-bones!'

Donald lifted his plate to the sideboard and the spoon flew over his head to the floor.

'That child say he finished?' demanded Mr Brown.

'I finished,' said Donald.

'It's all on his plate still,' said Mr Brown, and went on reading his paper.

'Velvet!' called Mally. 'It's a do, Velvet! Come back. Jacob hasn't got a bone.'

Velvet appeared in the doorway.

'Donald,' said Mrs Brown, turning full on him, 'have you told me a story?'

'It *was* a story,' said Donald gravely.

'Do you know what a story is?'

'No,' said Donald.

Mrs Brown removed him to her bedroom.

'Piebald's gone down the street again,' said Mi, putting his hair in at the door and disappearing. The four sisters rose and streamed from the room. Mr Brown glancing up once and half turning round, went on with his paper. Mrs Brown returned.

'Donald sorry?' said Mr Brown.

'He's thinking,' said Mrs Brown. 'He isn't sure. Girls gone?'

'That piebald of Ede's got loose again,' said Mr Brown. There was peace and silence.

The tiny window pane between the cineraria was filled with black and white and the piebald went back up the street at a hand gallop. After his metal feet the street rustled with running shoes.

'That animal'll knock down a pram one of these days,' observed Mr Brown. 'Seems to make for the sea.'

'Curious horse,' said Mrs Brown. 'Climbs out in the night when the moon's up.'

'Don't he jump?' said Mr Brown.

'Jumps a house,' said Mrs Brown. 'Sort of rodeo, so they say . . . Yes, Donald? What is it?'

'I'm sorry,' called Donald in muffled tones through the door.

Mrs Brown opened the door.

'I'm sorry I was sick in the night,' said Donald.

'Child'll make a lawyer,' said Mr Brown.

Meredith returned to the room.

'He went right through the poles they're hammering up for the Fair,' she said. 'Then down to the Post Office, an' slid about and up the Chalk Road back on to the Hullocks again. Mr Ede was just going by 'n his cart. Cursed.'

'He'll get into trouble if that horse hurts someone,' said father. 'Mi done his breakfast?'

'Had it early. He's got given a glass tongue. Ate it in his room.'

'Well tell'm I want'm at twelve for six sheep.' Mr Brown passed away through the slaughter-house door. Mi came in from the street.

'Six sheep at twelve, father says.'

'M'm. Piebald jumped a five-bar gate with a wire on the top. Sailed over.'

'Who says so?'

'Fellow.'

'Is it broke?'

'The gate?'

'No. The piebald.'

'Ede says it's as quiet as a lamb. Just can't bear to be shut up. Bit mad.'

Mi blew his nose carefully, polished it, replaced his handkerchief and went for the yard door.

'You got a bit a time?' said Meredith.

'Get on an' do your canaries. Gotter sweep my room.'

'Done my canaries. I'll come an' sweep yours.'

Mi sniffed and went off. Meredith caught up a broom which stood beside the wall.

'You put that down,' said Mi, who knew she had taken it without turning his head. 'S'yer ma's own.' The broom was meekly put back. Meredith followed him.

Mi's room was outside, next to Miss Ada. It was an old loose-box that had fallen into disrepair. He took great pride in it and kept it spotless. Just within the door, which was propped open for freshness with a garden rake, was a large hole in the floor filled with rotting wood. The wood round the edges of the hole gave way like toast and Mi had marked a white ring round the hole and written in paint 'Step further than this'. He took his own broom and began to sweep.

'S'got no hairs on it,' said Meredith, standing about and in the way.

No answer. Mi did not like criticism. He swept the dust of the room vigorously into a heap, then propelled it with his brush over a portion of the painted line and into the hole in the floor. Picking up an old milk bottle by the neck he rammed the dust horizontally under the floor boards.

'Now whadjer want?' he said.

'Hammer'n nails,' said Meredith.

'Go out of the room then. Thurs no call fer you to see where I keep things.'

Meredith went outside into the sunny yard and stood with her back to the wall on the far side of the door. Honourably she looked away and straight before her. Mi went to his bed and abstracted a hammer and tobacco box of nails from under his mattress.

'How big?' he called.

Meredith measured her thumb joint. 'Inch an' a half.'

'Whafor?'

'Hang my Roller cage.'

'Find a joist then. It's rubble and such in between.' Mi came to the doorway with the hammer and nails.

'D'you think . . .?' began Mcredith.

'No,' said Mi shortly. 'You get into yer own hot water fer puttin' yer own nails in the house. Yor pa's down the village.'

'I know,' said Meredith. 'S' why I'm hurrying.'

She disappeared with the hammer and nails, and Mi took down his shaving mirror and polished it with his handkerchief. He replaced a drawing pin or two on the corners of his series of 'Grand National winners' pinned round the walls, and set the kettle on to his Primus that he might scald out his milk bottle.

Velvet and Mally appeared in the yard and hung about.

'Where's Merry?'

'Hammering,' said Mi.

Silence fell and the kettle hummed. Mally and Velvet looked with envy from the yard into the loose-box-bedroom.

'Wish I had a room of my own,' said Velvet. 'So I could hang up pictures.'

Mi came to the door, and holding the milk bottle over the hole in the floor poured the scalding water into it.

'I've earned it,' said Mi when the last drop was in.

'Why?'

'Full-grown,' he said, and sucked the gap in his teeth. He looked at them, long and straight. They looked back.

'They're puttin' that piebald up to raffle,' he said at last, and yawned deceptively.

'Raffle!' said Velvet, 'Raffle!' A pause. Then – 'Anybody might get it?'

'Anybody with a shilling.'

'Cost ony a shilling? You got a shilling, Mally?'

'Nothing at all.'

'Nor I've got nothing . . .'

'Oh, a shilling's easy got.'

'But we ought to have five. Donald ought to have a chance.'

'You'll never get five!'

'That's whur yer wrong,' said Mi. 'I'll give you five. You kin pay me back in yer time. I got a tip from a perisher.'

'Oh, Mi darling! What perisher?'

'Togged up perisher that was swanky and windy and couldn't sit his horse in his best suit.'

'What'd you do?'

'Fellow hired Belton's May Day and went out galloping. Top boots, spurs and checks, an' a bowler with a string on it.'

'Where were you?'

'Just walkin'.'

'Oh Mi! You were sitting behind the haystack with the ghost!'

'Had to sit somewhere.'

'Tell us . . .'

'I saw May Day go out. Galloped out. Perisher'd never heard of walkin' or trottin'. Half the sky was dancin' up an' down under 'is bottom, so I legged up the other way an' come to the haystack.'

Pause.

'. . . an' he galloped round,' egged Velvet.

'I see him coming down towards the haystack, May Day blowy and sweaty an' the ghost waiting for them as jolly as a daisy.'

'Oh . . . Mi . . . YOU . . . SAW it.'

'IT? No, s'not my kind. It's a horse ghost. Perisher was red in the face an' lumbering along. Toes pointin' down and not even clutching with his calves. Not clutchin' with anything. Heaving like a sack. Stock all out of place under his ear, having a high old seven and sixpence worth . . . Whoop . . . went May Day when the ghost made a pass at her. Sprung right across the road an' the perisher fell *on* the ghost, far's I c'd see. Serve it right, too. Reel vicious horse that must've been that got killed there. To have a ghost like that. Why, you can't miss making a bit in that place. Every hiring fellow that comes down from London spins off at that haystack. You ony got to sit behind it and pick up the bits.'

'They don't all tip you, though.'

'Most do. This one give me five. Here you are!'

Mi pulled two half crowns out of his pocket and handed them to Velvet in trust for them all.

'Thank you awfully, Mi. I'll give it you back. Swear.' And she hooked both middle fingers over her index fingers and held them up.

'Witches' stuff!' said Mi contemptuously. 'Keep yer word and don't crack yer fingers. And see this, Velvet, I'm a fool to do it. That piebald's as big a perisher's the fellow that tipped me the five. 'M going up to look at him this afternoon and likely I'll be sorry when I see his murdering white eye.'

'Can we come too, can we come too?'

'You got yer muslins to iron.'

'MUSLINS!' said Velvet outraged.

'Yer ma's just rung 'em out of the suds. I seen 'em. For the Fair.'

'I'm not going to wear MUSLIN,' said Velvet with a voice of iron.

'You'll wear what yer told,' said Mi placidly. 'I'll slip up after dinner. Nearer one. I got them sheep at twelve. Sounds's if I won't get any dinner. See Donald . . .'

Donald was beautifully dressed in a fresh striped blouse and grey pants the length of a coat cuff. The insides of both ankles were fastened up with sticking plaster and his silver hair had just left the prongs of a damp comb. The brown of his arms was a mixture of coffee and silk.

'Whur's the stinkin' ants?' said Donald.

'What's that?'

'A stinkin' ant jus' stung me.'

'Wher'd it sting you?'

'On my thumb,' said Donald clearly, and held up his thumb.

There was no mark of any kind on the pink thumb.

'Say "stinging",' said Mally. 'Ants don't sting. It was a wasp.'

'Go on,' said Mi. 'Don't be s'old-fashioned. He'll say "stinkin' ant" till he says "stinging wasp" . . . and it'll all come natural.'

Mally looked down her nose at Donald. 'You're soft, Mi,' she said. 'You bin and killed something, Donald.'

'It wanted to be dead,' said Donald. 'A very little ant.'

'Throwing the blame on the ant!' said Mally. 'I thought as much!'

Donald made a pass with his foot. 'Thur's another one,' he said. 'They all want to be dead.'

'Nice excuse!' said Velvet. 'Stop it, Donald!'

'Every one of those ants,' said Mally, taking a deep breath and blowing out her cheeks, 'has got an aunt and an uncle an' little brothers an' . . .'

'This one hadn't,' said Donald, and ran away.

'S'awful to be so pretty,' said Velvet, looking after him. 'He's like an actress.'

'Actress my boot!' said Mally. 'He's a common murderer.'

'Likes to see things stop,' said Mi. 'Anybody's the same. You better go iron them muslins. Sooner you get them ironed sooner you see the piebald.'

'Be in towels yet,' said Velvet. 'Mine was too short last summer. It'll look like a ham frill this.'

'Got to get on,' said Mi. 'Frittering my morning away . . .' and disappeared.

'He won't go an' see that piebald without us?' said Velvet.

'What about the blasted muslins?' said Mally.

'Better go.'

'Here's Meredith! What's the matter, Merry?'

'Went down the street,' said Meredith. 'Looking at the rooks' nests. Dropped a splodge. A rook dropped a splodge . . .' She was wiping her eye furiously with her dress. 'Gummy,' she said. 'S'gummy stuff . . .'

'Get in under the tap,' said Velvet. 'It's lime. P'raps it's quick lime.'

Meredith ran blindly into the scullery holding her eye. The lime ran off at the touch of water.

On the scullery ledge was a board with four objects on it like babies in long clothes, old bath towels, used for keeping the best washing evenly damp. Mally cautiously undid the first.

'It's them,' she said, as though she had smelt a drain.

'What?' said Meredith.

'Muslin, ducky, for the Fair. Our muslins.'

'Muslin!' said Meredith, stiff with offence.

'Muslin,' said Mrs Brown from behind with a soft and heavy certainty. 'An' your white woolly pullovers on top. You'll be warm an' you'll be pretty. Get on upstairs and look over your stockings for holes.'

'STOCKINGS! We're not going to wear STOCKINGS!'

Mrs Brown sat down on the scullery chair.

'We'll get it all over,' she said. 'I'll run through it. You'll wear your long black Christmas stockings, WITH suspenders, fastened to them calico belts I bought you for the Christmas dance. You'll wear white petticoats that go with . . .'

'PETTICOATS!'

'Petticoats. That belongs to the dresses. (Or should.) You'll wear your muslins, an' your pullovers, an' your black lace shoes . . .'

'SHOES!'

'If you get a shock over everything, Velvet, you'll be ill an' you won't go at all. When you have muslins you have black shoes an' when you have black shoes you have stockings, or your heels rub . . .' (Edwina came through the street door.) '. . . an' you'll iron your muslins . . .'

'MUSLINS!' said Edwina, in exactly the same tone as the others.

'We've been through all that,' said Malvolia. 'Black shoes, black stockings, petticoats, suspenders, belts, pullovers . . . P'raps you'd like to sit down an' rest, D'wina? Go on, mother. We're to iron our muslins when?'

'Father's at the bottom of this . . .' muttered Edwina.

Mrs Brown reached for a long-clothes baby and unrolled it. 'Damp yet,' she said, trying it to her cheek. 'Soaking. They'll stay damp till the evening in the shade. You can iron them after tea. Go on and look over the stockings.'

Edwina, Malvolia, Meredith and Velvet passed through the little black door on to the stairs.

The canaries were singing and shouting in the breeding cages and the new wooden cage, recently put up by Meredith hung insecurely and crooked from the nail she had borrowed.

'You got it up,' said Velvet.

'It's all soft stuff in that wall,' said Meredith.

'Nail's going to come out,' said Mally – and they pulled out the drawers to look over the stockings.

Edwina held up her calico petticoat and measured it against her willowy figure. 'Dressed up in muslin!' she muttered.

'But I thought you liked dressing up,' said Mally. Edwina made no reply.

'Not dressed up enough is your trouble,' said Mally.

'It's time I had . . .' murmured Edwina, preoccupied and searching in a drawer . . . 'something . . . more . . .' and she found what she was looking for.

'I'll wear it over the muslin,' she said, holding up a tennis skirt of white flannel. 'It's a bit yellow. I've got a blue leather belt somewhere.'

'You'll make us look like a lot of dressed-up babies,' said Mally, half enviously. 'And mother won't let you.'

'I'll slip it on last thing,' said Edwina. 'Mother doesn't really care. It's father. The top'll look like quite a nice muslin shirt. I wish I could cut off the bottom.'

'Well, that's your trouble,' said Mally. 'My goodness, I wouldn't dare.'

'Where's it kept?' said Velvet.

'I had it in this bottom drawer,' said Edwina. Velvet turned and stared at her. After a pause she cleared her mind. 'I mean the piebald,' she amended.

'Oh, I meant to tell you!' said Edwina. 'They're going to raffle it tomorrow . . .'

'We know,' said Mally. 'Mi said so. And he's given us five shillings to have a ticket each. Even Donald.'

'*Lent* us,' said Velvet.

'I meant lent us. Where do we get the tickets?'

'They've got books at the Post Office. Books of tickets.'

'Let's go down and choose early ones.'

Edwina stuffed her skirt back in the drawer. The stockings lay in tight black balls on the bed.

'Come on, Meredith . . .'

'You go. I'll come in a minute.'

Edwina, Mally and Velvet clattered down the stairs and left Meredith stooping beside a cage.

Velvet put her head back in at the door.

'Shall I get yours or will you get your own?'

Meredith answered without looking round. 'The female's ill.'

'Which is it?' said Velvet, coming nearer.

'Africa,' said Meredith in a low voice.

Africa had been a male until she had been discovered to be a female. Now she lay in the palm of Meredith's hand, cloaking her eye with a little sagging hood.

'Is it the heat?' said Velvet, awed.

'I don't know,' said Merry. 'Get me the brandy. It's on the bottom shelf in the sideboard. In father's flask.'

While Velvet went for the brandy Meredith reached for her fountain-pen-filler, her left hand groping in a drawer, her eyes steady on the faint yellow bird.

'Draw the blind,' she said to Velvet who had returned. Velvet drew the blind behind the roaring cages and all song dropped like a flag when the wind has failed. There was a sickroom silence and anxiety.

'How much?' asked Velvet.

'One drop.'

But Africa died. She died in the palm of Merry's hand without a sound or a sigh or a movement. She seemed to miss a little breath and go smaller, and Velvet, startled, glanced round, as though a whiff of life had drifted out of Africa.

'I can't hold her now she's dead,' said Merry, her teeth chattering. 'Take her off my hand.'

'Tip her off,' said Velvet, wincing too.

'Go on. Take her! I'll scream.'

Velvet took her and laid her with distaste on the bed-table by Merry's bed.

'Horrible,' said Merry. 'It's a corpse. Poor little Africa. She's gone away.'

'I truthfully,' said Velvet in a low voice, 'thought I saw her go.'

'How?'

'When she went small. Just something.'

'What?'

'Air.'

'That was her spirit,' said Merry suddenly, looking at her intently. Velvet and Meredith stared at Africa.

'I should like her just not to be here,' said Merry savagely. 'I should like her to be all buried and finished.'

'Perhaps Mi will.'

'No, he won't. He'll say "Bury your own bird" .'

'Mother will,' said Velvet.

'Will she?'

'Yes, come on. Leave it there.' Velvet flipped up the blind again and all the canaries cantered straight into open song. 'Go on down to the Post Office an' I'll be down in a second.'

'Who's got the shilling?'

'Mally has,' said Velvet. 'They'll be waiting for you. Don't get my ticket for me!'

'No –' Merry ran down the street.

'Mother,' said Velvet, opening the scullery door. 'Africa's died.'

Mrs Brown turned. 'Merry know?'

'Yes, she died in her hand. Just now.'

'Where's Merry?'

'Gone down to the Post Office. But she can't touch Africa. She hates her dead. Could you bury her, do you think? She's on the table by Merry's bed.'

'I'll see to her,' said Mrs Brown. 'Bring her down.'

'I can't touch her either,' said Velvet. 'She's . . .'

Mrs Brown looked at her.

'You know when a thing's dead . . .' said Velvet uselessly. Then after a pause she went slowly upstairs and brought down the dead bird in her hand. Mrs Brown reached up to a shelf for a little cardboard box. She put Africa inside and shut the lid. Velvet raced down to the Post Office.

In the sultry midday, with the Hullocks steaming above them, a little group of parcel-posters and stamp-buyers was jesting over the book-tickets. Edwina and her sisters stood in the shadow, their eyes grave and full of choosing. They were weighing the flashing, unequal importance of numbers.

The blacksmith was having his joke.

'Stand up, gentlemen,' he shouted, 'the horse is yours! Shilling a go for a mad piebald gelding. Or is it a stallion, Mr Croom? Not clean gelded, eh? Thought as much. Mr Ede done it on the cheap an' left a chip.'

'Not a bad thing to have a horse for a shilling,' suggested Mr Croom. 'You can always sell it for something.'

'Not so easy done,' said the blacksmith. 'You got to feed it an' lodge it meanwhile.'

'Ede says it'll ride quiet,' said Mr Croom. 'He *says* it will. Anybody know?'

'I seen him ride it,' said a voice. 'Went along quiet an' dull. He had a basket on his arm too. An' he opened a gate and let the basket fall. Never turned a hair.'

'What's the matter with it that he wants to raffle it, then?'

'He can't tie it up an' he can't keep it in. Jumps any wall. Go sailing over the moon if you'd let it. Kink in its mind about being tied up or shut in. Ede's tired of catching it. Besides he's afraid it'll do a damage in the village. He bought it cheap in Lewes Market, but it's no good to him.'

Some tickets were bought but there was no rush on them.

Edwina walked out of the corner to the counter.

The raffle book was *one* to *two hundred*, got out in ink hurriedly by Mrs Ede.

'He'll likely make his ten pound on him,' said Mr Croom. 'That's more'n he paid for him at Lewes.'

Solemnly the four girls lined against the counter and gazed at the book.

'I've thought of forty-seven,' whispered Mally.

'But did you make yourself or did it come?'

'That's what I don't know.'

'I've got ten . . . printed on my brain, large . . . in red letters,' said Edwina.

Silence.

'It's like a visitation,' persisted Edwina in a whisper.

Silence.

'But perhaps I'm meant to avoid it,' she ended.

Each girl stretched her mind and tried to tremble to the finger of God.

'I'll have 119 please,' said Velvet unexpectedly and firmly to the postmistress.

She paid her shilling, and the other three watched her, envious and dismayed.

'What did you . . .' began Mally.

'I don't want to talk about it,' said Velvet, low, and walked out of the Post Office into the street.

The others followed her with tickets in their hands.

'We just took them anyhow,' said Edwina, rather cross. 'What's the good of thinking!'

'Have you got one for Donald?'

'Number One.'

'Well, there we are anyway,' said Mally. 'Let's go an' pin them in the Bible. It's dinner time.'

Meredith instantly thought of Africa. As they walked back towards the house Africa was like a yellow shade upon her mind. Where did she lie? Would she be visible again to the eye or was she packed up for ever? Mrs Brown called to them from the door. 'Wash your hands quick,' she said, 'it's hot dinner.'

'I'll wash mine in the scullery,' said Merry and fled through the sitting-room.

Velvet whispered to the others, 'Africa's dead.'

Mrs Brown turned off the scullery tap that Merry might hear what she said. 'Your little bird's buried,' she said. 'Cage is all cleaned an' I've put the cock in there. The greeny cock. But he's got no food or water yet. Run up an' see to him.'

Merry turned with streaming eyes and kissed her. 'I'll rearrange them,' she choked, and went upstairs to the bedroom.

They sat down to dinner without Mr Brown or Mi, and Mrs Brown brought in the joint. Merry joined them, a little flushed, but peaceful.

A squeaking and bleating came muffled through the wall.

'That's the last,' said mother. 'Father'll be in soon.'

'Row those sheep make,' said Mally.

Edwina got up to get the red jelly from the sideboard.

'We've taken five tickets, shilling tickets, for a raffle for the Fair tomorrow,' said Velvet. 'They're raffling that piebald.'

'The piebald?' said Mrs Brown, 'Ede getting rid of it? Well I'm not surprised.'

'But what'll father . . .'

'Time enough to worry when you get it,' said Mrs Brown. 'Got that jelly, D'wina? It's there behind the pickles.'

'Where's Donald?' said Velvet.

'Slep on. But he ought to be woke now. You get him, Velvet.'

Velvet got up and went out by the yard door. She pressed the spaniels back with her foot as they struggled and changed places, smelling the joint.

Jacob came wriggling and smiling round the wall. He was late in, having been down the village to the sea, watching the trippers unload from the charabancs.

The whole day's heat was shimmering in the yard. The

splendour of the heat stood upright like a tank of water. Dust moved in it and midges poured up and down. Immediately she faced the yard Velvet went into a vision. The bones and stones and boxes and dogs of the yard dropped away below and she was mounted on a cliff beside the piebald, on the hip of a cliff overlooking the sea. The sea was pale and a ship swam up in a haze on the sky. The piebald stared like a lunatic at the cobbled wall which bound his field. Velvet choked as she stared with him, and saw the grasses wave at the foot of the cobbles. The wall gave way as they cleared it and sank together, the sea rushing up. A gull's wing zipped and she saw the indigo shadow, and with her knees she felt the ribs spring in arcs from the horse's spine. His boundless heart rushed into hers. The soles of her feet cramped against the impending waters.

'I've woke!' called Donald from the shade where he lay, on a mattress in Miss Ada's unused cart – its shafts propped on an upright barrel. Velvet crossed the yard and opened the little door at the back of the cart. 'Get up,' she said, but the child only stared half-awake at the sky. She took him by his bare legs and pulled. His shirt left his pants and began to turn up over his arms.

'Can't walk. Carry me,' he said. His teeth chattered. 'I'm shivery,' he said, and bumped his heavy head on to her thin chest as she struggled with him.

'That's only sleep,' she said. 'It's dinner time. You've slept too long.'

Merry opened the sitting-room door. 'Are you coming?' she called.

'I've slept too long,' moaned Donald at the door, in Velvet's arms.

'Get down an' walk,' said Mrs Brown.

'Slept *too* long,' he wailed self-pityingly.

'A little tap-water an' you'll feel better,' said mother.

She took him and he wept a little and was carried away. He reappeared in a few minutes bright and silky. 'I slept too long,' he said in quite a different voice, engagingly, socially.

'Yes, we heard,' said Mr Brown who had come in. 'Get up on your chair now. Here's your plate.'

'The meat's sour,' said Donald instantly, putting his nose to his meat.

'Poor lot those sheep,' said Mr Brown. 'It's the drought. Bit ribby, weren't they, Mi?'

'Dog bin racin' 'em,' said Mi.

'It's sour,' said Donald, giving his plate a push.

Mrs Brown glanced over. 'He's got capers put on his. Take them off, D'wina.'

'It's you that's sour,' said D'wina to him, getting up and

stopping beside him. 'Oh . . . Mother, he's spat at me!'

'Spit came out,' said Donald, a little anxiously.

'Fractious,' said Mr Brown. 'Sit down, D'wina, and get on both. I heard Ede's going to raffle that piebald animal that got loose.'

There was no response. Everyone, thinking hard, ate silently.

'You oughter take a ticket, Velvet,' said Mr Brown genially.

'We've all . . . we've all taken tickets,' said Velvet softly, unable to believe her ears. Mr Brown's face changed. He had meant to make a joke.

'He'll be meat if you get him,' he said after a pause, and not genially at all.

Velvet's face flushed faintly.

'Cabbage is stringly,' said Donald, and created a diversion.

'He's possessed,' said Mr Brown vexedly. The condition of the sheep had annoyed him.

Edwina and Mally cleared the plates and brought in gooseberry fool. Velvet fetched the milk pudding from the oven. They started with fresh life on the fresh food.

'Want you s'afternoon, Mi,' said Mr Brown. The girls grew tense, and waited, spoons still.

''Bout five,' said Mr Brown, and the breath of anxiety was let out again, and the spoons moved on.

The chairs were pushed in. 'F'whatweave received . . . thank God!' they said as one voice and fled.

CHAPTER IV

The piebald cropped in just such a field, on just such a Hullock as Velvet had dreamed. There was the haze, and the ship. Mi, Edwina, Malvolia, Meredith and Velvet stood in a row leaning against the cobbled wall. There was a long and watchful silence. The wild thyme smelt warm and looked pink. The sea lay below, not blue but dove-grey. The coping of the wall was hot and rough.

'Stands marvellous,' said Mi at length.

Another long appreciative silence.

'See his bone . . .' said Mi.

Mi made a click with the gap in his teeth and turned to look at Velvet. 'What's that number of yours?'

'119.'

'Well there!'

'What?'

'You ought to have a horse!'

The piebald looked up and saw them. Stared. Then cropped again.

'Seems quiet,' said Edwina.

'Huh. No knowing. Think he's more than fifteen hands?'

'Think he's more,' said Velvet.

'See his white eye?'

They saw it. They saw everything. Their eyes, like birds' eyes, flickered over his startling patches of black and white. He was white in bold seas, and black in continents, marked in such a way that when he moved his white shoulders and his white quarters flashed, and his black body seemed to glide.

'Showy,' said Mi.

Velvet climbed the wall into the field.

'He'll be off!' said Mally warningly.

Velvet went among the hot grasses towards him. She knew him. She had already ridden him in her dream. He cropped, head towards her, but watched her coming. She walked steadily and straight and began to talk in low tones. He raised his head and looked at her, as firmly as she looked at him. She paused. He walked several paces towards her with confidence. No quirk or tremor or snort of doubt.

'See that!' said Mi, hanging against the wall.

They saw Velvet pat him and run her hand slowly down his neck on to his shoulder.

'She'll be that upset now,' said Mi, 'if she don't get him.'

Velvet moved away. The animal followed her, flashing and jaunty. He had a white mane, a long white tail, pink hooves, a sloping pastern, and he struck his feet out clean and hard as he walked.

'Isn't his neck thick?' said Edwina.

'Bit,' said Mi. 'Bin gelded late.'

The piebald, whose desires were gone, had kept his pride. He walked after Velvet like a stocky prince. Thick-necked, muscular, short and proud. He left her a few paces from the wall, and stood looking, then turned and cropped quietly.

'Gotter be back,' said Mi.

Velvet hung a moment longer by the wall, then all five in silence turned downhill. There was a wild snort behind them and the thunder of feet.

'He's off!' said Mi, turning sharp. 'It's set him off!'

The piebald had his white tail raised and his head arched like a Persian drawing. He was galloping down the field towards the corner.

'Stop! Stand! He's never going over that!'

The ground had dropped away so sharply at the far corner that the original builder of the cobbled wall, to keep his coping straight, had heightened the wall itself. It was five foot two at the end of the field, with a fine downhill take off. The horse sailed over like a dappled flying boat. It was a double spring. As he was high in the air he saw also to his hind feet and drew them up sharply.

'. . . AND to spare,' said Mi quietly, nodding his head. 'A horse like that'd win the National.'

'You don't mean it, Mi!'

'Gets his hocks under. Got heart. Grand take off. Then when he's up in the air he gives a kind of second hitch an' his feet tuck up so he's ony a body without legs. See him look before he took off? See his ears flitch forward and back again? You ony got to sit on him.'

'Oh Mi, why don't you ride?'

'. . . Got a nasty sort of look of Man-of-War too,' pursued Mi, unheeding.

'Who was Man-of-War?'

'Man-eatin' stallion,' said Mi.

'But a black and white horse like that doesn't look like anything to do with a race.'

'Ever hear of the Tetrarch?'

'No.'

'Looked like a rocking horse. Sorta dappled. Mr Persse his trainer was. One mornin' he was sitting eatin' his egg an' a stable lad rushed in an' screamed out, "That coloured horse can beat anything!" an' rushed out again.'

'And what did he win?'

'Didn't win anything so marvellous because they ran him as a two-year-old. But he sired twenty-seven thousand pounds!'

'How'd you know so much, Mi?'

'Used to read when I was up there,' Mi jerked his finger north, away from the sea.

'Why did the stable boy rush in?'

''Cause he won, didn't he, in the gallops in the morning.'

'The piebald Tetrarch?'

'He wasn't piebald. Not even grey. He was coloured. Grey and roan and white. Mottled. They got him for a mascot. Just for a stable companion. And he brought them a fortune.'

They walked down the slopes, wrapped in the eternal drama of the last being first.

'An' Mr Persse,' said Velvet, lifting her boy's face to the sky, 'he rushed out?' She wanted to sit again over the breakfast table with Mr Atty Persse. (The heavenly, escaping past –)

'He rushed out,' said Mi, warming, 'and he said: "Where's that goddam boy? I'll wring his neck!"'

'Why?'

'He had a feel the boy was right.'

'Well, and . . .'

'When you gotta good thing you keep it dark, don't you? Not shout all down the passages and right through the kitchen an' go back runnin' an' grinnin' like a fathead to the stables.'

'Mustn't anybody know when you think you're going to win a race?'

'Money passes,' said Mi. 'Fortunes. Thousands. Millions. It's like the City.'

'Do they race a lot in the North?' asked Velvet.

A landscape glittered behind her voice. There were icicles in it and savage fields of ice, great storms boiling over a flat countryside striped with white rails – a chess-board underneath a storm. Horses were stretched for ever at the gallop. Tiny men in silk were brave beyond bearing and sat on the horses like embryos with their knees in their mouths. The gorgeous names of horses were cried from mouth to mouth and circulated in a steam of fame. Lottery, The Hermit, the great mare Sceptre; the glorious ancestress Pocohontas, whose blood ran down like Time into her flying children; Easter Hero, the Lamb, that pony stallion.

'Race?' said Mi. '*All* the time.' And Velvet knew she was right.

'If I won that piebald,' said Velvet, 'I might ride him in the Grand National myself.'

'Girls can't ride in that,' said Mi contemptuously.

'Girls!' said Velvet, stopping still beside him so that they all drew up, 'who's to know I'm a girl?' She cupped her face in her two hands so that her straight hair was taken from it.

"Tisn't your hair,' said Mi, and his eyes fell on her chest. 'Flat's a pancake,' he said. 'You'd pass. There's a changing room though.'

'What'd you undress for?'

'Change your day things for your silks.'

'But you needn't undress to your skin. You could keep the same vest.'

'It *could* happen . . .' said Mi. 'It never has. You got to get your horse first.'

There was a silence as they walked.

'There he goes!' said Mi. The piebald was galloping below them, making as usual for the village. 'Heavy galloper. Plunges as he goes.'

'He's lovely,' breathed Velvet, simply. They started to run. Below them they could see a sweeper at the entrance to the village wave his broom at the horse.

The piebald leapt round him and galloped on. He disappeared

'Yes, but they think it's fresher if it comes tomorrow.'

'There!' Mally took her muslin dress and held it up by the puff sleeves.

It was stiff and fresh with ironing and almost stood by itself.

'It's like a paper bag,' said Velvet. 'Seems a pity to wear it. D'you want to start, Edwina, or shall I start mine?'

'I'm only wearing the top of mine. I've cut it off.'

'Gosh! You *have*? You've been an' cut it?'

All the three heads were raised towards Edwina as she took this step into the future. They contemplated her for a second then accepted her. Velvet got up and began to unroll her frock and lay it out.

'Ay . . . Merry. Look out! What's that . . . it's blood!'

Meredith shot one hand to her face. 'It's my nose,' she cried from under her hand.

'It's dropped on the muslin. Get me a rag!'

'Here's the ironing duster. Hold your head off the dresses! Lie down on the cold scullery floor. It's brick.'

Donald appeared in the doorway from the street and watched Meredith as she ran into the scullery holding the duster to her face.

'She hurt herself?' he asked.

'Her nose is bleeding,' said Velvet.

'I laugh when my nose bleeds,' said Donald.

'Your nose hasn't ever bled,' said Velvet briefly.

'I would laugh if it did,' said Donald, and went.

'Merry marked her muslin?' said Mrs Brown coming in from the scullery.

'Great drop,' said Mally.

'Put it under cold water,' said Mrs Brown. 'Not a touch of soap an' no hot. It sets it. It's Africa's made her nose bleed.'

'I'll go with the steak tomorrow then,' said Velvet.

'There's the Fair an' all. She better keep still.'

'What steak's that?'

'Father said Mr Cellini wanted a steak before breakfast.'

'Funny time,' said Mrs Brown.

'I'd like to go anyway,' said Velvet. 'I might see the chestnut.'

That night, before the Fair, they went to bed early.

'Africa!' said Meredith, wildly and suddenly in the middle of the night. And slept again.

Chapter V

Velvet's dreams were blowing about the bed. They were made of cloud but had the shapes of horses. Sometimes she dreamt of bits as women dream of jewellery. Snaffles and straights and pelhams and twisted pelhams were hanging, jointed and still in the shadows of a stable, and above them went up the straight damp oiled lines of leathers and cheek straps. The weight of a shining bit and the delicacy of the leathery above it was what she adored. Sometimes she walked down an endless cool alley in summer, by the side of the gutter in the old redbrick floor. On her left and right were open stalls made of dark wood and the buttocks of the bay horses shone like mahogany all the way down. The horses turned their heads to look at her as she walked. They had black manes hanging like silk as the thick necks turned. These dreams blew and played round her bed in the night and the early hours of the morning.

She got up while the sisters were sleeping and all the room was full of book-muslin and canaries singing. 'How they can sleep! . . .' she said wonderingly when she became aware of the canaries singing so madly. All the sisters lay dreaming of horses. The room seemed full of the shapes of horses. There was almost a dream-smell of stables. As she dressed they were stirring, shifting and tossing in white heaps beneath their cotton bedspreads. The canaries screamed in a long yellow scream, and grew madder. Then Velvet left the room and softly shut the door and passed down into the silence of the cupboard-stairway.

In her striped cotton dress with a cardigan over it she picked up the parcel of steak that had been left on the kitchen table and drank the glass of milk with a playing card on the top of it that Mrs Brown had left her overnight. Then she got a half packet of milk chocolate from the string drawer, and went out to saddle Miss Ada.

In the brilliance of a very early summer morning they went off together, Miss Ada's stomach rumbling with hunger. Velvet fed her from a bag of oats she had brought with her up on the top of the hill. There were spiders' webs stretched everywhere across the gorse bushes.

Coming down over the rolling grass above Kingsworthy, Velvet could see the feathery garden looking like tropics asleep down below. Old Mr Cellini by a miracle grew palms and bananas and mimosa in his. Miss Ada went stabbing and sliding down the steep hillside, hating the descent, switching her tail with vexation.

Velvet tied Miss Ada to the fence, climbed it and crept through the spiny undergrowth into the foreign garden. There was not a sound. Not a gardener was about. The grass was like moss, spongy with dew so that each foot sank in and made a black print which filled with water. Then she looked up and saw that the old gentleman had been looking at her all the time.

He had on a squarish hat and never took his eyes off her. He was standing by a tree. Velvet's feet went down in the moss as she stood. His queer hat was wet, and there was dew on the shoulders of his ancient black frockcoat which buttoned up to the neck; he looked like someone who had been out all the night.

Raising one black-coated arm he rubbed his lips as though they were stiff, and she could see how frail he was, unsteady, wet.

'What have you come to do?' he said in a very low voice.

'Sir?'

He moved a step forward and stumbled.

'Are you staying? Going up to the house?'

'The house.'

'Stay here,' he said, in an urgent tone which broke.

Velvet dropped her own eyes to her parcel, for she knew he

was looking at her and how his eyeballs shone round his eyes.

'How did you come?' (at last). She looked up. There was something transparent about his trembling face.

'On our pony,' she said. 'I rode. She's tied to the fence. There's some meat here for the cook, to leave at the back door.'

'Do you like ponies?' said the rusty voice.

'Oh . . . yes. We've only the one.'

'Better see mine,' said the old gentleman in a different tone.

He moved towards her, and as they walked he rested one hand on her shoulder. They walked till they came to the open lawns and passed below some fancy bushes.

He stopped. And Velvet stopped.

'. . . if there was anything you wanted very much,' he said, as though to himself.

Velvet said nothing. She did not think it was a question.

'I'm very much too old,' said the old gentleman. 'Too old. What did you say you'd brought?'

'Meat,' said Velvet. 'Rump.'

'Meat,' said the old gentleman. 'I shan't want it. Let's see it.'

Velvet pulled the dank parcel out of her bag.

'Throw it away,' said the old gentleman, and threw it into a bush.

They walked on a few paces.

Something struck her on the hip as she walked. It was when his coat swung out. He looked down too, and unbuttoned his coat and slowly took it off. Without a word he hung it over his arm, and they walked on again, he in his black hat and black waistcoat and shirt-sleeves.

'Going to the stables,' said he. 'Why, are you fond of horses?'

There was something about him that made Velvet feel he was going to say good-bye to her. She fancied he was going to be carried up to Heaven like Elisha.

'Horses,' he said. 'Did you say you had horses?'

'Only an old pony, sir.'

'All my life I've had horses. Stables full of them. You like 'em?'

'I've seen your chestnut,' said Velvet. 'Sir Pericles. I seen him jump.'

'I wish he was yours, then,' said the old gentleman, suddenly and heartily. 'You said you rode?'

'We've on'y got Miss Ada. The pony. She's old.'

'Huh!'

'Not so much *old*,' said Velvet hurriedly. 'She's obstinate.'

He stopped again.

'Would you tell me what you want most in the world . . .? Would you tell me that?'

He was looking at her.

'Horses,' she said. 'Sir.'

'To ride on? To own for yourself?'

He was still looking at her, as though he expected more.

'I tell myself stories about horses,' she went on, desperately fishing at her shy desires. 'Then I can dream about them. Now I dream about them every night. I want to be a famous rider, I should like to carry despatches, I should like to get a first at Olympia, I should like to ride in a great race, I should like to have so many horses that I could walk down between the two rows of loose-boxes and ride what I chose. I would have them all under fifteen hands, I like chestnuts best, but bays are lovely too, but I don't like blacks.'

She ran out the words and caught her breath and stopped.

At the other end of the golden bushes the gardener's lad passed in the lit, green gap between two rhododendron clumps with a bodge on his arm. The old gentleman called to him. Then he walked onwards across the grass and Velvet and the gardener's boy followed after. They neared a low building of old brick with a square cobbled yard outside it. The three passed in under the arched doorway.

'Five,' said the old gentleman. 'These are my little horses. I like little ones too.' He opened the gate of the first loose-box and a slender chestnut turned slowly towards him. It had a fine, artistic head, like horses which snort in ancient battles in Greece.

'Shake hands, Sir Pericles,' said the old gentleman, and the little chestnut bent its knee and lifted a slender foreleg a few inches from the ground.

'But I've no sugar,' said the old gentleman. 'You must do your tricks for love today.'

He closed the door of the loose-box.

In the next box was a grey mare.

'She was a polo pony,' he said, 'belonged to my son.' He still wore his hat, black waistcoat, and shirt sleeves. He looked at the gardener's boy. 'I need not have bothered you,' he said. 'Of course the grooms are up.' But the gardener's boy, not getting a direct order, followed them gently in the shadow of the stables.

The grey mare had the snowy grey coat of the brink of age. All the blue and dapple had gone out of her, and her eyes burnt black and kind in her white face. When she had sniffed the old gentleman she turned her back on him. She did not care for stable-talk.

In the next loose-box was a small pony, slim and strong, like a miniature horse. He had a sour, suspicious pony face. There were two more loose-boxes to come and after that a gap in the stables. Far down the corridor between the boxes Velvet could see where the big horses stood. Hunters and carriage horses and cart horses.

The gardener's boy never stirred. The old gentleman seemed suddenly tired and still.

He moved and pulled a piece of paper from the pocket of his waistcoat. 'Get me a chair,' he said very loud. But before the boy could move a groom came running swiftly with a stable chair.

The old gentleman sat down and wrote. Then he looked up.

'What's your name?' he said and looked at Velvet.

'Velvet Brown,' said Velvet.

'Velvet Brown,' he said and tapped his pencil on his blue cheek. Then wrote it down. 'Sign at the bottom, boy,' he said to the gardener's boy, and the boy knelt down and wrote his careful name. 'Now you sign too,' he said to the groom.

The old gentleman rose and Velvet followed him out into the sunlight of the yard. 'Take that paper,' he said to her, 'and you stay there,' and he walked from her with his coat on his arm.

He blew himself to smithereens just round the corner. Velvet never went to look. The grooms came running.

The warm of the brick in the yard was all she had to hold on to. She sat on it and listened to the calls and exclamations. 'Gone up to Heaven, Elisha,' she thought, and looked up into the sky. She would like to have seen him rising, sweet and sound and happy.

In the paper in her hand she read that five of his horses belonged to her.

Taking the paper, avoiding the running and the calling of the household, she crept back through the garden to Miss Ada. When she got home she could not say what had happened, but cried and trembled and was put to bed and slept for hours under the golden screams of the canaries. At four o'clock Mally burst in and cried:

'They've drawn! They've drawn! We've got the piebald!'

'Whose ticket?' said Velvet faintly.

'Yours, oh yours. Are you ill?'

'Mr Cellini's dead,' whispered Velvet. 'Just round the corner!'

Mally stood transfixed to the floor. 'They're bringing the piebald home,' she said, staring. She could not be bothered by the death of Mr Cellini.

Hearing a sound she ran to the window.

'It's here, it's down at the very door!' she called.

'Get mother,' said Velvet, who could not move because the room was swaying.

Velvet went to Mr Cellini's funeral. As an heiress. She did not bury him in her heart till then. The nights before she had seen him only smashed, but living. Seen his face with its looks. Could a look be smashed? That night before the funeral, the horses in her dreams galloped downhill. By the head down, like rockets. But when she had been to his funeral and walked in her winter black tarpaulin mackintosh, among his relations, her eyes like sad lights in her head and her bony teeth, veiled in gold, like a war chief's trophy across her thin face, then she knew he was still and folded and she could turn to the horses.

Mr Brown was quite agreeable to the horses. It was all in the local papers, and lovely pictures of the girls looking like three gazelles. And Velvet? Velvet looking like Dante when he was a little girl.

Mr Brown saw it was good for trade. 'You'll be wanting a field,' he said.

'But they've been kept in,' said Velvet.

'Keep them in you won't, my girl. And it's summer.'

'But next winter?' said Velvet.

'Next winter'll take care of itself.'

There were six horses now.

The strange piebald, won at the Fair, had been put that night by Mi into the Tablet Gully. In this narrow valley there was a tablet to a dead man, but the name had gone. The tablet said he died gathering moss in the snow, overwhelmed in a snowstorm and fallen down a mountain.

In all the ninety miles of the Hullocks there was no moss; there was no snow; no mountains to fall down, but only the curving breasts of hillsides. Still the legend of the nameless man remained intact, and here the piebald grazed, flashing like black and ivory in the dapple of the valley. He was six miles from the village and he had not yet attempted to break loose. He could not see a chimney or a roof from where he cropped, nor hear any sound but the sheep who filled his valley. The food was new to him, richer than in the high burnt-up fields above the village, and his attention was caught, and his nostalgia for the time assuaged.

Now that the excitement in the village had blown out, Mr Brown began, and well he might, to fuss about expense.

'A man who leaves a butcher's daughter five horses might leave her some money to keep them with,' he said.

'Why do you suppose he left them to you, Velvet?' asked Mally for the hundredth time.

Velvet looked at the table and said, 'It was a joke he made with himself at the last minute.'

'Just leave her,' said Mrs Brown calmly. 'Don't keep on asking, Malvolia.'

*

It was the green summer dawn of the day the horses were due to arrive. Velvet woke up and she could hear the birds' feet walking up and down on the roof.

'Swi . . . ipe!' said one canary in a very loud voice, and all the sisters woke.

At breakfast Velvet sat back in her chair, a little yellow.

'Chew your toast well,' said Mrs Brown, 'and don't drink your milk. It'll lay loose.'

'Is it eleven or half-past that they're coming?' asked Edwina.

'Don't talk about it,' said Mrs Brown. 'Leave the subject alone.' Velvet faintly chewed.

At nine she had a strong drink of peppermint, and some whitish powder of her mother's choosing. Sitting close to the kitchen stove she slowly recovered. Every now and then the sisters looked in at the door at her anxiously.

'Shall I ever grow out of it, mother?' asked Velvet once.

'Yes,' said Mrs Brown, like a palmist, 'when you're sixteen.'

The room, crammed with furniture, was faintly green as the light struck through the cactus window. The cactus pots were arranged on glass shelves. They were well cared for, of different sorts, and six of them were in peculiar flower. The street door was shut, the yard door was open. On one side of the room the mahogany sideboard stretched from wall to wall, with its bottles of vinegar, old decanters, a set of green wineglasses, salts, peppers, A1 and Demon sauces, and in the middle the Sheffield dish cover, thirty inches long, that covered the joint on Sundays. The Albert lamp, used at night in winter, stood on a table by itself. The dinner table, round, covered with a Paisley cloth, filled the centre of the room. The window on the street was blocked with cineraria. Motes of blue from the flowers floated on the belly on the dish cover.

Velvet held the shell-box of paper horses in her hand, like something to which she was being disloyal.

All the girls had on striped cotton frocks too big for their thin bodies. Edwina and Malvolia had belted theirs in with leather belts bought in the village, but the dresses of Meredith and Velvet hung loose on them.

'Half the village outside in the street,' said Mr Brown complacently, coming in with his pipe out of the sunlight. 'Seems to have got round.'

'Not surprising,' said Mrs Brown, 'with three reporters coming here.'

'This family's cut out for the newspapers,' said Mr Brown, putting his arm on her vast shoulder. Mrs Brown said nothing.

'Got your strong knickers on?' said Mrs Brown presently.

'Yes,' said Velvet.

'What's that for?' said Mr Brown. 'She's not going to ride this string of racers she's getting.'

'They're hacks. Little hacks,' said Velvet.

Mrs Brown rose.

'See to Donald,' she said. 'He's frittering his time.'

But at that moment, as they fidgeted, the door opened and Donald walked in, all buttoned up and shining and his brow as black as thunder.

'Who's buttoned you?' asked Mrs Brown.

'Mi's buttoned me,' said Donald savagely.

'Huh!' said Mrs Brown.

They measured each other.

'You forgot me,' said Donald.

Mrs Brown said nothing. Donald strutted down the room and out into the yard.

'Seems upset,' said Mr Brown.

Mi came in.

'I'll thank you not to button him again,' said Mrs Brown.

'Any sign of the horses?' said Mr Brown.

'Early yet,' said Mi, 'but the whole village is waiting on the Green.'

'Most of 'em's outside,' said Mr Brown motioning to the flower-window with his pipe. The flower-window was black with faces. 'Ask Mr Croom in.'

Mi opened the door and spoke through the crack of it. Mr Croom, the grocer, came in.

'Wonderful,' said Mr Croom, 'Velvet gettin' them horses.'

Mr Brown got up and looked at his watch, which lay under a tumbler on the sideboard. 'Getting on time,' he said, and Velvet, sitting at the stove, felt suddenly light and warm.

'Whur's the little chap?' said Mr Croom. 'Donald?'

'I'm here,' said Donald through the half-open yard door.

'I got silver an' gold for you,' said Mr Croom.

'More'n he deserves,' said Mrs Brown.

Donald came in brightly with his sweet smile.

'Silver an' gold,' said Mr Croom, holding out a net bag full of chocolate coins covered in silver and gold paper. 'Foreign,' he said, 'Dutch stuff. But Donald won't care.'

'Say thank you,' said Mrs Brown.

'Thank you,' said Donald, with his heart in his face. He took the bag and wandered away.

'Fine chap,' said Mr Croom.

'Cup of coffee, Mr Croom?' said Mrs Brown.

'If you're making any.' Mr Croom peered through the street window. 'Quite a stir in the village.'

'Yes,' said Mr Brown.

' 'Strordinary thing,' said Mr Croom. 'Like a tale.'

'Yes,' said Mr Brown again. 'Took to Velvet, I suppose.'

'Ever seen him before, Velvet?' said Mr Croom.

'Yes,' said Velvet faintly. 'Once. At the Lingdown Horse Show.'

'Better leave her,' said Mrs Brown. 'Turns her stomach.'

'Well, well . . .' said Mr Croom regretfully. 'Yes.'

Mr Cellini swam across the ceiling, frailer than memory, like a cobweb.

Mr Brown rose again and looked at his watch on the sideboard. 'Should be here,' he said.

'Where's your gold and silver bag?' said Velvet suddenly to Donald.

'I put it away,' said Donald.

'Don't you want it?' said Mr Croom, hurt.

'No,' said Donald. 'I might want it some day.'

'What you got there instead?'

'It's my spit bottle,' said Donald, holding up a medicine bottle on a string.

He walked a little further into the room and dangled the

bottle, showing a little viscous fluid in the bottom. 'That's my spit,' he said.

'He's collecting his spit,' said Velvet.

Donald applied his mouth at the top and with difficulty dribbled a little more spit into the neck.

'D'you let him do those sort o' things?' said Mr Brown to Mrs Brown.

'Take it outside,' said Mrs Brown. 'Here's your coffee, Mr Croom.'

Edwina, Malvolia and Meredith burst the street door open with the crowd behind their shoulders. 'Over the hill! You can see them!' Meredith panted, and all three disappeared.

Mrs Brown picked up Donald, his spit bottle swinging. 'Put your cardigan on,' she said to Velvet. 'Keep warm an' you'll be all right.'

They all went out, the crowd following them, and turned up the chalk road.

'Where's Mi?' said Velvet suddenly.

'Got a half dozen sheep to fetch,' said Mr Brown. 'Be here any minute.'

'Poor Mi,' said Velvet, and walked on, rapt with happiness.

Over the brow of the hill five horses moved down towards them.

'Ther's three grooms. My word, ther's three of them,' said Mally, who had joined the procession. The grooms were walking the horses, two horses to a groom, then one alone at the back. As they reached the foot of the grass slope and stepped on to the flashing chalky road in the sun, the black crêpe could be seen on the arm of each walking groom. They were bowler-hatted, and round each bowler a band of crêpe was tied. The head groom, walking in front with the grey mare and Sir Pericles, had a rosy face and a fine black coat of good cloth. The others wore dark grey.

The horses were halted at the entrance to the village.

The head groom produced a slip of paper. 'Miss Velvet Brown?' he asked. Mr Brown stepped forward, Velvet close behind. Her thin face shone, smile alight, frock ballooned under cardigan, legs bare and scratched. 'I'm Velvet,' she said.

She walked up to Sir Pericles, transfigured, touched him gently on his neck, took the rein from the groom.

'We'll go down to the house,' she said softly. 'I'll lead this one home.'

'Better let me,' said the groom. Velvet stared at him, shook her head, and walked on leading the shining horse.

'Daft today,' said Mr Brown to the groom.

'Mind she don't let him go then,' said the groom.

The procession went on, Velvet first with her horse, Mr Brown at her elbow, the horses and the village people following. 'Keep the boys back! Don't let them frighten the horses!' said the old head groom.

'Keep back there,' said Mr Croom mildly, and the boys ran and skipped. Edwina and Malvolia and Meredith went ahead, turning to look over their shoulders.

'Better stop!' called Edwina.

The procession drew up and halted as it reached the street. Half a dozen sheep had arrived unexpectedly from a farm for the slaughter-house, and Mi was striving to get the last three in. He ran about in his Sunday clothes, put on for the arrival of the horses. They could hear him cursing. The three sheep skipped, butted and ran. 'Yer poor slut!' yelled Mi to the last one, bounding like a hare to keep it out of the main road. He turned it, and the last of the sheep went dingily behind the great wooden door. With the clatter of delicate feet on brick the horses moved on till they reached the sunny square before the cottage.

Donald was swinging his bottle before the door. He had not kept up with the procession.

'Keep that child in!' called Mr Brown. But Donald swung his bottle gently, and Mrs Brown did no more than lay a finger on his head.

The horses were drawn up facing the doorway and the second groom took over the bunch of leather reins. They ran like soft straps of silk over his fingers, narrow, polished, and flexible.

'Better take this into the house and read it over,' suggested the head groom to Mr Brown, handing him a typewritten sheet.

Mr Brown glanced at it and called to Velvet. Together they went in at the door and sat down at the little fern table inside. Mr Brown pushed the ferns gently to one side and laid out the sheet.

'One chestnut gelding. 14 hands. Seven years old. *Sir Pericles*. 1 snaffle bit, bridle, noseband and standing martingale. 1 Ambrose saddle, leathers and stirrups. 1 pair webbing girths.'

And underneath this Velvet wrote 'Velvet Brown'.

'One grey polo pony. Mare. 15 hands. Nine years old. *Mrs James*. 1 straight pelham, etc. . . . martingale . . . soft saddle and sewn girths.'

And underneath Velvet wrote 'Velvet Brown'.

'1 child's pony, chestnut. 12.2 hands. Gelding. *George*. Snaffle bit and double bit. Soft saddle and sewn girths, etc.'

And Velvet wrote 'Velvet Brown'.

'1 cob pony, for hacking or cart. 13.3 hands, dark bay

gelding. *Fancy*. 1 double bit, etc. . . . . old leather saddle,
and harness for cart.'

'Velvet Brown.'

'1 Dartmoor filly, two years old, unbroken. 11 hands.
Halter only. *Angelina*.'

'Velvet Brown.'

When Velvet had written her name for the fifth time, carefully, in
ink, and with her breath held tight, her father touched her arm,
and they both returned to the sunlight of the street. Mr Brown
gave the paper to the head groom.

'What are you doing with them straight away?' said the groom.

'Turning them into a field of mine,' said Mr Brown.

The groom hesitated. 'Warm weather, but they've none on
'em been out at night yet. Won't hurt the little filly.'

'They'll have to be out now,' said Mr Brown, with a slight rise
of voice, as though he were being dictated to.

'Will they eat sugar?' said Mally.

'All except the grey mare,' said the groom. 'She likes apple.'

Mally brought sugar out of her cotton pocket. Meredith went
for an apple.

'Shall you be selling them, sir?' said the groom, a little
hesitatingly to Mr Brown.

'They're mine!' said Velvet suddenly.

'We've not decided anything,' said Mr Brown. Velvet's soul became several sizes too large for her, her mouth opened, and she struggled with speech. Mrs Brown's hand fell on her shoulder, and her soul sank back to its bed.

'I suppose you are fixed up with a man?' said the head groom tentatively. 'I have a place myself, but . . .' he made a gesture towards the other two grooms.

'I'm a butcher,' said Mr Brown firmly. 'My girl goes and gets herself five horses. Five! We've seven all told, with that piebald. If she has to have horses she must look after 'em. We've fields in plenty, and there's oats in the shed, and I've four girls all of an age to look after horses. Beyond that I won't go. I'll have no fancy stables here. I'm a plain man and a butcher, and we've got to live.'

'Eh, yes,' said the little old rosy head groom. 'Shall we unsaddle them and turn them into the field for you?'

'Saddles'll have to go in the slaughter-house,' said Mr Brown. 'Through with them sheep yet?' he said to Mi.

'Ain't begun,' said Mi.

'Well then, you can put the saddles in the sun here on the wood rail, and lead 'em to the field in the bridles. Head collars they have on 'em. P'raps you'd better leave the bridles here.'

The head groom went up to the girths of Sir Pericles, but Velvet's thin hand was on his arm. 'I'm going to try them all first,' she said.

Mr Brown heard what she said, though he made no sign. He looked at Donald, then at his wife. She made no sign either.

'Fetch your gold sweets now!' said Mr Brown heavily and with unreality to Donald, tweaking his chin, and retired from the whole scene towards the slaughter-house.

'Let's go round to the field,' said Velvet, with confidence, to the groom.

'Wait a bit,' said Mrs Brown. 'You'll have a little something first. Edwina, there's that bottle of port. Bring it out. And glasses. Mr Croom you'll join too, a drop won't do anybody any harm.'

Edwina and Mally brought out the fern table, a tin one, the sacred table that was never moved.

Velvet as the heroine, Edwina as the eldest, the head groom as the guest, and Mrs Brown as the hostess sat down at the table and sipped a sip from the thick glasses of port. The village stood round at a respectful distance, and Mally and Meredith walked among the horses. Sir Pericles drooped his neck and nuzzled by the head groom's pockets. The second grooms shared a glass between them. Then they all went up to the field to try the horses.

Velvet mounted Sir Pericles. She had ridden Miss Ada for

eight years, hopped her over bits of brushwood and gorse-bushes, and trotted her round at the local gymkhana. Once she had ridden a black pony belonging to the farmer at Pendean. She had a natural seat, and her bony hands gathered up the reins in a tender way. But she had never yet felt reins that had a trained mouth at the end of them, and, as she cantered up the slope of the sunny field with the brow of the hill and the height of the sky in front of her, Sir Pericles taught her in three minutes what she had not known existed. Her scraggy, childish fingers obtained results at a pressure. The living canter bent to right or left at her touch. He handed her the glory of command.

When she slid to the ground by the side of the head groom she was speechless, and leant her forehead for a second on the horse's flank.

'You ride him a treat,' said the groom. 'You done a bit of riding.'

'Never ridden anything but her old pony,' said Mi, his hair rising in pride.

'The mare here's harder,' said the groom. 'Excitable, and kind of tough.'

He shot Velvet's light body and cotton frock into this second saddle. Her sockless feet, leather-shod, nosed for the stirrups. The groom shortened the leathers till they would go no more, and then tied knots in them. Mrs James, the mare, broke into a sweat at once. She flirted her ears wildly back and forwards, curved her grey neck, shook her bit, gave backward glances with her black eyes, like polished stones in her pale face.

'Mind! She don't start straight! She'll leap as she starts, and then she'll settle. She was Mr Frank's polo pony an' she's not really nervous but she's keen.'

There was scum on the mare's neck already, and the reins carved it off on to the leather as she shook her head. Mrs Brown, holding Donald by the wall, watched quietly. Edwina, Mally and Merry sat on the gate.

'Hang on!' said the groom, and let go. Mrs James, with a tremendous leap, started up the field. Her nostrils were distended, her ears pricked with alarm. She thought she carried a ghost. She could not feel anything on her back, yet her mouth was held. Velvet, whose hand had slipped down to the pommel of the saddle at the first leap, settled more steadily and lifted her hand to the reins. Mrs James snorted as she cantered, like a single-cylindered car. She was not difficult to ride once the first start had been weathered. They rounded the field together; then Velvet got up on the pony George. George threw her as soon as her cotton frock touched his back.

'Get up again,' said the head groom and held the pony tighter.

'Walk him, walk him,' said the groom warningly. 'Trot before you canter or he'll buck!'

George stuck his head out in an ugly line, and Velvet tried gently to haul him in. The whites of his eyes gleamed and his nose curled. He snatched at the bit when he felt her pressure and stretched his neck impatiently. Velvet's lips could not tighten, there was too much gold; but her eyes shone. She twirled the ends of the long reins and caught him hard, first on one shoulder, then on the other.

'She'll be off!' said Edwina.

'Not she!' said Mi. 'It's what he's asking for.'

George curved his neck and flirted archly with his bit, then trotted smartly back to the gate. Velvet dismounted and turned to Fancy, the cob.

Fancy was no faster than Miss Ada, and somewhat her build. He trotted round the field sedately.

'That's the lot,' said the groom. 'The filly's not broke.'

'I must try George again,' said Velvet.

'You bin on the lot,' said Mrs Brown. 'Come home now.'

'But Merry and Mally . . .'

'The horses'll get all of a do,' said the head groom, 'if they get too many on 'em. Better let them graze now, and tomorrow they'll be more themselves.'

The horses were turned loose and the saddlery carried back to the slaughter-house, where it was straddled over iron hook-brackets among the sheep's bodies.

The head groom stayed to midday dinner. The two others went down to the inn. It was Irish stew, with dumplings and onions. As the groom ate, he gave Velvet advice on how to catch the horses. His hat with the crêpe on it was laid on the sideboard.

'They haven't been out since last summer, and they're sure to be a bit wild at first. But you want to be up there, sitting on the wall, and just feeding them and coaxing them for a bit before you try to catch them. Mrs James she's wily. Sir Pericles'll do anything in the world you tell him. He knows a lot and what he knows is all pure goodness. Mrs James is what you might call worldly wise. The pony's just pure cuss. He'll jump his own height if you can ever get him to believe in you. You can use a bit of stick on him. He's suspicious of kindness. But never touch Sir Pericles with anything. He'll break his heart and go sour. Fancy, she's no temperament. The little one, Angelina, wants playing with an' fondling, like you might fondle this dog here.' Jacob grinned and bowed.

'Nice dog,' added the groom. Jacob trembled with expectation. But the groom, pulling a piece of gristle out of his mouth, only laid it on the edge of his plate.

'You haven't asked about food, Velvet,' said Edwina. But Velvet, who couldn't manage dumplings and onions, looked more ready to be carried to bed.

'Food now,' said the groom. 'But they're to be out to grass entirely? Well, well . . . They'll just have to get accustomed to it. It's to be hoped they won't blow their bellies out the first day. But the grass is thin up there and that's a mercy. If they get colic you'll have to bring 'em in and sweat 'em and draught 'em. Whisky and rum together's the thing.'

'Half and half?' said Mi abruptly.

The groom looked at him. 'You'll be taking 'em on, I daresay?' he said hopefully.

'Mi won't waste his time,' said Mr Brown with authority. 'The girls must learn what there is to learn.'

'Leave it, leave it,' said Mrs Brown. 'It'll settle itself.'

'My plate makes me retch,' whispered Velvet to her mother.

'Grumble, grumble, grumble,' said Mr Brown, who had heard.

'Ho! I gotta huge *Huge* caterpillar in my greens!' said Donald, holding it up.

'It's dead!' said Mally. Velvet put her face in her hands.

Mrs Brown rose and took a plate off the sideboard. 'Put it there, Donald,' she said firmly, 'and not another word about it.'

'Let me see it,' said Merry, leaning forward. Mr Brown looked up, frowning. 'There's manners about caterpillars,' he said sharply. 'Put them aside and *say nothing*.'

'It's done me!' said Velvet through her hands. 'Can I go?'

'Yes you can go,' said her mother. Mr Brown looked up again. 'No good keeping her,' said Mrs Brown. 'She'll vomit.'

CHAPTER VI

'Donald yelling on the Green!' called Mrs Brown from the scullery.

Mi, with a bridle on his knees, in the living-room, rose and looked through the flower-window.

'Mally's got him up in front on Mrs James,' he said.

'S'e all right?'

'Can't see what's wrong with him. He's screaming awful.'

'Mally,' called Mrs Brown, opening the front door. 'Stop it. He's got a pin or something.'

Mrs James was cantering jerkily round and round the Green at what Mally believed to be a show canter. Donald, sitting on the edge of the saddle in front of Mally, had his arms over her arms and his bare legs were sinking beneath her knees, preventing her grip. He was scarlet in the face, his mouth was open, and he was screaming. His head jerked madly up and down as Mrs James bounded. With difficulty Mally pulled up.

'Can't get off,' called Mally (for Donald was half underneath her), then slid off in a heap with the child in her arms. Mrs James sprang away in fear and trotted into the yard. Donald, sobbing, began at once to search in the grass.

'Whatever's the matter, Donald?' said Mrs Brown from the doorway.

'Lost my sixpence. My chocolate sixpence,' screamed Donald, hysterically turning over every tuft.

'Good God, is that all?' said Mally, rubbing her knee. She got up and went after Mrs James.

'Lost his sixpence,' said Mrs Brown to Mi, closing the door and returning to the scullery.

'Ain't lost his nerve,' said Mi, polishing the bit.

'Lot o' work we get out o' you, Mi!' said the butcher, coming in from the shed. 'Place slimy with sheep stomach! Get on cleaning, do. Bits and leathers and irons and horses . . .' He disappeared again.

Mi grinned, put the bit on the sideboard and followed him. The little living-room was dark and empty. Jacob parted the fringe of the sofa-covering with his beaded nose and stole out, dragging his hindquarters after him with a yawn. He glanced round, grinned too, and leaped upon the sofa, turned round once or twice, scraped primevally with his foot and lay down.

Mi stuck his head back through the slaughter-shed door.

'Ha!' he said, and sprang for the sofa. Jacob was underneath again in a flash of white.

When the horses had been with the Browns a month, life readjusted itself and everything was easier than had been thought.

The horses had lost flesh a little in the dry, sea-blown field, and were very slightly out of condition. Mi knew it, but did not speak of it to Velvet. Velvet frowned, and put her fingers into small hollows on the haunches, but said nothing. On the whole it was as well, for, corned-up as the horses had been when they arrived, the four girls would have had much more difficulty with them.

In the mornings they rode them in the field, and Mi, when he could sneak away, constructed jumps out of old packing cases, branches and bean poles, carrying up his precious hammer and nails. In the late afternoons they cantered over the Hullocks high up above the sea, preferably just before sunset. Mi watched them go off with a queer look in his eye, a look old Dan had worn when he saw Araminty Brown strike out from the brim of the land. There are men who like to make something out of women.

Velvet and Edwina usually rode Sir Pericles or Mrs James. Mally liked her battles with George, and Meredith, who never knew sufficiently what she was doing, was safest and happiest on Fancy.

'What shall we do when the summer's over?' said Velvet one evening to Edwina, as they rode along a chalk track on a ridge. 'We can't keep Sir Pericles and Mrs James out.'

'It'll be murder,' said Edwina.

'Mother'll do something with father,' said Velvet.

While they cantered in a stream Merry always formed the tail. She went with a loose rein and trusted God. Fancy plodded along and minded his path. Merry liked the air whistling round her forehead, and the shifting clouds reflected on the Hullocks. She watched for partridge and thought of her canaries. The arrival of the horses had not disturbed her at all. The partridges rose and went skimming away sideways and downhill like falling arrowheads. The rooks tossed about in the sky like a tipcart of black paper in a whirlwind. The larks hung invisible and the hawk hung visible. But Meredith, glancing at them, knowing them, was reminded only of Arabelle, of Mountain Jim, of Butter and Dreadnought Susan. She was not romantic about wild birds. She liked her power over her little yellow flight at home.

'When we bring out Donald, what'll we start him on?' began Velvet. (This was a favourite theme.) Donald was to ride, youngest, in the under-eight. He was to ride well, for the sake of their honour, but capital might also be made of his youth and his silver hair. He was to ride home up the village, carrying the silver cup he had won as best-boy-rider in the under-eight. But what on? That was the everlasting question.

'George is the narrowest.'

'George would have him off in a second.'

'Do you suppose . . .' began Meredith, but nobody listened to her. Mating was her mania. She was certainly going to talk about mating.

They walked their horses slowly down the chalk road leading to the village and reached the field.

'Who's got the key? Meredith, you had the key.'

Meredith fumbled under her cotton frock. Not one of them had riding breeches.

'It was in my knicker pocket,' she said, turning her brown knickers almost inside out.

'You've lost it!' they all said instantly. Edwina got down and, undoing a bit of wire, took the gate off its hinges and opened it from the wrong side.

'I've got it!' said Mally suddenly, fishing in her knickers.

They rode up to a little lean-to allotment-shed with a padlock where they kept the saddlery and the rubbers. The horses were rubbed down and turned loose, and, wiring up the gate's hinge, the girls sauntered back along the road to the village.

'Let's see that schedule again,' said Mally.

Velvet drew it out of her pocket. They came to a stop and sat on a flint bridge over a stream. The setting sun picked out the flints like pieces of glass.

'"Novices jumping,"' said Velvet, pointing to an item many times underlined. The whole programme was ready to drop to pieces.

'*Children's* Novice jumping,' corrected Edwina.

'Well, of course! Sir Pericles couldn't do anything else. It'll be three foot.'

'Three foot six, Mi says.'

'Are you sure?'

'Well, you know what he is. He never likes to be wrong.'

'Find out how he found out, anyway.'

'George can jump three foot six.'

'Easy, if he wants to,' said Mally.

'About money,' said Velvet. 'We ought to look at it that way. There's more to be won in the jumping than in potatoes or bending. But there's most to be won in the hurdles races. Most of all. Pounds.'

'But we . . . You wouldn't do that?'

'I don't know,' said Velvet. 'It isn't so awful. It's only low hurdles and a hustle.'

'Don't you remember the way some of them crashed last year?'

'There's no need to crash like that,' said Velvet. 'It's the men who crash, not the women.'

'Why is that?'

'I think they must be wilder,' said Velvet.

'They win more too,' said Mally.

'Sometimes women win,' said Velvet in her clear voice, lifting her boy's face just a little.

'Would they let you?'

'Oh, yes, in gymkhanas. It's the size of the horse that counts. It doesn't matter who rides. It's "Open". It doesn't say "Adults". See in this one? First prize £3.'

'We'll just have to borrow our entries, and pay them back out of prizes.'

'But if we don't get any prizes?'

Nobody answered.

'Who can we borrow from?'

'We haven't paid Mi yet for the tickets for the raffle. And there's sixpence owing on Mars Bars and twopence on Crunchies.'

'Those are only shillings!' said Velvet impatiently. 'We are going to win pounds. We must just borrow again.'

'Couldn't we sell something?'

'We ought to sell Miss Ada,' said Meredith.

There was a silence like the silence of wasps before attack.

'I wasn't thinking!' said Meredith hurriedly.

'I should think not!' said Mally.

'But there's something in it,' said Edwina. 'We've got too many horses. If we sold the piebald we'd have money to pay for all the other horses.'

'If anybody ever sells the piebald,' said Velvet slowly, 'I might as well die.'

'Well, it's borrow or sell,' said Edwina. 'Come along. We've got to feed them still.'

The sky green, the sun almost gone, they returned, buckets of oats mixed with chaff carried between them. They pulled branches of reeds and switched the horses off as they tried to steal each other's buckets. George ate with the whites gleaming in the corners of his eyes, and, as he finished, his ears went back. Then with a rush he stormed another bucket, and the evening rang with the clatter of iron shoes, girls' curses, and zinc buckets overturned. Mrs James ate steadily and could lash out if interrupted. Sir Pericles was nervous and would rather not eat at all than be hurried. Fancy threw his bucket over, mixed his oats with earth. Angelina got the leavings. Unbroken, she was definitely out to grass and was only a crumb-picker, like a dog.

The stars came out as they watched the horses eat.

'Mrs James, Mrs James,' said Velvet suddenly, with love. And the mare laid her ears back at such nonsense.

'Why do you love her?' asked Meredith.

'She is like mother,' said Velvet.

'Oh . . . How?'

'She is,' said Velvet. 'Aren't they wild and lovely in this field at night. Look how their eyes shine! Look at Angelina's! Got kitten's eyes.'

'Come . . . up, Mrs James!' said Mally, tugging.

'What's a matter?'

Mally had the mare's off-fore in her hands. 'Shoe gone. I thought so. Now there'll be shoeing bills. Had you thought of that?'

'That's upkeep. Father'll pay,' said Edwina.

'Yes, but pay and pay, and there'll come an end. There's nothing coming in on these horses,' said Mally.

'At Pendean . . . at Pendean . . .' said Velvet, stammering and desperate all at once.

'You won't make a fortune anyway. And you may break your neck. Mother won't let you do it.'

'If I get the entry money, I'll enter. She won't know till I'm down at the starting post.'

'Come along,' said Edwina, holding the gate.

The horses who had finished hurried after them. They were shut out at the gate and hung their heads over into the dark.

'Cat in the ditch!' said Mally as they walked. They all saw the two fiery points among the dark weeds.

'Shush!' said Edwina, jumping suddenly to the brink of the ditch. The eyes winked and blew out.

'Cats' eyes shine like thieves' lamps,' said Velvet. 'What's for supper?'

'I just bin wondering,' said Meredith.

'It's the two lobsters father brought!' said Mally suddenly. 'Mother said she'd do 'em hot . . .' They ran, buckets clanking.

The spaniels, pressed against the door, yelped as Mally pushed them aside.

The living-room smelt alive with hot lobster. A red, entrancing smell.

Edwina snatched a little parcel that had come by post from off the sideboard.

'What's that!' said Velvet and Mally instantly.

'Mine,' said Edwina. She shot up the stairway to the bedroom. All three streamed after her.

'I wish to God I had a room of my own!' panted Edwina, turning on them at bay from the dressing table, the parcel in her hand. 'I shan't . . . I won't undo it.'

'Hey!' called Mrs Brown. 'Father's come! Come on down. Never mind washing. It won't stand a minute.'

In a few seconds they were all grouped round the table as keen as the dogs outside.

Mi appeared from nowhere.

The lobster was borne in on a vast dish, surrounded by a bank of rice. It was chopped up, thickened with flour, buttered, and boiling hot.

'Where's that sherry?' said father, diving for the cupboard. 'There was a drop.'

'You'll cool it down,' objected Mrs Brown.

'Poof!' said father. 'Where's the damn thing? Here it is . . .' He got the bottle and poured half a glass over the lobsters. 'Turn it over then.'

Mrs Brown took up a spoon and turned the steaming lobster in the sherry. The helpings were ladled out, a lot of rice and a fair share of lobster. They ate.

'God, it's good,' said Mally.

'You don't need to keep on saying God,' said Mr Brown, with his mouth full. 'Just be quiet.'

'Poor Donald,' said Velvet.

'Sleeping like an angel,' said Mi.

'Empty angel,' said Mally. 'No lobster inside him.'

'Stir him up if he had!' said Mi. 'My word . . .'

At the thought of Donald stirred up with lobster to worse excesses they fell still again and continued to eat.

'No dog eats shellfish,' said Mr Brown sideways to Jacob, who was bowing at him.

'How d'you know?' asked Mally.

'Kind o' law,' said Mr Brown. 'My father always said it to his dogs.'

'Give him a bit an' see.'

'Can't spare any,' said Mr Brown.

Jacob mooned under the table.

'Father, Mrs James's lost a shoe,' said Velvet.

The storm broke swiftly over the supper table.

'Oats an' shoes an' soon there'll be bits o' saddlery . . . nothing to show for it . . . nothing but pleasure and a lot o' girls being spoiled for school . . .' The storm blew in a wind of indignation and as it blew Velvet was conscious of her father's case. It was a good one. There was no benefit to him in the horses. The lovely creatures ate, and were sterile. They laboured not, and ate and ate, and lost their shoes. Velvet had no answers and no comfort to offer. And all her promises were child's promises and air until she could carry them out.

When supper was over and cleared, and father was standing in the street with his pipe, she pulled out the gymkhana schedule from the dresser drawer, and bent her strange face over the yellow paper.

Mechanically her hand went up to rock the gold binder and lay it in her lap.

'You *would* choose tonight!' said Edwina, giving her a shove with her elbow.

Velvet stared at her.

'Get your plate in,' said Edwina. 'You always do it when he's angry.'

Velvet stared at her still. A gust of loyalty to her father shook her heart. Edwina had a way of talking . . . She eyed Edwina sideways. Edwina was rough, and she looked as fine as wire. Something about the beauty of the antelope face caught Velvet's attention. Suddenly she wondered if Edwina would save her if she were drowning. Then studied the schedule again.

'Seven two-and-sixes,' she said finally.

'Make it eight. That's a pound,' said Mally. 'Wherever d'you suppose we're going to get that from?'

'Let's look again and see if there's anything we can leave out,' said Meredith.

'No point in doing that,' said Velvet. 'It's just as difficult to borrow seventeen and six as a pound.'

'Queer idea,' said Mally.

'Why queer?'

'Thinking saving doesn't matter.'

'We got nothing,' said Velvet. 'We got nothing, have we?'

'Nothing.'

'Then we might as well ask for what we want as ask for less.'

'Who you going to ask?'

'Don't know,' said Velvet. 'I'll have to see. Let's work it through once more.'

There was a rustle by the door and she put her plate in.

'Let's go to Miss Ada.'

They filed out across the yard, and stood and sat by Miss Ada's manger.

Miss Ada stood droopingly and sour. She had not seen much of them lately.

'Give her something to brighten her up,' said Edwina. 'She's looking a crime.'

Velvet pulled up her frock.

'You've always got sugar in your knickers,' said Mally. 'How does mother let you have so much?'

'I buy it.'

'*Buy* it?'

'I promised Mr Croom I'd pay, after the gymkhana.' She fumbled. 'Here's a bit.'

Miss Ada took it in her exasperated manner, and turned her back on them.

'"Children's Bending,"' read Velvet. 'That's Mally. On George. "Children's Potato Race." Me on Mrs James. "Children (Novice) Jumping." Me on Sir Pericles . . . and on the piebald.'

'The piebald'! The three voices snapped in the stall like whipcracks. 'The piebald! But you've never ridden him.'

'I shall have ridden him. By then. Remember how he jumped the wall?'

'Yes, but . . .'

'I shall have ridden him. I'm going over tomorrow afternoon.'

'We'll all go. Tomorrow afternoon,' said Meredith.

'I'll ride him quietly up and down the valley. We'll take Sir Pericles and change the saddles. His ought to fit the piebald. There's nothing wrong with the piebald, except that he hates being shut in square fields with walls. Or else he likes jumping walls. Where's the list? There's the Threadneedle Race. That's me.'

'Who'll thread your needle?'

'Mother.'

'Then you'll have to tell her you're racing?'

'At the last minute. She'll do it. What is the fuss about racing? You've got to sit on and go round. It isn't even like a professional race, where they catch their legs in yours, if you're an amateur, an' throw you off.'

'How d'you know?'

'I read about it in the Li'bray.'

'Where'd you get the penny?'

'On tick again,' said Velvet wearily. 'There's an old book there on the National.'

'What National?'

'The Grand National,' said Velvet, with an undertone in her voice like a girl in love.

'The next's a Wheelbarrow race,' said Mally reading.

'We can't all do everything,' said Velvet, 'because of the money. We must choose. Anyway, we've worked it out. We've eight half crowns.'

'Where?'

'I mean that's what we're going to borrow.'

'When's the closing day for the entries?'

'Friday,' said Velvet. 'I must get the pound by then.'

'Bed yer ma says,' said Mi, putting his head in at the door of the stable.

In the dark, when the light was out, Mally remembered. 'What was that parcel, D'wina?' she asked.

'Hell!' said Edwina, settling herself angrily further into the clothes. 'Not a minute by myself . . . *Never* by myself!' she whispered into her pillow, and the tears of growth and self-pity heated her eyes.

Very soon they were all asleep, and the dreams waved like palm leaves over the room.

Chapter VII

The sun poured down on the beach. The Hullocks blazed, hot and grey with burnt grass in the late gymkhana summer. Horses were everywhere, creeping over the dun hills, silhouetted on the skyline like plumes, plunging down the skyline to the sea. Donald came in to midday dinner, shoeless, with painted toenails.

'What's he got on his feet?' said Mally, Velvet and Meredith all together, with gimlet eyes and sharp voices. Donald climbed on to his chair and placed his ten scarlet toes on the table.

'D'wina did me,' he said. He looked pleased.

'Where's D'wina?'

'Up in your bedroom.'

Down came Edwina, blowing on her last finger. She held up her two hands, ten drops of deep crimson madder at the tips.

'The parcel!' she said tauntingly, and with triumph. 'Wet still. Don't touch!'

There was a silence.

'Have you got stuff to get it off?' asked Velvet in a cold voice.

'I'm not going to get it off.'

'Gymkhana's Friday week.'

'Well?'

'D'you think you're going to ride Mrs James with those red nails?' said Velvet.

'Why not?'

'Men have played polo on Mrs James,' said Velvet, choking, 'an' you . . .'

'Coming!' called Mrs Brown from the kitchen, with the dish.

'Godamighty look at the boy's feet! Who's dolled 'm up?' said Mr Brown from the street door.

'I got PAINTED feet,' said Donald with satisfaction. 'D'wina done it.'

Mr Brown paused and looked at D'wina. He saw her nails and still he looked. She shuffled a little and took her seat at the table. Mrs Brown came into the room with the dish of oxtail, glutinous, steaming, crusts of toast swimming.

Mr Brown sat down and began to help with the food. Mi slipped in and took his seat. Jacob caught the door on his shoulder and squeezed in, squirming, as it closed. Mally, Velvet, Merry, everyone was silent. When the food was all around Mr Brown observed that Donald's toes were one thing. Then he paused. Velvet waited, almost in pity, for what was to fall upon D'wina.

But father was strange. He only said, 'I'm not against yer fingers, Edwina. Looks kind of finished to me. Yer getting on too. Time you worried about your appearance. Donald's toes is just silly.'

'What's he done to his toes?' said Mrs Brown, eating.

Donald arranged them again upon the tablecloth. His mother looked at them and went on with her dinner.

'Looks like my garnets,' she remarked. 'An' can you count 'em, Donald?'

So it was left to Velvet to undo Edwina. She clinched her spirit and knit it up again. When dinner was over she waited for Edwina in the bedroom where she knew she would come to look again at her bottle of nail varnish.

From the height of the window, beyond the canary cages, the immortal Hullocks browsed, burnished and lit, at two in the afternoon. Bowed like silver barrels they were set in rows endwise to the sea. Like pigs, like sheep, like elephants, hay-blond with burnt grass. Velvet's mind stuttered like a small candle before the light and the height and the savage stillness of the middle afternoon. As she gazed her heart rolled slowly over, a wheel on which something is written. Edwina seemed to her small and distressed. The piebald horse, the light of her mind, walked slowly across her imagination. She leant upon a cage. Merry opened the door and saw her.

'Looking at my canaries?' she asked, warmed to her marrow, like a mother whose baby is patted.

'No,' said Velvet turning round. Then seeing Meredith's face – 'I was at first, and then I looked outside at the Hullocks. We're going over to the piebald as soon's Mally's washed up.'

'What are you going to do about D'wina's nails?' said Meredith, and came towards the cages.

'Nothing,' said Velvet. 'She can have her nails if she likes.'

'And ride Mrs James?'

'If she likes to,' said Velvet. 'It's a disgrace to us but she can.'

'I thought you minded so.'

Velvet said nothing. Then she poked her finger in at Mountain Jim. 'Will he sit on it?'

'On mine he will!' said Meredith eagerly, and opened the cage door. Mountain Jim bowed and fluttered his wing tips. Then descended to her finger and twisted his layered neck and cocked his easy head.

'You like them better than the horses, don't you?' said Velvet wonderingly.

'Nobody else wants them,' said Meredith. 'And they're small. They're like a doll's house.'

'Why, there's a new one!'

'Mi bought it for me,' said Merry in a small, touched voice, 'because of Africa. This morning. That new mate got it for him.'

'What mate?'

'The plumber's mate. The boy with the glass eye. The cat got it an' it's got no tail, but Mi says rub it with oil an' it'll grow. Hair oil he says. He's going to give me a teaspoonful of his.'

'Does Mi use hair oil?'

'No, he doesn't use it, but he bought it.'

'Merry,' said Velvet, 'nobody's thought what we're going to wear at the gymkhana.'

'Our knickers.'

'Yes,' said Velvet, pondering. 'Yes, our knickers. Every other child will have jodhpurs. I suppose they'll *let* us ride? In knickers?'

'Oh, I should think so,' said Meredith, cleaning out the drinking pots with her finger. 'Look at Butter bowing!'

Butter opened her wings and bowed from her perch.

'She can't make up her mind to go from perch to perch without doing that,' said Meredith. 'She laid another useless egg this morning. Just drops them about.'

'Are you sure it's useless?'

'I put it in water an' it floated. It's sterile.'

'Does Mi say –'

'That's what Mi says. Float 'em. No good if they float.'

'Mi comin' with us to the piebald this afternoon?'

'It's such a long way to walk,' said Merry. 'If only he would ride.'

'Nothin'll ever make him,' said Velvet. 'He won't even talk about it.'

Donald came round the bedroom door, with naked feet and painted toes. He carried a postcard in his hand. 'You gotta postcard. From Aunt Em.'

'For me?' said Velvet.

''Sfer Meredith.'

Meredith took it. 'She's at Brighton. Just her love . . .'

'Thurs a picture,' said Donald. He looked at it. 'What is it? It's a church.'

'No, it's a palace,' said Meredith, reading the printed inscription. 'It's the Pavilion, at Brighton. "Where George the Fourth lived," it says.'

'Who's George a Fourth?' asked Donald.

'Was a king . . . lived in this palace.'

'Whur's he now?'

'Oh, he's dead. Ages ago.'

'Who died 'im?'

'Nobody died him. He just died.'

'Well, whur's he now?'

'Well, dead, Donald. Like everybody. Everybody dies.'

'Why?'

'Well, they do. You will an' I will an' old people do.'

'Do what?'

'Die.'

'Who died that king then? Who died him, I say?'

'Velvet,' said Meredith exasperated. 'You tell him. I got to finish these canaries.'

Velvet considered Donald with a mild expression. He was frowning. His lovely face was angry.

'Where's your spit bottle?' she asked.

'Ts'full,' said Donald, his whole face lighting with radiance. 'I'll get it, shall I?'

'Yes,' said Velvet, 'only hurry up.'

'You didn't do much,' said Merry.

'He didn't really want to know,' said Velvet. 'He just wanted to be angry. Bin smacked or something, downstairs. He knows all about death. Look how he trod on those ants.'

'Perhaps he didn't like a king being dead. A king's not like an ant. He's coming with his beastly bottle.'

Donald fell on the top step and his bottle was smashed. It had been the work of weeks. The stairs ran with spit and blood and tinkled with broken glass. The house was rent. Mr Brown, Mrs Brown, Mi and all the sisters picked him up.

Mally cut her knee kneeling on the glass. Edwina read to Donald, who had to have a stitch in the ball of his foot. Mrs Brown kept Merry to help her with the washing.

In the end Velvet took Sir Pericles and rode alone to Tablet Gully.

In Tablet Gully the piebald cropped, moving from tuft to tuft in sun and shadow, and flashing as he moved. The bone of his shoulder, thrown up by his stooping neck, rippled under his sliding skin. His parti-coloured mane hung forward over his neck, and his long tail tipped the ground.

He swung round with the sun. His teeth tore evenly as he worked. Now his quarters could be seen, slightly pear-shaped and faulty, but strong. His hocks, too thick, but straight and clean, waded in the burnt grasses. He lifted a sloping pastern finished with a pink hoof, and bit a fly off his leg. The clouds reared overhead, the legendary gully with its dead man's tablet was heavy with steady sun and shielded from the wind.

Among the scabious flowers on the north slope sat Velvet, steady as a gorse-bush, cross-legged, and watching the horse.

She had tied Sir Pericles to a gate in the valley behind her.

Sitting like a Buddha, dreaming of the horse, riding the horse in dreams. A piece of cake and a Mars Bar beside her in a paper bag, and the insects hummed and the mauve August flowers hardly moved. Just to look at him her heart beat violently with ambition. Her strong and inexperienced imagination saw no barriers. She was capable of apprehending death and of conceiving fame – in her own way, not for herself but for her horse. For a shilling she had won this wild creature that did not know its strength. In this valley, tucked away, she had got glory. What she meant to do made her heart beat afresh. She looked steadily at the piebald as though she pitied him. Eating his grass, prince, with his kingdom waiting for him! Her hand stole out and pulled the Mars Bar from its bag, and she sucked its heavy stump, made from milk chocolate, toffee and nuts.

All the Hullocks were creeping with dowdy animals at livery. But here in Tablet Gully moved on its clever legs this living horse. Pulling gently at a blister on her heel she rode him in her mind. She would dazzle the world with this spot of luck, she and the creature together, breathing like one body, trying even to death, till their hearts burst. She would place her horse where he belonged, in history. She clasped the Mars Bar like a prophet's child, with both hands.

'Leaders have been cut from coaches, to do it . . .' she whispered as she rose. 'Even horses out of carts. Why not him?'

A halter made of rope lay behind her and picking it up she walked gently down the valley holding it behind her frock. The piebald stared at her, interested. He loved humanity, and had it not been for the exceptional grass in Tablet Gully would have been off to the village long before this.

Frankly he watched her come, nostrils slightly distended and both calm eyes upon her, the blue eye, and that white eye where the pied colour streaked across his cheek. She paused beside him and slipped the halter over his head. He shook his neck to free it from flies and came with her willingly.

They reached Sir Pericles, who snorted at the sight of them and danced his hindquarters, looking from side to side, catching his soft nose on the reins. How could his mistress walk so out of valleys leading horses? He was intrigued, and excited, jealous, pleased to see her again. Velvet loosed and mounted him, and the piebald walked sedately at their side, striking out his forefeet in his own peculiar gait.

They reached a field not far away, enclosed by a stone wall, and Velvet changed the saddle and bridle, tying Sir Pericles with the halter to the gate. She mounted the piebald, and walked and trotted him quietly in large circles. His mouth was a mixture of lead and rubber. He had no notion how to obey the bit but imagined that to turn his neck was all that was wanted. He would trot onwards with his neck turned on one side like a horse that has no face. Velvet had to rock him with her knees to get him out of his orbit, and even then it was no more than a bewildered stagger to one side. She set him into a canter. It was clumsy and gallant, and accomplished with snorts. He flung his powerful white head up into the air and nearly smashed his rider's precious plate. Sir Pericles watched. The flashing picbald snorted excitedly round the field. Above him sat the noble child, thin as famine, bony as a Roman, aquiline nose and domed white forehead, tufted loonily with her cotton hair. Velvet, with her great teeth and her parted lips, her eye sockets and the pale eyes in them, looked like a child model for a head of Death, an eager bold young Death. She was thinking of something far outside the field. She was thinking of horses, great horses, as she sat her horse.

Turning in a flash in the middle of the field she drove him on with her knees. They went at the wall together. Over the grasses, over the tufts and mounds, both knitted in excitement, the horse sprang to the surge of her heart as her eyes gazed between his ears at the blue top of the flint wall. She bent slightly and held him firm and steady, her hands buried in the flying mane firm on the stout muscles of his neck. She urged him no more, there was no need, but sat him still. He was a natural jumper. She did not attempt to dictate to him. They cleared the wall together, wildly, ludicrously high, with savage effort and glory, and twice the power and the force that was needed. Velvet felt his hindquarters drop when they should have hitched. But there was so much space to spare that the piebald could afford it. Nevertheless it was an intemperate and outlandish jump.

She rode him back to his own valley and loosed him, then returned home alone on Sir Pericles, parading in dreams. As she approached the village she was outlined against the sunset, on the brow of a Hullock. Stirrups short, angled knee and leg etched on the side of the saddle; childish, skeleton hands waving with the ebb and flow of the horse's mouth on the reins; hands that seemed knotted and tied like a bunch of flowers with streamers going from them, swinging together, knuckle to knuckle, thumb to thumb, while she sat erect above them, her face held on the wand of her body. The straw hair floated and stared above the wide-open eyes.

Sir Pericles walked like Velvet sat. His soft mouth held the snaffle as a retriever carries a bird. Yet he arched his neck as though his bit were a bit of thorns, and his long, almond, Chinese eyes looked both backward and forward at once. He seemed to be watching from either end of the agate stuff that was his window, watching Velvet's leg, watching the horizon before him. The oxygen in the evening air intoxicated him. In the eye of little Sir Pericles something soft and immortal shone.

Velvet had laid down the piebald and her ambitions and was thinking comfortably of the coming gymkhana. In her mind she rose at white-painted gates and fences. Her knees crisped with her thoughts in the saddle and she leant forward. Sir Pericles never altered his tossing walk. His head and tail, both like plumes, flirted, and he walked within her dream with a spot of gold upon his eyeball.

It was not the silver cup standing above the wind-blown tablecloth that Velvet saw – but the perfection of accomplishment, the silken co-operation between two actors, the horse and the human, the sense of the lifting of the horse-soul into the sphere of human obedience, human effort, and the offering to it of the taste of human applause. All this she had learnt already from the trained mouth and the kneeling will of Sir Pericles.

And as the dim sense of this understanding sighed up and down her body it entered too into Sir Pericles' nerves, and through his nerves to his comprehension. Velvet lived her round of jumps, lips parted, the sunset shining on her golden mouth. She rose and fell at the triple bar, the water-jump, the gate, the imitation wall. She heard the hands, palm on palm, threshing the noise of applause. Sir Pericles dreamt it too, a wild dream beyond his understanding, but to be recognized when the taste came again.

His hoofs came down sweetly on violets, grass and knitted thyme, clanking on a flint, breaking the crisp edge of a wheel rut. He took in everything, behind, before, and from the body astride him. Below, the chimneys were smoking up like poplars and a light was lit in the cobbler's shop.

They sidled together down the steep grassy banks towards the village.

'Velvet!' said Mally out of the darkness by the bottom gate.

'That you, Mally? Open the gate.'

'Who's wired it up like this?' Mally wrenched at the twist of wire. She opened it and horse and child passed through. 'The piebald's out again. Nobody knew you bin riding him but us. Came thunderin' down the street ten minutes ago.'

'Where's he now? Father angry?'

'Went down to the sea as usual, an' slid about. Went crackin' up a side street. Father doesn't know. Better not let him. He's bin carrying on about the horses. It would be the limit if he found the piebald had started cracking down the street again.'

'F'e broke a leg!' said Velvet in a voice of horror. 'F'e did! Might. Easily.'

'You can't go after him now. It's pitch. Thurs stars coming.'

Sir Pericles gave a whinny. There came a sharp, near answer, and the piebald stalked out of the shadows, gleaming in the dusk.

'He's here!' Velvet's marvelling whisper, as she slipped off Sir Pericles and held out her hand. The piebald came nearer, breathing hard.

'Mount, mount!' said Mally. 'Get on again! He'll follow. He won't think you want to catch him.'

'What'll we do with him?' said Velvet as she scrambled back.

'I'll go an' get a halter and we'll try an' put him . . . Put him in Miss Ada's box tonight and put her in the toolhouse!'

The piebald followed, threshing his head, snorting the pleasant village smells, till they reached the yard of the cottage. He dropped his neck for the halter like a horse born in a kitchen. Soon Miss Ada stood among the spades and shovels.

'Poor old darling Ada,' said Velvet, as she pushed the shovels to safety behind a wooden case. 'Get half the bedding from the loose-box, Mally. The piebald won't miss it. He's never had any before. I'll get Ada some oats to make her happy.'

'What'll father say . . . about the piebald being in?'

'He won't know. I'll take him back early in the morning.'

'Bet he neighs in the night. We'll shut both doors. He might try and jump the bottom one. Let's give him . . . What'll we give him?'

'Just hay,' said Velvet. 'He's not accustomed to oats.'

'D'you know . . .' said Mally suddenly, pausing with an armful of hay.

'What?'

'He'll be worse than ever after this. He'll be coming back every night to get a night's lodging and a supper! You never saw . . .'

'What?'

'The way he came down the village street, slipping and sliding and snorting and his eyes shining.'

'He's like a prince!' said Velvet.

'Eh?'

'Just a thing I thought,' said Velvet. 'I pretend he's a prince.'

At supper everyone ate with memories behind them. Edwina had been kissed by Teddy, for the first time. Her nails had shocked and enchanted him. Merry had oiled the canary's stump, and was worrying about what she should call him. She had got a list of gods' names, and a birthday list of girls'. It was so hard to know the sex of canaries.

Mally and Velvet were thinking of what they had got in the stable, the prince who might kick up a row in the night. Donald was asleep now, stitches in his foot, blood and spit mingled in his dreams. He yelped from time to time in his sleep like a puppy.

'Whur's Jacob?' said Mr Brown suddenly as he ate.

'After they bitches,' said Mi, with resentment.

'Seem bad this August.'

'Bitches? Terrible they are. Crown's got one an' Ede's got one. That Jacob he . . .' Words failed, and slightly redder than before Mi continued to eat.

As the door opened for the pudding's entry they heard the impatient hammer of a hoof on wood. Mr Brown continued to munch his bread. Mi sat up and his eyes flickered upon Velvet's face.

'I'm not hungry any more. Can I get down, mother?' said Velvet.

'Say your grace,' said Mr Brown.

'F'whatayave receivedthankGod,' said Velvet, pushing her chair in, and went out in the dark. At the corner of the yard and the road four apple trees were enclosed by a broken fence. They were laden with little sweet apples and the ground was littered with the wind-blowings. She gathered two handfuls and went to the stable with them.

Mi hung about the yard all the evening, whistling for Jacob and looking down the road. Once he opened the top portion of the loose-box and looked in, grinning.

'Gettin' on all right?' he enquired. Velvet was sitting on the manger.

'He's quiet while I'm here,' said Velvet. 'But I can't stay here all night. Where's father?'

'Gone down to finish the bills,' said Mi. 'I thought he better.'

Later in the evening Mally, swinging on the gate by the apple trees, saw Jacob coming up the empty road.

'Bitches good?' she asked him, flinging him a block of lichen off the gate post.

'Succulent,' said Jacob, making a half circle round her.

'Go an' tell Mi about it!' said Mally.

Jacob went, bowing and grinning. Mi walloped him and gave him his supper.

Later in the night the house was quiet, the piebald quiet (for he had Velvet in her nightgown sitting on his manger), the moon rose steadily. At two o'clock the moon began to sink. Mi came to the stable door and looked over the top. He wore his sleeping clothes, several old sleeveless jerseys and a pair of shorts.

'Get to bed now,' he said. 'I'll do a bit.'

Velvet lowered off the manger. 'Here's six quarters left,' she said, pointing in the manger. 'Give him a piece every time he seems restless.'

'What is it?'

'Apples,' said Velvet. 'I bin feeding him bits all night.'

'You'll make him loose,' said Mi. 'Where's the sacking pieces?'

'In the corner. An' ties. Ties off the hay bales.'

At five the sea was running up with a gale behind it and pounding in the sewer. The day broke in flashes of light and the elms soughed in the wind. The piebald's tail and mane were flung about as Mi led him out into the yard, his hooves bound up in sacking. Velvet met them in the road.

'How'd you wake?' asked Mi.

'An't bin asleep,' said Velvet. 'I just heard the wind. Isn't he good!'

'Perisher,' said Mi.

'Oh no,' said Velvet. 'Oh no. Wait while I get a bridle.'

She returned with a snaffle-bridle belonging to Sir Pericles, one which they had brought in to clean the night before.

'Gimme a leg up, Mi,' and he jumped her on to the warm, round back.

'Key of the field's behind the manger. Come up an' help me get Sir Pericles. I got to ride back on him.'

Mi walked beside her up the road to the field in the gale.

'Blowing awful up there,' he said, looking to the Hullocks.

'Seaweed's smelling like drains,' said Velvet, looking at the wild and shining east.

"'Tis drains,' said Mi sniffing. 'Lot a' nonsense they talk about seaweed. You had anything to eat?'

'No, I forgot.'

Mi grunted with disfavour. 'Fer a sickly girl you give yerself something to do!' he said.

'An't sickly. M'wiry,' said Velvet. 'Shove the gate wider. I'll stub my knee!'

Sir Pericles trotted down gladly, tail flying.

'Halter's under the stone in the corner,' said Velvet.

Mi picked it up. Sir Pericles came willingly enough. The two horses hustled clumsily through the gate.

'Good-bye,' said Velvet and went off across the reedy ditch, riding the piebald and leading the chestnut.

'Why don't you ride the other?' shouted Mi, but his voice blew back into his mouth as he called into the gale coming off the sea.

He watched the horses go up the chalk road and break into a canter on the crest. His old mackintosh flapped on his bare legs and the wind tore at the roots of his red hair. 'If she were a boy . . .' he said longingly to himself. With that light body and grand heart he would get her into a racing stable. He knew of many up north. He had friends here and there. She'd be a great jockey some day. Fancy wasting those hands and that spirit and that lightweight on a girl. 'No more'n a skeleton,' he said. 'An' never will be, likely. She'd ride like a piece of lightning. No more weight'n a piece of lightning.' He thought of her mother . . . and of his old father. 'Velvet an' her. A feather an' a mountain. But both the same.'

Boom . . . went the sea on the cliffs. The savage blow came up the valley. Mi hated water. Brought up by the Channel trainer he had edged back inland as soon as he could. He couldn't stand the waves and the empty trough that sucked and soaked along the lip of the beaches. It turned his head, and he went up the village whenever he thought of the sea. 'How she ever!' he thought, with his mind's eye fixed sharp on Mrs Brown. Great, wallowing woman, half submerged, water pouring backwards and forwards over her shoulders, threshing across the water like a whale. A stormy dawn when she had landed. 'Bet old Dan was pleased,' he thought. 'Wasn't many swimming the Channel those days.'

His mind went back to Velvet. He too, like her, was longing to place his dream in history. This child, Velvet, was good for something.

He turned back to his bed, shivering, Velvet in his thoughts.

And hungry, sick, delicate, blown so that she could hardly

breathe, Velvet in the grip of horses and of the gale went on across the blunt and unprotected Hullocks. Great skies slipped out of the folds, unfurled, and stood a thousand miles above her. The sight battered against unseeing eyeballs, was drunk into the marrow of something older than her brain. Flags and pennons and beacons waved above the high land as she sat below, thinking in slow brown drops of thought, sure of her future, counting her plans, warm in expectation, glorious butcher's – Velvet, eyes cast down upon the moving shoulders of mortal horses.

CHAPTER VIII

Mi raised thirty shillings for the gymkhana. He borrowed it from his girl for Velvet's sake. That is to say he treated love worse than he treated adventure.

'Your girl,' said Velvet, frowning in thought. 'Which girl? Didn't know you had a girl.'

'Nor I had. Met her at the dance last night,' said Mi. 'Pleased as Punch, she was. Lent me the money too.' So Mi behaved badly, and Velvet knew it. But neither she nor Mi cared when they set their minds firm.

On the day of the gymkhana, about mid-morning, it grew suddenly very hot and the rain came down in sheets. Inside the living-room, polishing the bits, it was like the tropics. The girls' faces were wet. Rain came down outside on full leaves, making a rattle and a sopping sound. Everything dripped. The windows streamed. The glass was like glycerine.

'Oh, Lord,' said Mally, 'oh dear, oh damn!'

'We've only two mackintoshes. Velvet's has stuck to the wall in the hot cupboard. Won't it rain itself out?'

'The grass'll be slippery. What about their shoes being roughed?'

'We've no money,' said Velvet, 'for roughing.'

'If Mi had a file . . .' said Mally.

'A file's no good. You want nails in.'

'I'm sweating,' said Edwina, 'can't we have a window open?'

She opened the yard window and the rain came crackling in over the cactus.

'Hot's a pit in here!' said Mi, coming in from the yard, and taking off his dripping coat. 'The yard's swimming. Everything's floating.'

'Will they put it off?'

'The gymkhana? No, it'll be over soon. It's a water-spout. There's a great light coming up the way the wind's coming from. Your ma going to serve the dinner early?'

'Yes, at twelve,' said Edwina. 'We better clear now. Put the bridles and things in the bedroom. Better father doesn't see too much of it!'

'He knows, doesn't he?' said Meredith.

'Yes, he knows, but he doesn't want to think too much about it.'

At dinner they had sardines instead of pudding. Mrs Brown always served sardines for staying power. Dan had dropped them into her mouth from the boat as she crossed the Channel.

Donald considered his on his plate.

'I'll take your spines out, Donald,' said Meredith.

'I eat my spines,' said Donald.

'No you don't, Donald. Not the big spine. The little bones but not the big one in the middle. Look how it comes out!'

'I eat my spines I say,' said Donald firmly with rising colour, and held her knife-hand by the wrist.

'But look . . . they come out lovely!' said Merry, fishing with the fork. The spine of the slit sardine dangled in the air and was laid on the edge of the plate. Quick as lightning Donald popped it into his mouth with his fingers and looked at her dangerously.

'I crunch up my spines, I like them,' he said.

'Leave him alone,' said mother.

'D'you eat your tails too?' said Merry vexedly.

'I eat my tails and my spines,' said Donald, and the discussion was finished.

At one the rain stopped and the sun shone. The grass was smouldering with light. The gutters ran long after the rain had stopped.

*

'Keep up on the hog,' said Velvet, as the horses moved along. 'We don't want 'em splashed. Gutters are all boggy.' They were well on the way to the gymkhana, held in the football field at Pendean.

'We look better in our mackintoshes!' called Mally. 'I'm glad it rained.'

'I'm steamy,' said Edwina. 'Merry, you can wear mine. You'll look better.'

'I'm all right. I don't want it, thank you, Edwina.'

But Edwina was struggling out of her mackintosh. 'You'll look better. You're all untidy . . . Put it on!'

'I don't want it!'

'You're a bully, D'wina,' said Mally. 'You jus' want to get rid of it an' not sweat.'

They turned up a chalk road between a cutting and in a few minutes they could see below them the gathering of horse-vans in the corner of Pendean field, the secretary's flagged tent, white-painted jumps dotting the course, and a stream of horses and ponies drawing along the road below.

The soaking land was spread below them, and the flat road of the valley shone like a steel knife. Getting off their horses they led them down the chalk path between blackberry bushes, and in ten minutes of slithering descent they were at the gates of the gymkhana field.

'Competitors' passes,' murmured Edwina and showed their pasteboard tickets.

They picked out a free tree in the field and established themselves.

'Here's someone's programme!' said Mally. 'Squashed and lost. Sixpence saved!'

They crowded round to read it.

After endless waiting the band arrived. Then the local broadcaster rattled up, mounted on its ancient Ford, and settling into its position against the ropes began to shout in bleak, mechanical tones . . . 'Event Number One! Event Number One! Competitors in the Collecting Ring, please . . . PLEASE.'

Instantly the field was galvanized. Children and ponies appeared from behind trees and hedges and tents. Mally mounted George and rode towards the ring.

In five minutes it was over and Mally was back again. George had had no idea of bending. Nor Mally either. They had broken three poles on the way up and were disqualified.

'We haven't practised!' said Mally, trying to carry it off.

But Velvet, busy saddling Mrs James, made no reply.

'Here's Jacob!' said Edwina suddenly. Jacob sprang lightly against Mrs James's flank and grinned. 'Mi must be here.'

'Event Number Two!' shouted the Voice, and Velvet mounted,

and made for the Collecting Ring. Seeing Pendean Lucy waiting at the gate for the first heat, she thrust up beside her. The bar fell and Velvet, Lucy and three others, two boys and a fat little girl, were let out to the potato posts.

'You know what to do?' shouted the Starter, his flag under his arm. 'Leave the posts on your right! Take the furthest potato first! . . .'

Velvet tried to take it in but the trembling of Mrs James distracted her attention. Mrs James had broken already into a sweat of hysteria that had turned her grey coat steel-blue.

They were lined up, the flag fell, and Mrs James made a start of such violence that Velvet could not pull her up at the fifth post. Six strides were lost before they could turn. Lucy was cantering down the posts with her potato and Velvet heard the jingle of the bucket as the potato fell neatly into it. The heat was over, and Mrs James, too big, too wild, too excited, too convinced that she was once again playing polo, was left three potatoes behind when the winner had drawn up beside the Starter. Pendean Lucy won the first heat.

'Five shillings gone . . .' muttered Velvet with humiliation as she trotted slowly back to the tree. Mi was there standing beside Sir Pericles.

'Five shillings gone, Mi,' said Velvet aloud to him.

'It's a gamble,' said Mi. 'Keep yer head. Afternoon's young.'

'Jumping . . .' said Mally. 'It's the jumping now. Which you jumping first?'

'Sir Pericles.'

The blazing sun had dried up the burnt grass and the afternoon shone like a diamond as Velvet sat on Sir Pericles in the Collecting Ring. Mi wormed his way between the crowds against the rope. Lucy came on her roan pony, but the pony refused at the Gate. Twice and three times, and she trotted back disqualified. A schoolboy in a school cap quartered in purple and white, rode out. His almost tailless pony jumped a clear round. Jacob wriggled with excitement between Mi's legs.

'Number Sixteen!' called the Broadcaster.

Sixteen was Lucy's elder sister, a fat girl in a bright blue shirt.

'Blasted girl!' said Mi under his breath, as the blue shirt cleared the first and second jumps. His heart was in his mouth, but he spat whistlingly and joyfully between his teeth as the pony landed astride the wall, and scrambled over in a panic, heaving the wall upon its side.

It seemed they would call every number in the world except Velvet's.

'Break her nerve, waiting!' grumbled Mi. He could see her cotton hair bobbing as she sat.

A small girl came, with pigtails. A little shriek burst from her throat each time her chestnut pony rose at a jump. The plaits flew up and down, the pony jumped like a bird. A clear round.

'Hell!' said Mi. 'Two clear rounds.'

'Number Fifteen!'

Out came Velvet from the black gap between the crowds. Sir Pericles arched his neck, strained on his martingale, and his long eyes shone. He flirted his feet in his delicious doll's canter and came tittupping down over the grass. Velvet in her cotton frock stood slightly in the stirrups, holding him short – then sat down and shortened her reins still more. Mi's stomach ran to soup.

'Got her stirrups in her armpits . . .' sighed Mi approvingly. 'Little swell!'

There was nothing mean, nothing poor about Sir Pericles. He looked gay as he raced at the first jump.

'Too fast, too fast!' said Mi, praying with his soul.

The horse was over safely and had his eyes fastened on the next jump.

'Haul 'im in, haul 'im in!' begged Mi of the empty air. 'He'll rocket along . . .' He saw Velvet's hands creep further up the reins, and her body straighten itself a little. The horse's pace decreased. It was the double jump, the In-and-Out. Sir Pericles went over it with his little hop – one landing and one take-off. Mi saw Velvet glance behind – but nothing fell. And the Gate. The Gate was twelve paces ahead.

He cleared the Gate with one of his best jumps, an arc in the air, with inches to spare.

'He'll do the wall,' said Mi with relief.

He did the wall, but a lathe fell at the stile. Half a fault. She was out of it then. Mi yawned with fatigue. He had held his breath. His lungs were dry. Jacob was gone from between his legs. He looked round.

'Bitches . . .' he murmured vaguely, then turned again to the ropes to wait for the piebald.

There were no more clear rounds till the piebald came, and when it came a murmur went up from the villagers who stood in the crowd.

'Jumping *that* animal!' said a voice.

'Why that's the one she won at the Raffle!'

The piebald strode flashing into the sun. He paused, stood still, and gazed round him. Velvet's knees held him steadily, and she sat behind his raised neck without urging him on.

'I don't expect anything . . .' she whispered. 'Do what you can. Keep steady. You're all right.'

'You next,' said a man at the bar of the Collecting Ring. 'You waiting for anything?'

'I'm going,' said Velvet quietly. 'He just wants to look round.'

Mi saw them come down the grass, the piebald trotting with a sort of hesitation.

'He's in two minds whether he'll bolt,' thought Mi.

'Showy horse . . .' said a spectator.

'Butcher's girl . . .' said another. 'The youngest. Got a seat, an't she?'

The piebald's best eye was towards the crowd, his white eye to the centre of the field.

The trot broke hesitatingly into a canter, but the horse had no concentration in him. He looked childishly from side to side, hardly glancing at the jump ahead.

'He'll refuse,' said Mally, who had arrived at Mi's side. But Mi made no answer.

Sir Pericles had jumped like a trained horse. The piebald's jumping was a joke. Arrived at the jump in another two paces, he appeared to be astonished, planted his forelegs for a second, looked down, trembled, then leapt the little bush and rail with all four legs stiff in the air together. Dropping his hindquarters badly he came down on the rail and broke it in two.

'Two faults,' said Mi.

'Only two for breaking that?'

'Hind feet. Only two.'

Again the piebald trotted, flashing, his grass-fed belly rounded, and his shoulders working under the peculiar colour of his hide.

'Why don't she canter 'im?' said a voice.

Mi turned on the voice. 'First time he's seen anything but his own grazing. It's a miracle if she gets him round.'

'The In-and-Out'll finish him,' said Mally under her breath.

The piebald jumped willingly into the In-and-Out, then paused, and remained inside.

A shout of laughter went up from the crowd.

'Oh . . . poor Velvet . . .' murmured Malvolia, agonized.

The piebald attempted to graze, as though he were in a sheep pen, and again the crowd laughed.

'She's handling him gentle,' said Mi. 'She's trying to keep him thinking he's a winner. She's backin' him, see . . . I don't believe he's ever backed a pace before.' The piebald had backed two paces till his quarters lay against the first jump of the In-and-Out. With a light heart he responded to his rider, and with a spring he was out again and cantering on.

'Do they count that as a fault?'

'I don't know,' said Mi. 'Watch out . . . now . . . It's the Gate.'

The piebald broke the gate. He would have liked a stout, stone wall, but this flimsy thing that stood up before him puzzled him and he did his goat-jump, all four legs in the air at once,

and landed back upon the lathes and broke them.

'That horse is breaking up the field,' said a voice.

Mi glared. 'He's knocked his hock,' said Mi, 'that'll learn him.' For the piebald limped a pace or two. It learnt him. Unlettered as he was he had no thought of refusing. He saw the friendly wall ahead, and taking it to be enduring flint he went for it with a glare of interest, ears pricked and eyes bright. The wall was three foot six. He leapt five. For a second it seemed to the crowd as though the horse had nothing to do with the wall but was away up in the air. A little cheer went up and hands clapped in a burst.

'Don't she ride him!' said the voice. 'It's that Velvet girl. The ugly one.'

'What, that kid with the teeth?'

'That's who it is.'

Mi knew that Mally's beauty stood beside him and he resented it. He half turned his shoulder on her. While Velvet sat the piebald he thought her the loveliest thing on earth. Like Dan, his father, he hardly saw the faces of women.

'Hullo, she's missed the stile!'

'Did he refuse?' asked Mi, keenly.

'I don't think she saw it,' said Mally. 'She simply rode on.'

The judge waved his stick and called to a Starter. Velvet cantered, glowing, radiant, to the exit gate. The man who held the exit spoke to her and pointed. Velvet looked behind her, paused, then shook her head.

'Not coming . . .' shouted the man to the Steward.

After a brief pause . . .

'The last Competitor,' announced the Broadcaster, 'did not complete the round.'

'Why ever didn't she?' said Mally, as she and Mi left the rope to fight their way round to the tree. They scrambled out from the crowd and ran.

Velvet was standing looking at the piebald as though bemused. Merry, her face happy with pride, was holding the horses.

'Marvellous, Velvet, to get him round!' said Mally, coming up. 'Why didn't you jump the last jump?'

Velvet turned and looked, and Mi could see how her face was shining.

'I thought I'd better not,' she said gently.

'Why?'

'He did the wall so beautifully I thought he'd better end on that.'

In a flash Mi felt again what she was made of. That she could take a decision for her horse's good and throw away her own honours.

'It was the right thing to do,' said Mi.

Edwina arrived. 'What made you miss the Stile?'

Velvet said nothing.

'People near me thought you'd funked it,' said Edwina half indignantly. 'You must have bin asleep to go and miss it.'

'She's no more asleep 'n my eye,' said Mi. And Mi's little eye, like an angry sapphire, raked Edwina till she shuffled her shoulder and itched.

'It's you, Edwina, now!' said Mally looking at the torn programme. 'On Mrs James. Bending.'

'A lot of chance I have!' said Edwina. 'Mrs James'll break every pole.'

'She gets rough and excited,' said Velvet.

'But it's Adult!' said Merry. 'They won't have nippy ponies. It'll be easier.'

But the Adults were seated on the smallest ponies they could ride. They looked like giants on dogs. Every grown-up was riding his sister's pony, and Mrs James, galloping like a wild animal, nostrils blowing and eye rolling, broke all the poles she could break. Edwina led her back without a word, disgusted and silent.

It began to rain. Merry put a sack round her shoulders and pulled out the *Canary Breeder's Annual*. Edwina left them and went towards the tent.

'She got any money?' said Mally, looking after her keenly.

'Can't have,' said Velvet. 'She was broke yesterday.'

'P'raps she's got twopence for an Idris. Wish to God I had a crunchie,' muttered Mally.

'Kandy Korner's got a stall here,' said Merry, reading. 'What's happening now?'

'It's the tea interval,' said Velvet gloomily. They had won nothing. They had made not a penny. They owed Mi thirty bob.

The rain slid, tapping, through the branches, and swept in windy puffs across the field.

It made a prison for them, it pressed them into a corner of life, a corner of the heart. They were hung up. Velvet was hung up in life. Where was she? A butcher's daughter, without money, in debt, under suzerainty, an amateur at her first trial of skill, destined that night to a bed of disappointment among the sleeping canaries. She did not think like that. But cared only that the piebald had jumped one jump as she had dreamt he might jump, with power, with crashing confidence. He was ignorant but he had no stage nerves. Of her own powers she had no thought.

Staring out into the lines of rain lightly she lifted her hands and placed them together in front of her, as though she held the leathers. So acute was the sensation of the piebald beneath her that she turned with surprise to see him standing under the dripping branches. A look of simplicity and adoration passed into her face, like the look of the mother of a child who has won honours. She had for him a future.

The rain came down in long knitting needles. Backwards and forwards blew the needles, as the wind puffed. Wet horses, wet mackintoshes, wet dogs, wet flapping of tents, and then as the storm was rent a lovely flushing of light in the raindrops. Wind blew the sky into hollows and rents.

'That Violet that Mi met, she's at Kandy Corner,' said Merry. 'Serving with them for a week on appro.'

'We can't borrow from her if she's only on appro. She'll get into trouble.'

'Mi,' said Velvet, looking round the tree, 'you round there? Is it dryer there?'

'No.'

'Your Violet's with Kandy Korner. Got a stall down here.'

Silence. Displeasure.

'You couldn't touch her for another twopence.'

'Not till I see daylight with that thirty bob.'

Edwina had gone off with one of the mackintoshes. The saddles were heaped under the other. Merry, Mally and Velvet flattened themselves, shivering, against the tree-trunk.

'There's mother!' said Velvet suddenly.

Across the field, swaying like a ship at sea, came the red and yellow meat van.

'She's brought tea!' said Merry.

'She'll thread my needle!' said Velvet.

Mally ran out into the open and waved. The van nosed and swayed towards them.

'Father's driving! If he stops . . . He'll never let you race, Velvet!'

'Stop him buying the programme if you can! Here, tear ours . . . give him the wrong half! Then he won't buy another.'

Velvet snatched up the programme and tore a little piece out with her thumb-nail. The van drew up under the tree. Mi opened the door and the giant bulk of Mrs Brown descended backwards.

'We've done nothing, mother! Nothing at all!' said Mally.

'That's bad,' said Mrs Brown. 'Here's your tea.'

'I'm not stopping,' said Mr Brown, from the wheel. 'There's a sugar box in the back. Pull it out for your mother to sit on. You're wet through, the lot of you. You ought to come home.'

'Coats is soppy,' said Mrs Brown. 'How's your vests?'

'Dry,' said Velvet, edging away. 'Dry's a bone.'

'You stay for one more race or whatever you call it,' said Mr Brown, 'an' then you'll take them hosses home. I'll be back to fetch mother.'

'But we've PAID . . .' began Velvet in horror. The self-starter whirred and he was gone.

'Does he mean it, mother?'

'You're dripping,' said Mrs Brown, cutting up a Madeira cake. 'Mi, come round here an' get some food.'

The cake grew wet even as they ate it.

'What's the next?' said mother. 'Gimme the list.' She studied it for a moment.

'That's next, mother,' said Velvet, pointing.

'Was your name in it?' asked Mrs Brown looking at the hole.

'Yes . . . it was. 'Tis.'

There was a long pause and Mrs Brown slowly stroked her chin. Mi looked down on her old felt hat in which a pool of rain was settling. Velvet ran one nail under the other and shot out a piece of earth.

'I'll thread your needle,' said Mrs Brown at last.

Velvet looked into the heavy eyes and smiled. The eyes blinked with the violence and worship of the glance.

The voice of the Broadcaster came roughly through the wind and rain.

'Event Number Five,' said the Voice . . . 'Competitors for Event Number Five . . . go to the Collecting Ring.'

Sir Pericles was saddled in a moment, and Mrs Brown rose to her feet.

'Where'd I stand?' she asked.

'Mi'll take you. Mi! It's right far up there.'

Mrs Brown walked like a great soldier up the field.

In Velvet's heat she was the only child. She rode out of the gate of the Collecting Ring with four others – two livery-stable-men from Worthing, a grizzled woman with short hair and a hanging underlip, and a young man in checks on a hired horse with poverty streaks.

'I've plenty of chance,' she thought, 'I'm lighter than any of them.' All the horses were dripping and began to steam with excitement.

'Be slippery at the corner there,' said one of the livery-stable-men.

They reached the starting post, and the sodden Starter came down towards them.

The faces, shining in the rain, looked back at him. The young man in the check suit lay up on the inside against the rail. The woman with the hanging lip scowled at him and edged her horse nearer. Velvet came next, and on the outside the two stable-men. The flag was raised. Before it could fall the young man made a false start. While he was getting back into position the grizzled woman took his place.

'Don't shove!' said the young man, but the woman made no reply. Up went the flag again and the bounding of Velvet's heart swept Sir Pericles forward.

'Get back . . . that child!' shouted the Starter.

Velvet swung Sir Pericles back behind the line and brought him up. The flag fell again neatly as she got him square. She drove for the centre of the first hurdle. Out of the corner of her eye she saw the grizzled woman's horse run out. The young man in the checks she never saw again. Perhaps he never started. As she landed she saw a horse and man on the ground beside her. The heat was between Velvet and one livery-stable-man.

Sir Pericles, the little creature, brilliant and honest, never looked to right or left but stayed where Velvet drove him, straight at the middle of each hurdle. He fled along the grass, jumping as neatly as a cat, swung round the sharp, uphill corner towards the table where the sewers stood, Velvet kicking the stirrups free, neck and neck with the livery-man on a blue roan. The roan drew ahead. The sewers' table neared. Velvet flung herself off as they drew up; her feet ran in the air, then met the ground and ran beside the horse.

'What have you got off for?' said Mrs Brown calmly, as she began to sew.

Velvet glanced with horror at her rival, leaning from his saddle while a tall girl sewed at his sleeve. 'Oh . . .' she breathed. She had forgotten the instructions. She had had no need to dismount.

But Mrs Brown's needle flashed in and out, while the blue roan fidgeted and danced, and the tall girl pivoted on her feet.

It was an easy win for Velvet. She was in the saddle, off, and had time to glance behind, before the roan had started. She heard his galloping feet behind her but he never caught her up and Sir Pericles went steadily down the grassy slope, jumping his hurdles with willing care.

A burst of clapping and cheers went up.

'Stay in the field!' said a Steward. 'Wait for the other heats to be run.' Velvet sat alone in the rain, in a cloud of steam from the excited horse. One by one the winners of the three heats joined her.

The first was a boy of about nineteen, with a crooked jaw. Steaming and shining and smiling he rode up to her on a brown horse with a hunter-build, long tail and mane.

'You did a good one!' he said to her.

'I'd only one to beat,' she said, 'and even then it was the button that did it.'

'That's a beautiful little horse,' said the boy. 'He's *neat.*'

They turned to watch the finish of the next heat.

They were joined by a fat little man in a bowler hat, a dark grey riding coat and soaking white breeches. He took off his bowler as he rode towards them and mopped his shining bald head. His horse was a grey.

'What a horse . . .' he said as he rode up. 'I hired him. Couldn't hold him fer a minute. Just went slap round as though he'd got a feed at the winning post. I'll never pull it off a second time, not unless he chooses to! Lands on his head too, every time. Not a bit of shoulder.'

'The saddle looks too big for him,' said the boy. 'It's right up his neck. But he's a grand goer.'

'It's right up his neck, an' so'm I,' said the little man, dismounting. 'It's the way he jumps. Next round I'll be down and off and rolling out of your light! Here's the last! It's Flora Banks!'

'Who's she?' said the boy.

'Tough nut from Bognor,' said the little man under his breath.

Flora Banks wore a yellow waistcoat, had a face like a wet apple and dripping grey hair. She rode astride a bay horse that looked like a racer, lean and powerful and fully sixteen hands. Velvet's heart sank.

'My poor Flora,' said the little man calmly, bringing out a

match, 'you've got an overreach. You're out of it!'

The Tough Nut was off her bay in a second, flung her cigarette into the grass and knelt and took the bleeding forefoot tenderly in her hands. The big bay hung his head like a disappointed child. He was out of it. She led him, limping, away.

'Makes us three,' said the little man, mopping his head. 'Two really. I can't last another round. You go it, little girl, an' get the fiver. Hi, they're calling us.'

Down went the three horses to the starting post, reins slipping in cold fingers, rain whirling in puffs. Velvet's breath would not sink evenly on the downward stroke. She shuddered as she breathed.

'Lay up against the rails, little girl,' said the bowler hat. 'I'm so fast you can't beat me whatever you do, but I'm coming off. Where's that Starter? Goin' to keep our hearts beating while he drinks his coffee? Hi, where's that Starter? The blighter's drinkin' coffee!'

The Starter burst out of a little tent wiping his mouth and ran through the raindrops, that suddenly grew less. The miraculous sun broke all over the soaking field. The freshness was like a shout. Velvet shaded her eyes, for the start was into the west. Water, filled with light, shone down the grass. The flag was raised and fell.

The boy on the brown horse got a bad start. Velvet and the little man rose together at the first hurdle. Velvet had the inside and the grey lay behind her. At the second hurdle she heard him breathe, then lost him. At the slight curve before the third hurdle he had drawn up on her inside, between her and the rail. She had lost her advantage.

Suddenly the boy on the brown appeared on her left. Both the grey and the brown drew ahead and Velvet strung out a near third. Like hounds over a wall they rose, one, two, three over the fourth hurdle and went sweeping round the uphill curve to the table.

Mrs Brown stood like an oak tree. Velvet galloped and drew up in a stagger beside her, throwing the single rein loose on Sir Pericles' neck. She stooped and hung over him, kicking both feet free from the stirrups to steady him. Trembling, panting, his sides heaving in and out he stood, his four feet still upon the ground, like a bush blown by a gale but rooted. Mrs Brown's needle flashed.

Velvet was off, stirrups flying, down the grass hill, the blazing light no longer in her eyes, going east. First the grey, then the brown, were after her. At the fifth hurdle the grey passed her, but the brown never drew near. The grey was wound up to go. Its hind quarters opened and shut like springs in front of her. She saw it rise at the sixth hurdle just ahead of her, and come down almost upon its head. It slowed. As she drew up she saw the little man was done, stretched up unnaturally on its neck. He took a year falling. She passed him while he was still at it – jumped the seventh and eighth hurdles and whispered to herself as the noise went up behind the ropes, 'A fiver . . .' And the piebald's glistening future spread like a river before her, the gates of the world all open. She pulled up, flung herself off Sir Pericles and glanced down at his feet.

He was all right. And the Steward was examining her button . . . That was all right too! Here came the sisters . . . The little man in the bowler, unhurt, was leading his horse down the track. Mrs Brown . . . Where was mother? Mi was by her side.

'Lead him off! Don't stand there! You look daft,' said Mi lovingly, and his little blue eye winked and shone. 'Good girl, Velvet!' said Mr Croom as she neared the exit. And hands patted her and voices called.

The ruthless voice of the Broadcaster was gathering competitors for the next event.

'Thirty shilling is yours, Mi.'

'You'll have to give me forty. I want ten to get me teeth out of pawn.'

'You put them in again?'

'I had to. Hadn't nothing.'

'How is it they're so valuable, Mi?'

'Mass o' gold. My old Dad got 'em done. He said, "You always got money on you if you got gold in your mouth." I can raise ten shillings on them most towns.'

'You whistle better without them.'

'Yes, I do,' said Mi. 'Where's that Jacob?'

It was the evening, before supper. They had turned the horses into the field after a good meal, and the piebald in with them. He had shown no sign of kicking. He trotted happily about among the new companions, his tail raised in an arch and his nostrils blown out with excitement. Velvet leant on the gate and Mi stood beside her. The others had gone home before them down the road, clinking the buckets.

'Sir Pericles was lovely,' said Velvet for the twentieth time. Mi was tired of grunting assent. The reddest sun that ever sank after a wet day went down behind them and sent streams of light through rushes and branches. Mi shaded his eyes to look for Jacob, that thorn in his side.

'Was The Lamb really only fourteen-two?' asked Velvet casually.

'Some say fourteen-two. Some say fifteen.'

'Smallest horse ever won the National, wasn't he?'

'Won it twice.'

'You ever bin round there?'

'The course? Know every stick. Been on it hundreds a times.'

'What's the highest jump?'

Mi gazed into the field. He stuck his chin towards the piebald. 'He jumped as high as any today.'

'I thought he did,' said Velvet, low and happy.

There was a long silence. The fields rolled uphill. The hedge at the top of the field was indigo. Sir Pericles was cropping, like a tawny shadow against it. The piebald, disturbed and excited, cantered the length of the hedge, neighing. Sir Pericles looked up, kicked gaily at the empty air, and cantered too. Mrs James rolled an eye and laid her ears back.

Evenings, after triumphs, are full of slack and fluid ecstasy. The air swims with motes, visions dip into reach like mild birds willing to be caught. Things are heavenly difficult, but nothing is impossible. Here stood gazing into the field in the sunset the Inspirer, the Inspired and, within the field, the Medium.

Under his boil of red hair Mi's thoughts were chattering 'Why not?'

And beside him Velvet looked, throbbing with belief, at her horse.

'Pity *you* don't ride,' said Velvet at last.

'The rider's all right,' said Mi mystically.

'What rider?'

'You.'

A pause.

'There's jockeys from Belgium,' said Mi following the insane thread of thought, 'no one's ever seen before. Who's to know?'

'You think he could do it?'

'The two of you could do it.'

'Mi . . . oh, Mi . . .'

Pause.

'Who'd you write to? Fer entries.'

'Weatherby's.'

'Where are they?'

'Telephone book. London somewhere.'

'Weatherby's.'

There are evenings, full of oxygen and soft air, evenings after rain (and triumph) when mist curls out of the mind, when reason is asleep, stretched out on a low beach at the bottom of the heart, when something sings like a cock at dawn, a longdrawn wild note.

Velvet and Mi dreamed a boldness bordering on madness.

The race was being run in stage light, under the lamps of the mind. The incandescent grass streamed before Velvet's eyes.

There was an unearthly light around the horses, their rumps shone. The white of the painted rails was blue-white like ice. The grass snaked in green water under the horses' feet. There was a thunder rolling in the piebald like a drum. His heart, beating for the great day of his life.

'Weatherby's,' said Velvet again. The word was a gateway to a great park. You could touch it, crisp, crested, full of carving . . . *Weatherby's*. Green grass, white rails, silk jackets. Through the arch of Weatherby's.

'Who's to know I'm a girl?' said Velvet, very very far along the road.

Mi was not far behind her.

'Just wants thinking out,' he said. His belly felt hollow with the night air. 'Supper, Velvet.' Slowly they left the gate and walked towards the village.

'Once I caught a dove,' said Donald, sitting up to supper on the gymkhana night.

'Oh no,' said Mrs Brown absently.

'I did,' said Donald. 'It was in . . . July. When you was in France.'

'Never bin to France but once,' said Mrs Brown. And suddenly the soles of her feet tingled with the sting of Calais cobbles, slipping, slipping under her tired weight. Memories surged up.

In the air tonight, this gymkhana night, when little Velvet had touched the tail of glory, there was something abroad.

'It was on the roof,' said Donald.

(Coming up out of the water in the early dawn after a gale . . .)

'I put a ladder up. A man gave it to me. I caught it in my hand.'

Silence . . .

'I EAT it,' said Donald quietly, and looked round.

'Poor dove,' said Velvet kindly, as nobody said anything.

'It said I could eat it,' said Donald.

(The water had been kinder than the beach. She had been exposed in front of thousands, dripping, huge, shapeless, tired. She had been held up by her soaking legs and chaired to the hotel. The battle with the water had been pure and dark, but in the morning she began to wonder why she had done it. Dan had been pleased. It was for Dan that she had done it. He had made a warfare between the water and her strength and courage. She had never thought of the crowds on the beach, the cameras, and newspapers. She had a sense of honour and chastity as sharp as a needle, and she had been outraged. Great burning virgin as close as an oyster and dark as the water at night. Stupid, fierce, honourable, strong and courageous. She and Dan could have opened a new world together, he directing, she enduring. She could have been a great mare whom a jockey rode to victory.

Dimly behind the hooded eyes of the innocent and savage mother those aspirations washed.)

'It was that dove that made me sick . . .' said Donald.

'Shut up with that dove,' said Mr Brown, reading his paper.

Chapter IX

After three days of gale the sea's surface lay in an oily, moulded condition, yellow as clay, folds thick as treacle and casting shadows. Gulls tipped in the dun valleys and rose on the crests. No water broke. The clouds tumbled and heaved, subsiding, and shadows like the shadows of creatures streaked the sea.

After imprisonment of wind and rain the washing flew in banners down the gardens. Velvet mouched about the village, basking, her clothes and face dappled with sun. Little boys carried tyres to the yellow sea and floated in them. The village stank of seaweed.

By the head of the shore stood a singing mendicant, mouth yapping aimlessly, emitting a thread of aged sound.

Edwina walked lightly down the street with Teddy. Teddy carried his beach gramophone and Edwina's bathing dress. They waved to Velvet leaning on the cobbled wall and went down the gap to the beach. They did not want her and she did not want them, there was nothing sad about that.

There are pleasures earlier than love. A may tree, a cat's back will evoke them. Earlier than love, nearer heaven. As Velvet leant on the wall and heard the cries of Teddy's gramophone she would not have changed her bliss for theirs.

She turned and saw Meredith coming towards her and the two watched the gulls idly, side by side.

'I could eat,' said Meredith yawning.

'M'm,' said Velvet. She held the money bags.

After she had given Mi the forty shillings she had put three pounds in the Post Office Savings Bank. But Mr Brown, pleased with the performance at the gymkhana, had given her five shillings. She had wanted to bank this too but there had been outcry among the sisters.

'Come on, Velvet,' urged Meredith. Velvet pulled out two shillings, and laid them in a crack on the top of the wall. One of the shillings she put back again.

'We'll have one between us.'

'Doughnuts?'

'We can't eat six doughnuts each.'

'We'll have,' said Merry, 'one doughnut each, one candlegrease bun, one crunchie, one Mars . . .'

'I should be sick,' said Velvet decidedly.

'Perhaps sixpence between us is enough. One doughnut each, and one crunchie.'

'You go an' get 'em. An' bring me back the sixpence.'

Velvet lolled happily on the hot wall, just tickled and touched awake by the idea of approaching food. The juices in her mouth got ready. An aeroplane flew over her head, spewing advertisements in smoke. She turned on her back with her shoulders over the wall to read what it wrote.

'Buy Nougat Nobs' she read, written across the pale blue seat of God.

'Did you see the aeroplane?' said Merry suddenly beside her. 'I got Nougat Nobs instead of crunchies.'

'Well you can have 'em,' said Velvet. 'It'll bust my blessed plate.'

'Thanks,' said Merry contentedly, not protesting.

Meredith somnolent, loved her food, lived in dreams, loved her canaries, was inaccurate, incurable, and never quarrelled.

Standing against the sunny wall she was soon over-eaten, and undid the ends of her hard leather belt. The screaming of the canaries never really ceased for Meredith. As she ate slowly her head was full of yellow wings. Dreadnoughts and Rollers and Hartz Mountain and mating. Mating was her preoccupation.

If you mated a Hartz Mountain to a Roller . . . or a Yorkshire Dreadnought – What about the green streaks on the wings? Would they be increased if Mountain Jim were mated to Arabella? She leant back against the wall to ease her stomach and dreamt on. A child, when it is over-eaten, does not get a clouded brain.

In her mind the mating always took place safe and sure and certain, and with instant results. She saw a long line of descendants almost simultaneously created. She felt the power of the Patriarch, looking down her family line, and rambling, slow and vague she told a story to herself. Her memory tracks were scored by the noise of their songs wherever she walked. Constantly she was eased by dreams and sensations of flight. Some day she would construct a real aviary, real trees inside the wire netting, and would walk inside the bird house and call the birds off the branches on to her shoulders.

'Where's that sixpence?' said Velvet suddenly.

Meredith handed her fourpence.

'I got an extra two doughnuts,' she said. 'I was simply frightfully . . .'

'What?' said Velvet.

'Hungry,' said Merry.

There was a long, sun-warmed, friendly silence.

'I wish I could eat like that,' said Velvet with a sigh.

'You're nearly the youngest. You're weak,' said Merry, fallacious tags of breeding in her mind. 'You can breed a hen right out.'

'Mother's not bred out. Just look at her!' said Velvet, irking. 'And Donald's not weak!'

'I shouldn't think strength matters,' said Merry yawning. 'It's guts.'

'Mother says I'll get over being sick,' said Velvet. How often had she had assurance from the calm and rocklike eyes. Above the paunchy cheeks, eyes that held neither anxiety nor alarm. Mrs Brown watched the growth of Velvet as God might watch a sapling's growth; without concern, with unheeding conviction. She would grow, she would cease to be sick. Like Merry, if Mrs Brown had been asked what her hope and expectancy in life was for Velvet she would have answered 'guts'. It was what Dan Taylor had required of her, endlessly, all through the night. Against the tide too. Father must see to the fal-lals and the gold plates. She, Dan's Araminty, only wanted staying power.

'You weren't sick at the gymkhana,' said Merry. 'I forgot to expect you to be.'

'I prayed an' prayed,' said Velvet.

'D'you think that's any good?'

'Not much. Because I always do it. But I don't dare leave it out.'

Merry flicked a grain of flint down towards Edwina's head. It missed. Edwina stretched herself in the sun below the wall and put her arms behind her head.

'Don't,' said Velvet. 'She'll make a row. We're so comfy.'

'Pity she's getting a sort of enemy,' said Merry.

'It's because she's in love.'

'But why . . .?'

'It just turns you. Like drink.'

In happy silence they watched the silver enemy below them, her ash hair pillowed on her coffee arms. Teddy looked at her like a gooby. She flung a word to him now and then, and the gramophone, pushed into a hollow in the cobbles, sang on. 'It's lovely, that noise,' said Velvet dreamily, and licked the last stub of nougat.

There was a sound of hooves behind them and three horses came round the corner from the livery stables, setting out for the Hullocks.

Merry and Velvet swung round and leant, backs to the sea, on the wall to watch.

'What's the matter with people who can't ride?' said Merry.

'Dunno,' said Velvet.

They watched the riders intently.

'Nothing's right,' said Velvet.

'Look as though they were kneeling,' said Merry. 'Their knees are forward and their feet are back . . .'

'You can see miles away on the Hullocks,' said Velvet half shutting her eyes. 'They heave as the horse heaves. They have enormous legs, all loose.'

'It must be awful,' said Meredith, 'to ride like that.'

The horses disappeared and sun and sparrows took their place.

'Must be awful,' said Velvet after a while, 'to be a livery horse.'

Merry slid her feet into the sunny dust. It rose in a roll round the toes of her shoes and she said nothing.

'It's not what they're born for.'

'What are they born for?'

'They're simply born,' said Velvet rather suddenly, 'to try to get to know what one person thinks. Their backs and their mouths are like ears and eyes. That's why those horses move like that and hang their heads down from the wither like a steep hill.'

'What horses?'

'The livery ones. They've got broken hearts.'

'How d'you know?'

'Oh,' said Velvet, 'I can see. It's like seeing the dead go by.'

'You once said you'd go in a livery stable when you grew up.'

'I could never go in a livery stable,' said Velvet.

The sun shone and warmed her. Velvet was in a state of abeyance, of waiting. She was a pond which stood empty but was certain of the mysterious, condensing dew.

'I'm going home,' said Velvet, after a pause.

'I'm waiting here,' said Meredith.

Velvet left Meredith and slouched up the street. She looked in the shoe shop with an urge of heart. 'Butcher's Velvet,' thought Mr Ede, and crossed the street to speak to her.

'Piebald didn' do too bad at the Pendean,' he said, stopping and looking at the shoes. He was hardly prepared for the beaming eyes that turned on him. 'He's beautiful, Mr Ede,' said Velvet earnestly. 'I hope you'll never feel bad you let him go.'

'Rough animal,' said Mr Ede, embarrassed. 'Bit mad p'r'aps. You done wonders to him. Wouldn't stay in any field of mine.'

'He's settled down nicely,' said Velvet. 'He's a very boyish horse.'

Mr Ede passed this over as fanciful. He thought she looked queer too. Delicate and spiny. And all them teeth. In truth Velvet could look like a fairy wolf gone blonde. She had this look as she turned back upon the shoes. Ede left her and Mi touched her on the shoulder.

'Looked up Weatherby's?'

' 'Tisn't in the telephone book.'

'Just write "Weatherby's. Racin' experts. London,"' said Mi. 'Just ask for the rules of entry.'

'What'll I say?'

But Mi was in a hurry. He didn't know.

Her mind began its letter across tan and silver heels, plaid bedroom slippers and sea-shoes of canvas. She moved homewards, carrying disjointed words like broken crockery in a napkin.

The spaniels were sitting, sunning, round the door, Wednesday's joint disturbing them already. The bitch laid her nose from time to time to the bottom door-line and drew long breaths and rolled her yellow eyes. The chained house dog flew out silently, choked on the end of his chain and fell back.

The sitting-room was empty, mother in the kitchen. Velvet pulled her lesson books from the dresser drawer and found a sheet of foreign writing paper that had laid in the grammar book for months. The ink bottle was on the cactus shelf, the pen beside it.

She sat and wrote swiftly, for fear of being disturbed:

'Dear Sirs,

'I am an Owner of a Horse. Please could you send me the Rules of entering for the Grand National Race?

'I am, Sirs, Your obedient Servant,

'V. Brown.'

There was a bit of blotting paper in the meat ledger, an envelope in the dresser drawer. In five minutes she was going back down the street with the letter stamped with a three-ha'penny stamp, the letter addressed according to Mi's advice.

She and Mi met at the midday joint. She whispered: 'I've done it.'

'Written it?'

'An' posted it.'

He seemed surprised. She could not eat.

'I don't like cabbage,' said Donald.

He was not answered.

'I don't like it but I eat it,' he said looking at Velvet.

'You're a marvel,' said Mally.

'Yes, I am a marvel,' said Donald. 'I don't like cabbage, I don't like food, but I eat it. Velvet doesn't.'

This provocation blew over.

'Eat your food, Velvet,' said Mr Brown after a suitable interval. 'That plate sitting softer?'

'Much,' said Velvet. 'But I'm not hungry.'

'I'm not hungry either,' said Donald, 'but I eat my food. I eat it all up, even when I'm not hungry.'

'I don't like to see a great slice of English leg left like that,' said Mr Brown. 'If you can't eat it lift it back.' The slice was returned to the dish. Velvet thought, as she chopped up her cabbage and hid it round her baked potato, that the box at the post office had just been cleared.

'You girls bin eating snacks?' said Mr Brown, looking at Meredith's plate.

'I got gristle,' said Merry hurriedly, pushing with her fork, and dividing plot from plot.

'Doughnuts,' said Mrs Brown placidly. 'They look like it.'

'Pay for 'em or put 'em down?'

'Pay for 'em!' said Merry indignantly.

'I'll have no putting down,' said Mr Brown. 'Hand me that plate, Merry. You're behaving like a customer.'

Meredith got up and carried her plate to him.

'That's not gristle, that's fat,' said Mr Brown. 'You just carry that back and eat it up. If snacks in the mid-morning's going to spoil a leg for you, you better have no more of 'em. Ten sheep coming at four, Mi.'

'Right,' said Mi.

'To be killed?' said Donald.

'Yes,' said Mi.

'Why killed?' said Donald.

'To make meat for you.'

'For me?'

'I said so.'

'I want to see 'em be killed,' said Donald.

'Well you can't,' said his father.

'Do they break an' fall down and die?'

No answer.

'Who dies them?'

'I do,' said Mr Brown. 'And Mi.'

Donald looked at his father without the slightest disfavour but with added respect.

'If there's a sheep's head for tonight give it me while it's warm, Mi,' said Mrs Brown. 'You can't cook it so tender once it's chilled down.'

CHAPTER X

When the answer from Weatherby's came it contained terrible difficulties. Velvet took it to Mi.

'Oh God,' said Mi when he looked at the blue entry form. 'I oughta known. It brings it all back.' Mi's wicked knowledge of the North came over him in floods. 'There's this to be done . . . an' that . . . and this and that . . . See if we can't get round it. You'll be disqualified in the end in any case, my girl. Might as well be disqualified all round. All you want is the chance to do it. I wonder if we're dotty.'

'Who could you ask?'

'Ask!' said Mi. 'Ask the churchwardens. You leave it to me. It's Lewes races tomorrow. I'll be over there and have a talk. You get on with the animal. Leave a lot to me. An' don't talk!'

'I never!'

Mi glanced at her a moment. He had been absorbed in his thought.

'No, you don't,' he said. 'But D'wina'd hand it on to Teddy, and Merry'd forget she wasn't to speak . . . An' it may never happen. You'd best just get on with the animal if you think such a crack of it.'

'Don't you?'

Mi heaved a big breath, first in then out of his lungs. 'I think more of you,' he said in the end.

'I'm nothing without him,' said Velvet.

'Get on now,' said Mi. 'An' don't keep asking me how I'm getting on. What's more there's another thing. You might have a shot at the Tindles jumps in the mushroom valley.'

'They're all wired up.'

'Yes, well I'd unwire 'em. Take some pliers. They're a lazy lot over there now the horses are gone. There's no one in the valley before seven.'

September passed and October came. Velvet by now had grown bolder. She no longer rose in the dawn to fetch the piebald to the mushroom valley but took him in the red-haired Autumn under cold afternoon moons of October, on dew-drenched grass. The mushroom pickers cleaned the valley before dawn. No one came down from Tindles, the hill village of the Derby winner. The old man was old, old. His horses gone, his men lazy. He warmed his toes and looked at his Derby cup but kept indoors between the sideboard and the fire.

Velvet grew so bold she ceased to replace the barbed wire over the jumps. The great brushwork barriers stood up free and clean and twice a week the piebald leapt them from end to end of the field. Sometimes Mi came with a bamboo rod and caught him a flick on his belly or his hock as he flew over.

One day when his work was over he came in the evening with a spade and dug a pit before one of the jumps and dragged logs to lie at the lip of the pit to make the Pie take off earlier. He came back with Velvet in the morning early and she and the horse leapt the contraption. After which Mi filled it in again and threw sods on it.

'They'll think we've buried someone,' said Velvet. 'You do take a lot of trouble, Mi.'

'Know what he's just jumped?' said Mi, straightening his back.

'What?'

'Jumped the third on the National. Third jump's a ditch an' fence. Same as this one. I wrote to a chap on the railway up there for the measurements.'

'Railway?'

'Truckline. Runs on the raised embankment alongside the Course. You o'ny got to run down and measure.'

Now the piebald jumped as he had jumped the five-foot wall when they had first seen him, hitching his quarters up behind him and leaving inches to spare. Not a twig on the jumps moved except from the wind of his passage. Velvet lay on his neck like the shadow of an ape and breathed her faith into him.

One evening before supper, Mi and Velvet sat alone under the Albert lamp. Velvet read the accounts of races. The Cesarewitch. Prophecies about it beforehand.

'". . . the conditions will be ideal for all except the mudlarkers",' she read aloud. 'What's that, Mi?'

'Dud talk o' mutts,' said Mi.

'"Munition started so slowly he was always tailed"?'

'The same,' said Mi.

'And "he galloped the opposition down in grand style".'

'And the same,' said Mi.

'Oh no!' said Velvet. 'I like that! It's what I'll do. I'll gallop the opposition down. It's grand.'

'If you like,' said Mi.

'I do,' said Velvet.

Silence.

'We gotta call him something,' said Mi.

'What? The piebald? Can't we call him The Pie?'

'If you like. It's a mutt name.'

'I'll always call him The Pie. But if he's got to have something grand . . .'

'We gotta choose the name and choose racing colours and send up and ask Weatherby's if they'll pass 'em. Sooner the better. They'll print 'em in the Calendar.'

'I'll have black and pink,' said Velvet.

'You'll look awful.'

'Could we call him Unicorn?' said Velvet slowly.

'That's the sort,' said Mi. 'Longish. Historical.'

'Is Unicorn historical?'

'Seems to me.'

'He could just be Unicorn for the race?'

'Yes he could. But he'll be put down Unicorn for ever in the history books.'

'On'y if he wins, Mi . . .'

'Win or no he goes down. Some of those books put every runner that ever ran. Starting with the "Lottery" year, with Jem Mason up. That was eighteen thirty-nine. Seventeen starters.'

'You know a heap.'

'Any chap knows anything knows the first Grand National.'

'Lamp's smoking, Mi.'

Mi turned it down.

'An' Mi?'

'M'm.'

'I don't like Unicorn.'

'Well, think of something else.'

'I'll never like anything but The Piebald. It's his name. He's got to go in the books like that.'

Mi looked up. The thin face opposite him had grief in it.

'They weren't all so grand,' he said at last. 'There was Jerry M. and Shady Girl. An' Old Joe won it in eighteen eighty-six. An' there was Hunter an' Seaman and Miss Lizzie, an' the Doctor, an' The Colonel . . . Why there was The Colonel! He won it twice. You call him The Piebald an' it won't hurt. It'll do fine.'

Velvet gave him a look of love. 'Thank you, Mi,' she murmured.

'Here, take the papers,' said Mi, 'an' look at 'em.'

'Gotta enter his sire and his dam,' said Velvet, poring over the Rules.

'Well, that's that,' said Mi yawning.

'Whad'you mean that's that?' said Velvet. 'He's got a sire and a dam somewhere, hasn't he?'

'Orphan. Horse is an orphan. Here, hand me the Rules!'

Mi drew the lamp nearer and leant his face deeply upon the little page. 'In entering' . . . m'm . . . m'm . . . 'he shall be described by stating a name,' . . . We gotta name. Settled. 'The age he will be at the time of the race' . . . 'Blacksmith says he's six. Might be more. We'll put "aged".'

'That's a horrid word.'

'It's fine. It means grown up. No more o' them silly years. We'll put "aged".'

'What's next?'

'The colour' . . . (they'll cough a bit when they read he's a piebald) 'and whether a horse, mare or gelding, and the Calendar or Stud-Book names of his sire and dam. That's where they get us!'

'Oh Mi . . .'

'Wait a bit! "If the sire or dam has no name in the Calendar" . . . wait a minute, wait a minute . . . "or if the pedigree or the sire or dam be unknown, such further particulars as to where, when, and from whom the horse was purchased or obtained must be given as will identify him." That's us all right.'

'What'll you put? You can't put about the shilling an' the raffle.'

'Make 'em sit up.'

'Too much. They'll sit up and see me!'

'You're right, yes. Pity though. Been a bit a fun. We'll put "Bought from Thomas Ede, Farmer," an' the date. Previous bought in Lewes Market . . . .'

'That reads odd.'

'You aren't asked to state all the buys. We'll leave it at Ede.'

'Anything else?'

'Not that I can see.'

'S'sh! Here's the others!'

Donald had out his jigsaws. He was doing a map of the world in big simple pieces. He could not get it started because two bits of the margin were missing. He begged and pleaded and nagged, 'Will you help me? WILL you help me?'

Merry helped him most. Mally stuck in a piece or two. Edwina bent over him and played the mother till she got bored.

'There's India!' said Edwina, skipping from mother to teacher.

'All the pink bits, Donald, belong to England.'

'What's England?'

'Us.'

'There's a pink bit and there's . . . LOOK Donald . . . there's a . . .'

'D'you know,' said Donald looking at her with his earnest charm, 'in my black socks I've got HOLES!'

'Goo!' said Edwina laughing suddenly. 'An' you haven't any black socks either . . .' and looking up she saw Teddy's face under the light of the lamp outside. She was gone with the swoop of a moth through the door.

'Will you help me?' began Donald again, leaning towards Mally. Mally flicked a slice of wood towards him. 'There's England and France in that bit.'

'What's France?'

'Over the water,' said Mally, chucking her thumb over her shoulder. 'Over the sea.'

'I seen France once,' said Donald.

'No!'

'I seen France once an' all the houses were slipping down in the water.'

'Huh!' said Mi. 'He doesn't know it's land. Thinks it's built on the Channel!'

'Bed, Donald,' said Mrs Brown in the doorway.

'I'm busy,' said Donald. 'We're all busy.'

'Get on, Donald,' urged Mi.

'Why do they have supper'n not me?' said Donald, feverishly searching for a piece of wood.

Lewes races had long gone by. Mi had made his arrangements. He had met a friend here and a friend there and had a talk or two and borrowed a bit, had his week's wages in advance from Mr Brown, and finally had paid a visit to Croydon. Edwina didn't notice, Merry didn't ask, and Mally, her nose twitching, didn't know enough to go upon, though sometimes she prodded like a person prodding with a stick in mud who thinks a treasure can be seen.

One day Mi came to Velvet after supper. He whistled her out of the living-room with a suck of his tooth and a cock of his eye. 'Sign this,' he said in Miss Ada's stall, the private sitting-room of their lives. Miss Ada ate her bedding undisturbed.

'What is it?' said Velvet.

'It's a Clearance,' said Mi. 'You put "James Tasky" here.'

He had his pen in his hand and a glass bottle of ink.

'Who's James Tasky?'

'He's you. He will be you in a post or two. Just ask me nothing. Sign what I say.'

Velvet wrote at the bottom of the paper 'James Tasky', balancing the paper on the lip of the manger. Mi produced three inches of blotting paper from his pocket.

'Now . . .' he said with satisfaction. 'Now we post it . . . see? An' we get a licence . . . see? An' the real Mr Tasky's not even in England. What a catch!'

'Where is he?'

'Being sick on the Baltic, I shouldn't wonder. He told me all about it. Horrible sea the Baltic. Water's shallow and bumps on the bottom an' comes up again. How people can go in ships beats me.'

'We gotta have the name in by the second Tuesday in January,' said Velvet.

'Say that on the form?'

'Yes.'

'Well, we'll have it in. We've put our backs in this now, and our shirts an' all. What d'you call it? About that horse? Putting it what?'

'Putting The Piebald in history,' said Velvet. 'I think of that whenever I feel giddy and it stops.'

'Well I'm putting you in history. See? Like my old Dan put Araminty Potter. It's a foreseen thing. Like God might a thought of. Believe in God, Velvet?'

'Yes, and no,' said Velvet. 'Yes, and no,' and sighed.

'Shouldn't have asked,' said Mi cheerfully. 'Private. Come along now and get a stamp out of your mother for me. I'm done this week to a penny.'

Christmas came and went. The Piebald's muscles grew tauter. One evening in the first days of January, Mr Brown took Edwina and Mally and Meredith to the pictures. Velvet would have gone but she felt shivery after tea. When they had left the house Velvet and her mother and Mi sat alone. Mrs Brown did a patience, Mi cut a piece of cork to fit a bottle, Velvet did nothing, the wind howled round them, the carpet rose against the door. The spaniels lay heaped in Miss Ada's stall.

'Bus'll be near blown over,' said Mi. 'They'll catch it going in.'

Mrs Brown laid out another card. Jacob shivered and recrossed his delicate fore-feet.

Mi looked at Mrs Brown as he cut his cork and knew the moment had come to include her. When he looked at her he saw a pillar of fire. He put aside the great dun-coloured coating, the enormous thighs, the shoulders which bore a pack of muscle like a yoke across them. He saw instead those mysterious qualities that made him say of any uncouth, unwieldy, unmanageable horse, 'He's got heart.' By heart he meant a heart that would stay.

'There's a horse,' he said, feeling his way to break the silence, 'over at Pendean would carry you.'

'Never bin on a horse,' said Mrs Brown.

'Makes no odds,' said Mi indifferently – but he would not let the silence close again.

'Should tell yer Ma 'f I were you, Velvet,' he said in an odd voice. 'Now's your minute.'

Velvet looked up. Mrs Brown laid out her cards unmoved.

Velvet watched her own feet. 'Piebald's fit,' she mumbled, 'to run in the National.'

Mrs Brown ruminated, laid down her cards. Said:

'What about it?'

'Thought of runnin' it,' said Velvet.

'You did?'

'M'm . . .'

'The Grand National with them jumps?'

'M'm. . . . Thirty jumps.'

'Stiff,' said Mrs Brown.

Nobody spoke. Mi cut his cork. His fingers stuck and slipped. Velvet would never disobey her mother.

'What'll it cost?' said Mrs Brown.

'A hundred pounds to enter. And money for a horse-box. An' me night's lodging. (I gotta see it).'

'What do you win if you win?'

'Oh,' said Velvet vaguely, 'thousands and a cup. But it's not that, it's for the horse. Besides, if they find out they'll disqualify me. It's only for the horse.'

'What makes you think it can win?'

'It can.'

'Can it, Mi?'

'Shouldn't wonder.'

'Well,' said Mrs Brown, and gathered up the cards into a neat pack. Her peasant's eye, half shrewd, half visionary, inspected the idea, and the features of her big face not stirring she moved her head with elephantine majesty. Then she rose and going to the sideboard took out a key from a drawer. She left the room and was heard above walking in her own.

Velvet closed her eyes. Her feet were cold.

'My feet are cold, Mi.'

'Keep still. Lie still.'

Mrs Brown came back with a box, her lips moving as though she were talking to herself. Unlocking the box on the table she counted out money, old-fashioned money, gold. Gold sovereigns.

Mi leant forward. Velvet sat up. Mi knew what they were.

'Your prize? What you won?' said Mi, quiet.

'Kept it,' said Mrs Brown. 'Thought I might. Thought I would.'

'Look at it,' said Mi. 'Never seen such a thing since I was a lad.'

Mrs Brown's thick fingers built castles with the coins.

'There's a hundred. Twenty fer expenses.' She looked straight at Velvet. 'I gotta fancy, Velvet, that you pay your entry in this.' She tapped the castles.

'Pay in the gold itself?' said Mi.

'It'll bring you luck,' said Mrs Brown.

'Weatherby's'll think it odd,' said Mi.

'You got a thing you sign?' said Mrs Brown.

'Yes,' said Mi. And fumbled in his coat pocket.

Mrs Brown took the blue form and read it.

'Not there,' said Mi, 'that's the Grand Military. Next page. Top a' page seventeen. "Liverpool – continued," it says.'

Mrs Brown read in silence.

'Queer,' she said at last. 'Queer thing. I had a feeling.'

'What?' said Mi.

'An' see there,' said Mrs Brown, handing him the form and plunging her finger on it. 'See what it says. "Sov. Ten sov. each. Fifty sov. extra." There's the wording clear. They can't go back on it. You use them sovereigns. I had a fancy they'd come in.'

Velvet hung softly against her mother, putting her arms round her shoulders. Mrs Brown took her suddenly on her lap. Mi was so affected he called Jacob into the yard. But before he went he hit his lips three times with his index finger at Velvet behind her mother's back. She stared at him vacantly and he shook his head and closed the door.

'Who'll tell father?' whispered Velvet.

'I'll tell your father,' said Mrs Brown rocking her.

Of this discussion Velvet heard nothing. When the battle was over she was given no more than the result. But in the deep of the night, forces were involved that stirred Araminty Potter to love and to fury, and finally to love again. In meeting a hard, but as it turned out a brittle, opposition from her husband, Araminty rose like a sea monster from its home. After her years of silence she grunted with astonishing anger, and William, powerless and exasperated, stung like a gnat upon a knotted hide. That something which was obstinate and visionary and childish bound Mi and Velvet and her mother together, and in the night Araminty, in doing battle for their dreams, fought too for her own inarticulate honour.

The difference ran to its end, they were shaken profoundly, and slept in friendship at dawn. Mr Brown rose next morning, spiritually bruised, feeling that he was going to be made ridiculous, but acquiescent.

The first effect of this discussion was that The Piebald stood in Miss Ada's stall and Miss Ada found herself once more among the tools (which she shared at night with the spaniels). Velvet took her gymkhana money out of the bank to buy oats, and what she could not buy her mother saved from the housekeeping.

The horse was walked endlessly uphill. There was not a steep hill-surface for miles around that Velvet had not sought out and ascended. The faulty, pear-shaped quarters of The Piebald swelled with muscle. Clipped out, he shone blacker and whiter than ever, his long tail and mane washed in the vinegar suds from Edwina's hair-rinsing, his pink albino hooves scrubbed with a nail brush and polished. He grew to look like a newly-painted rocking horse, freshly delivered.

On the first Monday in January Mi took the whole entry money of a hundred pounds in gold sovereigns in a bag up to London. He went to Messrs Weatherby in Cavendish Square, walked up the stone steps, pushed the doors, and stood at a wooden counter not unlike a bank. A tall man asked him off-handedly what he wanted.

'Entry. Fer the Gran' National,' said Mi, pulling out the completed form, dumping the heavy bag on the counter, and pushing it towards the man.

'What's that?'

'Th'entry money,' said Mi.

'Ten pounds. Have you brought it in silver?' said the man superciliously, touching the neck of the bag with his fingers.

'Ten? I've brought a hundred. In gold.'

The man drew the bag towards him and opened it. He peered inside with astonishment. 'What's this? Sovereigns?'

'A hundred sovereigns,' said Mi.

The man looked at Mi consideringly. He indicated a stool. 'Will you wait?' he said. He was away a moment, then returned with a companion whose air was even more exalted and critical.

'Do I understand,' said the second man, 'that you have brought a hundred sovereigns in pre-war gold to pay for an entry for the Grand National . . . Race?' He brought out the word 'race' as though it were the crime which Mi had committed.

'Yes, sir,' said Mi cheerfully and simply and shifted his feet and leant on the counter. 'It's quite simple, sir. I thought you'd like it best jus' as it was. I didn't know where best to change it into paper an' as this is as good's a bank' (the man's eyes lightened just a shade) 'I thought I'd bring it here.'

'To what horse does this refer?'

'It's a piebald horse. Property of Miss V. Brown. She owns it. Her father's a butcher down . . . The address is here.' He smoothed out the form.

'Who is the trainer?'

'Privately trained, sir.'

'Not by the owner?'

'Well, yes, by the owner. Yes, sir, trained by her since she's had it.'

'How do you come to bring up this money?'

Mi paused a moment and sucked his tooth.

'It's a fancy of Miss Brown's mother, sir. She had the sovereigns tucked away for years. Kind of store, sir. She had a fancy it would bring the horse luck if she paid the entry money with the sovereigns.'

'I'm afraid we can't do deals in gold. This is worth more than a hundred pounds.'

'You mean I get some change back?'

'You would if we took it. But we can't have anything to do with the price of gold at the present rate. That is not our business.'

'I don't think,' said Mi slowly, 'that Mrs Brown wants any change. A hundred sovereigns is a hundred pounds to her. She's old-fashioned. She's set on paying the entry with this hundred pounds here in this bag, sir.'

'There's another thing,' said the man. 'You don't need to pay a hundred now. It's ten sovereigns now, fifty sovereigns extra if left in after 30 January, with an additional forty sovereigns if left in after 13 March.'

'Sovereigns,' murmured Mi. 'It says "sovereigns", and these are sovereigns.'

'Well that's the . . .' (the gentleman looked acid), 'the wording dating from the original . . . er . . . inception of this form.'

'Clear enough,' said Mi. 'Sovereigns it says. I don't want to make difficulties, sir, but I've brought you sovereigns, haven't I?'

'I think you had better wait,' said the gentleman, and he and his companion disappeared. Mi sat on the stool again and eyed his bag. He read the antique sporting notices. There was a ginger and green notice, stiff with discoloured varnish, about paying for the weights in the weighing room. He frowned at it. He had never heard of such a thing. Then he saw that it was dated a hundred years ago.

After a long interval the gentleman returned, alone.

'The sovereigns will be accepted,' he said curtly, 'but there is no need to deposit more than ten as yet.'

'I'd sooner leave the lot,' said Mi obstinately.

'The reason for the division of the entry amounts,' said the gentleman, disliking Mi more and more, 'is in case the horse becomes by a later date unable to run.'

'This horse'll run,' said Mi.

'You cannot foresee,' said the gentleman, 'acts of God.'

'M'm I can,' said Mi, 'm'm I can. You take the lot an' stack it for me. Safer here. I might get it lifted off me on the way home. You got a fine big place here. You got room for ninety sovereigns stacked away. You can give me a paper for it. They need me at the butcher's down here. 'Tisn't easy to keep making journeys. You'll need the lot before we're done.'

Again the gentleman disappeared and a very exalted head was put round the lintel of an inner cubicle and two very shrewd and dwelling eyes inspected Mi.

Finally a receipt was handed to him, the bag and form taken from him and Mi was ready to depart.

'Who's your rider?' said the gentleman, almost sociably at last.

'Foreign chap,' said Mi instantly. 'Comin' over later.'

'He'll have to get his Clearance, you know,' said the gentleman, 'from his own accredited Jockey-Club.'

'Yes, sir,' said Mi quickly. 'Yes, thank you, sir.'

'What's his name? Do we know him?'

'Tasky. James Tasky.'

'English?'

'Mother's English. Chap's half Russian.'

'From which country then does he get his Clearance? There is racing of course still in Russia.'

'Mr Brown's working it all out,' said Mi. 'I'm just the hand down there. I know what I hear them say, that's about all.'

'Well, good-day then. Just a minute. You'll notice on that receipt "Received one hundred sovereigns in gold sovereigns, value to be decided by Coutts's Bank when the final payment is due". That means you get an amount returned. You'll explain that to the Owner, please.'

'Right, sir. Good-day, sir.'

Mi was out in the airy light of Cavendish Square and he ran his hand across his brow.

'Mother nearly bitched it with 'er whimsies,' he said.

It was March. The days of March creeping gustily on like something that man couldn't hinder and God wouldn't hurry.

'What about me jacket?' said Velvet in her whisper, somewhat hoarse, again and again.

'*Leave* yer jacket!' said Mi testily. 'I keep telling you. Leave me thinking of it.'

'I can't sew, remember,' said Velvet warningly.

'Think I don't know that! My sister's sewing it.'

'Your SISTER! You gotta sister!' Velvet sat bolt upright.

'I gotta sister. I got two.'

'You never told us!'

'I'm no family man,' said Mi shortly.

'Your old Dan . . . your old father's dead?'

'He's dead!'

'You gotta mother?'

'Dead too. But where I sprung from an' what I left behind's my business.'

'But your sister's my business. She's sewing my coat.'

'And well she can do that for me,' said Mi, reflecting. 'I never asked her for a penny. I got her her job. Bin there years.'

'Where?'

'Sews for a tailor at Newmarket. Does the tailored shirts. I sent her that top of yours yer ma said was past darning.'

'The top of that cotton dress what mother used the bottom for knickers?'

'That's the one.'

'Well, it was too small, anyway. I hope she makes it bigger. What about the stuff?'

'Black an' pink I told her. She's in the way of getting the stuff up there. She'll get the cap made, too.'

'And the breeches and the boots?'

'You leave it to me up at Aintree. That'll sort itself up at Aintree. Overnight. The valets go round with spares in their cases.'

'Valets?'

'Fellows that look after the jockeys. Press up their clothes an' do their boots. There's a gang of them go round the race meetings.'

'Now,' said Velvet at last, as low as low, 'there's another thing.'

'M'm?'

'Mother,' said Velvet. And the spinning air seemed to stop round them in anxiety.

'It's a thing I'm thinking of too,' said Mi. 'Worries me.'

'Yes,' said Velvet. 'D'you know, Mi?'

'What?'

'I couldn't do it f'I didn't tell her.'

The telling was done at the shop at night. Mi arranged it when Mrs Brown was totting up. She spared the electric and totted by candlelight.

'You gotta pretend I'm not your child,' said Velvet, long

after bedtime. She dragged up her words as though the roots were deep.

'You was nineteen when you swum the Channel,' said Velvet. 'I'm fourteen but my chance's come early. You mustn't think I'm your child. I'm a girl with a Chance.'

Her mother's throat clicked. She blazed into fire without moving an eyelash.

'Mi's in the street, waitin',' said Velvet. 'It's him an' me.' (She paused at the gasp her mother gave.)

'We're out on it together,' went on Velvet, not knowing the terror that cooled her mother's fire. 'We think . . . I think . . .' (coming up closer and speaking very low) 'I kin *ride* the horse.'

'Almighty God,' said Mrs Brown, mild and reverent. She was thanking Him that her child was her shining Velvet. Not all messed up with love. Not all messed up with love an' such. That Mi was to Velvet what Dan had been to her, that stuff grander and tougher than a lover. Now what was this suggestion that was like a wild dream?

'In the race, Velvet?'

Velvet described the machinery, Mi's plans, Mi's devices.

'If I'm found out then they'll send me home. Father'll be angry. Just as likely I won't be found out. Well then, we'll do our best. The horse is great. He's like a Bible horse.'

The interview was over, except the silence and the thinking.

'I don' want to speak to Mi about it,' said Mrs Brown at last. 'Tell him not to speak to me about it. Not a word. It's a weight on me. It's a terrible . . . I can't be but your mother, Velvet . . . To think Mi shoulda lent himself to this.'

Then at the very end . . . 'I'm all ashake. Let there be no whisperin' an' talking. I must put it from me an' pray to God.'

Velvet left her. The candle guttered but the totting did not continue. Later the heavy woman walked home.

CHAPTER XI

March ran two thirds of its days.

Mr Larke, the chemist, called in to fetch his meat book. 'I'm hair-washing,' called Mrs Brown from the scullery. Mr Larke stood in the scullery door critically.

'Two drops a' camomile is what you ought to add,' he said.

'Bleach 'em?'

'Bleach 'em.'

'Bleached enough already.'

'When I say "Bleach" I should say "Bring out the colour" .'

'Vinegar's what I use,' said Mrs Brown.

'So I can smell,' said Mr Larke.

'I got your last week's book made up,' said Mrs Brown, rinsing Edwina, 'it's on the sideboard by the apples. Now Velvet. Edwina, you go and rub your head an' Mally'll give you a hand.'

Edwina came staggering back into the living-room, her head and face blindly wrapped in the bath towel Mrs Brown had popped over her. 'My back aches,' she grumbled. 'I wish I could wash my own.'

'Velvet!' called Mrs Brown.

'I'm coming . . .'

When Velvet reached the scullery Mrs Brown looked at her. 'I won't risk it,' she said. 'Might make you squeamish, bending. I'll brush it through with a wet brush an' you can sit by the fire an' comb it.'

'I'm taking the book then,' called Mr Larke loudly. 'It's a great day for you all. Anxious. I'm not a racing man myself but we've all got our eyes on you, Velvet. There's a bit of money on you in the village.'

'Thank you,' said Velvet, through the brushing.

'Say it louder,' said Mrs Brown.

'Thank YOU,' shouted Velvet.

'Right,' said Mr Larke. 'Where you stopping?'

'Hotel,' shouted Mrs Brown. 'She's doing it slip-slap. (Why don't he go? Makes you testy all this popping in an' good-wishing) . . .'

('There he goes,' said Velvet. 'I can feel the draught on my legs.')

'I'm dry!' shouted Edwina. 'Can I go?'

'You can't be dry. Come here an' let me feel.'

Edwina came in.

'Damp all roun' your glands,' said Mrs Brown, feeling. 'You don't go down the street like that.'

'Teddy's just . . .'

'Teddy kin wait.'

'He can't.'

'Anybody kin wait, Edwina,' said Mrs Brown brushing hard, 'for a pretty girl.'

Edwina suddenly smiled all over her light-built face. She went back to the living-room.

'Isn't she getting grown-up,' said Velvet.

'You're all on the edge of it.'

'Not me.'

'There you are!' said Mrs Brown, laying down the brush. 'You fluff up with a bit of water.'

'It'll all be down again flat in an hour.'

'Greasy scalp,' said Mrs Brown. 'Get Meredith down for me. She's with the birds.'

It was the last evening before the start at dawn. Velvet and Mi were travelling to Aintree in the horse-box. The last evening meal. Donald was allowed to sit up. Taps came on the door as they ate and friendly voices called in. The whole village had of course long known that the piebald horse, won for a shilling, was going to be run in the Grand National. Velvet's Grand National. 'Gran' National Velvet,' Mr Croom called out to her in the street. 'Good morning, Gran' National Velvet!' and two boys outside the sweet-shop had clapped their hands. 'Got any tips for the National?' called the postman.

'The Piebald!' said Velvet with her shy look.

'Yes they're going up to Liverpool tomorrow,' said Mrs Brown at the door twenty times. 'Mi an' Velvet are going in the horse-box.' She filled the doorway with her body and behind her shadow Velvet sat. It was a soft March night between a pair of howling gales, a black, cold trough of peace, pierced with stars. Stars that above her mother's head as she stood in the open street doorway seemed like Christmas trees, slender, growing into the sky. The Albert lamp on Edwina's hair, her father's folded neck, her mother's majesty and silence, Donald's film face and dear, disgusting habits, the sideboard, heavy, loaded, bottles of ink, dish covers, salmon tins, apples, vinegar bottles, Merry's bird-absorbed face, Mally's loyal and sharp eyes, Mi's grin, Mi's slouch, Mi's way of coming through the door, Mi's shadow, the lying Jacob, the bitch-seeking, pleasure-loving, self-indulgent Jacob, agreeable dog, sensitive, agreeable dog . . . these things (not in words), but in the burning warmth of the present, swelled her leave-taking heart. She had a wordless premonition that this was an egg into which it was impossible to re-enter. When the shell had burst, it was burst forever. She felt this only as a dog howls for packing, mournful and simple and going, going, gone.

Going, going, gone, full of stars and cacti, and yellow canaries screaming in the morning.

'What d'you want, Velvet?'

'I'm getting my shell-box.'

In silence they watched her fetch her box and put it beside her plate.

Edwina laughed suddenly.

'Coo lummy, Velvet! Paper horses just before the Grand National!'

'Beastly pair o' words,' muttered father. 'Get 'em from Teddy . . .'

'H'm . . . Teddy uses better words 'an that!'

(Warm bickering of family life. Fathers and daughters . . .)

'Can I see wot's inside that box?' said Donald.

Velvet's face lightened. Donald should look at them tonight. He had never set his fingers on them before.

'Have you finished, Donald? Come an' sit on my lap.'

'I kin climb up. Don' you help me.' He walked up the bars of her chair like a ladder and bumped himself down on to her lap from the arm.

She opened the lid and a little shell fell off.

'You've dropped a shell!' (burstingly.)

'I must stick it back.'

'Let me look!'

'Ssh, wait . . .' Velvet put her thin finger inside and hooked up a race-horse.

'Hullo! This is Grakle!' she said. 'Who's been changing them round? Who's touched my box?'

'I did,' said Merry in a small voice, 'I did, Velvet. I'm sorry.'

Velvet looked astonished. 'I don't mind, Merry,' she said. 'I didn't think you ever cared about them.'

'It was yesterday afternoon,' said Merry. 'The canaries were so alive. You can't *do* anything with them. I took your horses out to exercise. I just took out the National winners and jumped a bush behind Peg's Farm.'

'Show me, show me,' hammered Donald, leaning over the box and poking his fingers inside.

Velvet put her hand over his fingers. '(In a second, Donald . . .) but I'm glad, Merry. I'd love you to take them out. Which ones did you take?'

'Tipperary Tim an' Sergeant Murphy and Manifesto. Doesn't Manifesto look lovely with his ears forward and the shine on his shoulder? He's a right-facing one. Where'd you cut him from?'

But Velvet bent her head suddenly over Donald. She had cut

him from a library book down at the schoolhouse.

'*Now* pull them out!' said Donald.

'All the National Winners are on top,' said Velvet, groping. 'The ponies are underneath. There's a tiny . . . there's a Shetland . . . Here it is. Look, Donald! Isn't he fat and like a kitten?'

'I like real horses,' said Donald, unmoved.

'Good, good boy,' said Mally.

'Oh there's my darling Chestnut Fourteen-Two!' said Velvet, half mourning over them. 'Oh why haven't I looked at them for so long?'

'Can't do everything, Velvet,' said her father, twisting his chair round so that he could read better under the lamp. 'You got your things packed up?'

'They're ready,' said mother, clearing away the last dish.

'I'm going to bed,' said Mi. 'We're off at five. Won't do her no good to sit up.'

'She won't,' said Mrs Brown. 'She'll go in half an hour.'

'On top o' my food!' said Velvet indignantly.

'Food or no,' said mother.

'Plate all right?' said father.

'Sitting fine,' said Velvet, who knew this was a gesture of love.

'Let me see that Manifesto,' said Mi, standing in the doorway. Velvet picked the horse out.

'Won twice,' said Mi. '97 . . . an' 99.'

'How'd you know all that, Mi?' said Mr Brown from his lamp and paper.

'Dunno,' said Mi. 'There it is. What a shoulder . . . eh? What a horse . . . eh? Looks too clever to win.'

'Shouldn't they be clever?' said Edwina.

'Jumpin' thirty jumps when they can stan' still . . .!' said Mi. 'He did that Course eight times. Greatest National horse ever was. Why, he won it twice.'

'I can't understand you, Mi,' said Edwina. 'You just said he wasn't clever.'

' 'Tisn't everything to be clever,' said Mi, and disappeared to bed.

'How come Mi never to ride?' said Mr Brown into his newspaper.

'Tell me some more,' said Donald.

'I wish we could all go to Liverpool,' said Mally.

'Cost too much,' said Mr Brown. 'Yer mother plumpin' her prize-money on Velvet that's one thing! We can't spend no more – just in the air.'

'Bed for you, Donald,' said mother.

'Tell me one more horse 'fore I go.'

'There was once a horse called Moifaa,' gabbled Velvet, looking at her mother.

Mrs Brown nodded. 'Just tonight. Just a quick one.'

Donald swung round his eyes and hooked them upon Velvet's lips.

'Moifaa was sent from New Zealand in a ship.'

'Where's that?'

Velvet pointed to the floor with her finger. 'Same as Australia. Down there. Th'other side.'

'M'm . . . m'm . . .' said Donald greedily, waiting.

'The horse was sent right round the world and the ship went down near Ireland.'

'How d'you know?' said Mally, listening like Donald.

'Mi told me. An' the ship went down an' the horse swam to an island off the coast, and the island had salt grass an' there was nothing to eat an' the horse walked up an' down the seashore looking out to sea an' neighing.'

'An' what?'

'Screaming for help.'

'The horse did?'

'Yes. An' fishermen were fishing an' they rowed near an' saw him. A horse standing neighing on an island where there'd never bin a horse. Never bin a cow. Never bin anything. It gave 'em the creeps an' they went home.'

'Did they leave him there?'

'Left him there all night with all that grass an' all of it salt an' all that water an' all of it salt, and him used to a good stable and lots of men. He musta bin scared stiff. He was a great big ugly horse, seventeen hands high, an' I bet he was a brave horse.'

'Did he die?' said Donald, his eyes blazing.

'No, he didn't die.'

'Yes he did. I KNOW he did.'

'You can't know because he didn't. He was fetched by a steamer or something . . .'

'He DIED,' said Donald with a blazing, inner look.

'He didn't, he didn't. He won the National.'

'He died on that island,' said Donald like a fanatic. 'I was there.'

'You weren't. What a story! You weren't born.'

'I was born, I was born . . .'

'You were a star,' said Edwina annoyingly.

'I wasn' a star I was born an' I was there an' that horse died. He died on that salty place an' I saw 'im die and he lay down an' his eyes . . .'

'Hysterics,' said Mrs Brown calmly and whisked him up. 'He's never any good when he's missed his hour.' Donald went to bed weeping and was asleep in ten minutes.

'You didn't wash him, mother!' said Mally, scandalized, on her mother's return.

'Wants sleep, not washin',' said Mrs Brown. 'Now Velvet!'

'Just after Donald? Not NOW?'

'This minute.'

'I must put my shell-box away.'

'Put it away.'

'I'll put the racehorses in at the bottom.'

In went Manifesto, Tipperary Tim, Sergeant Murphy, Ally Sloper, Why Not, and Shannon Lass, – five right-handers and one left. Then the Shetland, then the four ponies, and on the very top of all the prize among her findings (another theft from the Free Library book) the little grey stallion, the Lamb (by Zouave – dam by Arthur).

'There they are,' she said with a sigh, and shut the lid.

'Cheer up, Velvet,' said Mr Brown.

'Feels mixed up,' said Mrs Brown. 'Get on, Velvet, don't hang about.'

Slowly Velvet climbed the wooden stairs to bed. Her head seemed hardly to have touched the pillow when mother, dressed in her pink dressing gown, shook her in her bed. Dizzy she rose, and shivering dressed, then swallowed the hot cocoa, and holding a piece of cold sausage in her fingers climbed into the lobby of the horse box which had arrived in the dark before dawn. Her suitcase was stuffed in after her, Mi arrived, carrying another through the dark yard, a spaniel yelped from Miss Ada's tool shed, and the box was off, The Piebald already housed by Mi twenty minutes earlier.

'We're off, we're off!' whispered Velvet.

'Tscht!' said Mi. 'You stow it till it gets light,' and he settled himself on the straw to finish his night's sleep.

Endless journey in the horse-box till the south gave way to the north, bit by bit, and the day broken by fresh packets of sandwiches.

'Don't we stop *anywhere*, Mi?' said Velvet as the hours crawled on.

But Mi was full of thought. There was a frown on his forehead and an edge to his tongue, and now and again he glanced at his large suitcase.

The horse-box driver, hired from Worthing, was a stranger, a glum fellow who seemed to have no interest in horses, the Grand National, the countryside, or the passengers he carried. His eye was glazed on the road ahead of him, and his mind was mesmerized by hours on the clock and miles to be covered, and the relation of these to each other.

Five miles outside Aintree they paused and broke the journey for a pot of tea. Mi glanced at Velvet and rose.

'You off?' said the driver, half asleep over his cup.

'Girl got an aunt here,' said Mi gruffly. 'Takin' her to her aunt.'

The driver slipped his legs out and lay back deeply in his chair. His eyes closed.

It took Mi twenty minutes to get Velvet's hair chopped perfunctorily in the lobby of the horse-box. It was the back by the nape of the neck that took the time. He bent down and crushed the sweepings in among the straw with the horse.

'Whiter'n straw,' he muttered. 'Looks like stubble.'

'Won't he come any minute?' said Velvet anxiously.

'Any minute,' said Mi. 'Can't be helped. Got nowhere else to do it. Pull up them trousers and give me yer skirt.' The aged little skirt, the width of a schoolboy's pants, was stuffed into the suitcase.

'Where'd you get 'em all?'

'Don't talk. Hurry. Slip your arm in the braces, they're all ready.'

A hard white collar, slightly soiled, and a spotted tie, hung on a nail.

'Can you manage 'em?'

'Yes, I expect. Is there a stud?'

Mi took his own from his neck, and tied his handkerchief in its place.

'You manage 'em an' I'll go an' talk to him if he wakes.'

'What'll I do when I'm finished?'

'Slope round the back an' wait about. When we've gone get some tea or ginger an' sit in there. Here's a shilling. I'll be back in a couple of hours, near. Then we'll take the tram into Liverpool an' go an' have a look at the Adelphi. Look sharp now.'

The little man who emerged from the back of the horse-van was very much thrown together. As he walked he seemed to settle down; he turned up his coat collar to hide the badly-tied tie, and jammed his greasy hat more confidently over his brow.

Mi and the driver emerged, the engine started, the horse-box moved away.

The skies, which had held off, now lowered and broke. Rain fell and the little man stirred his cold tea endlessly, fencing the occasional questions from the landlady.

The landlady had no sort of doubt.

'It's a girl,' she said to her husband in the kitchen.

'No business of ours,' said her husband.

'None,' she agreed.

The inn was empty, the rain thudded, the white-faced clock tocked on, no customer came in. When Mi pushed the door open and dropped down upon the mat Velvet woke with a jerk from a cold half-sleep.

They started up the road, Mi carrying the heavy suitcase, Velvet the small papier-mâché one she had brought. The trams began half a mile away, but by the time they reached them rain was entering their collars and wallowing in their shoes.

Climbing on to the hard seats they jolted off, huddling close together for warmth, the little sturdy man with the red hair and the lad with the greasy Homburg hat.

'What's the Adelphi?' said the lad, low.

'Toff's place,' said the other. 'Maybe it's too toff. I've forgot. There's the Stork too. We'll walk round and see.'

'Be wet. Walking round.'

'Couldn't be wetter.'

'Funny, that chap driving off with my hair.'

'Turn your head round this way and let's look.' Mi inspected the nape of the neck under the Homburg hat. 'I'll have to trim it better,' he said, 's' choppy.'

CHAPTER XII

Drenched with rain they stood at the portals of the Adelphi. Mi laid his hand on the little man's shoulder. 'Mind the porter!' he said in a whisper. 'Stand back here behind the concrete. I gone an' forgot. This place is too swell.'

'Feet are sopped,' said the little man.

'This rain's like ink. It's a bad start off. Stop a minute . . .'

'Ah,' said the little man and looked hungrily through the revolving doors. 'Coo lummy,' he whispered, 'aren't they gay in there! It's all looking-glass!'

They were on the arrival terrace of the Adelphi above the dripping Square, rustling with the noise of falling rain and overflowing pipes. The trams nosed by, the wet lamps flashed, 'Ovaltine' went in and out, the grey buildings were polished with water.

'See the toffs go in,' said Mi as the taxis drew up. 'Gawd, ther's Lord Derby!'

'Where?'

'Crossing the hall, see? Why . . . he's got Tommy Weston with him.'

'The big man?'

'No, his Lordship's the big one. Let's go to the Stork.'

They trudged away in the rain, Mi carrying the bigger suitcase, which seemed to be melting at one corner.

'S'chap wantsa room,' said Mi. 'He's a foreign. Name Tasky. I'm not looking for one for myself. I'm lodged.'

The Stork took them in.

Velvet stared at him.

They went up the stairs to a small room at the back.

'How'd you mean you're lodged?'

'Tsch! Talk quiet.'

They reached number seven, went in, and Mi shut the door. It was a bare room with a small bed and a sixty-volt electric light.

'I don' need a room. See? I got to do some nosing round. There's chaps I'll see an' chaps I'll listen to. I might go round to th'Adelphi.'

'The Adelphi!'

'Why not? Place is full o' chaps like me. Not on the top level. Round the pantries. You can see things if you cross the hall purposeful from time to time. Nobody asks. There's the telephone lobbies. Head lads doing a bit of telephoning. Michael Beary'll be chatting about I daresay.'

'Who's he?'

'Dear God, Velvet!'

'Eh . . . I'll never get my feet warm,' said Velvet, sighing.

'Get undressed an' I'll poke round an' get you a hot bottle.'

'But . . . Me being a lad . . .'

'Yepp. Beat your feet with a brush, then. I'll do it.'

'Rub 'em.'

'Beat's better. Where's the brush?'

Velvet knelt down and undid her suitcase. 'I didn't bring a brush,' she said desisting suddenly. 'I thought my hair, now it's off . . .'

'I done it not so bad,' said Mi with pride. 'It's white skin where the hair used to hang. I'll snip it cleaner in the morning.'

'Can't we get something? It's the one place that shows, when I've got that cap on. How much money you got left?'

'Precious little,' said Mi. 'Enough fer your room an' gettin' out there. You get into bed an' I'll come back in ten minutes.'

Velvet lay shivering in bed, too tired to turn out the devouring light which blanched her under its beams. The bones of her forehead were sore when she pressed her head in her hands.

Mi returned. He carried a tiny glass full of a brilliant green liquid, placed it carefully on the mantelpiece and took out from under his coat a gin bottle which he had filled with boiling water.

'There goes one an' six,' he said. 'We gotta be careful.'

Velvet opened her eyes.

'Got this in the yard at the back,' said Mi, shoving the gin bottle under the bed-clothes and near her feet. 'Filled it myself. That's peppermint drink on the mantelpiece. Alcohol. It'll keep till the morning. It's mint 'an' spirits. Now you go to sleep an' I'll look in some time in the night.'

He went out and shut the door, leaving the light still on. Velvet slept fitfully beneath its glare, unaware of what was amiss. At three Mi looked in but she was still and he closed the door. At five he came in and found her awake. It was yet deep night, the light on and the window pane black.

'Streaming outside,' he said. He looked white and tired. Then, turning to the mantelpiece, 'You've *drank that stuff*!'

'I thought I was going to die,' said Velvet, sitting up and looking bright, 'n'hour ago. The room was going round. I got up an' drank it off. S'marvellous. Have you got another one an' six case I feel worse?'

'I might have,' said Mi, sitting down on the one hard chair. 'Don't you go taking to drink.'

'Drink? Is it drink?'

'Told you it was spirits.'

'Well I forgot. I was bad. It's saved me. Just look at that black rain on the glass. They won't put the race off, will they?'

'The going'll be heavy as lead. Now see, Velvet. You ready to listen to a lot o' things?'

'Yes, Mi.'

'Well an' ready? Cos I got a lot to say.'

'Yes, Mi.'

'Well, first here's a map of the Course. I got it from a chap. You oughtoa walked round with me this morning but it's so wet an' if I get you tired you'll be no use. Besides it's best you do without seeing what the other side o' Becher's is like.'

'When did you see it?'

'When did I see it? Didn't I tell you I know it all up here like my thumb? One time I used to shift coal on trucks on the line alongside Becher's. You can't see much on the National, there's such a crowd, but the Liverpool Autumn Meeting in November you got all to yourself. You can stand up there an' see the ambulance come an' see the men standing there with ropes ready an' all.'

'Ooh, Mi, ready for what?'

'Ready to lug the horses out of the drop.'

'Ooh – Mi.'

'Huh! It's not going to happen to you! You got The Piebald jumping under you. Don't you forget that. All I mean is don't be surprised when you ride at Becher's, an' don't think you've jumped over the lip of a quarry, 'cos it isn't a quarry and you'll stop dropping in the end an' if you're not surprised the horse won't be.'

'Yes, Mi.'

'Now. We'll take the jumps all round. Same as if you were walking round which you should be.'

Mi pulled his chair up to Velvet's bed and flattened the thin paper map on her sheet.

'Plan of the Liverpool Racecourse,' it said. 'Distance of Grand National Course about four miles 856 yards.'

'Now then,' said Mi. 'Just listen. You start . . . *here* at the corner. It says "Paddock" just behind.'

'Yes, Mi.'

'(An' don't keep saying "Yes, Mi".) Don't fuss too much about your start. It's no odds getting off in a tear-away. What you got to do is to jump round and jump clean and go as fast as you can when you know what you're doing. But wait till you know what you're doing before you hurry. Mind you, he doesn't know nothing about racing. He won't be hard to hold. I know you got him under your thumb. Now . . . First you cross a road. On tan.

The tan'll fly up in your eye. Keep 'em shut across the road. Then the first fence. Plain fence. Then the next. Plain fence. You done just as big in the mushroom valley. There's nothing in them, but don't you despise 'em. Many's come down in the first two. There won't be much tailing there. You'll be all clustered up.

'Then comes a rail, ditch, and fence. I'm not saying it isn't an awful whopper for them as stands at the sides an' looks. It looks awful from the truckway. But it won't look so bad to you, you won't know it. You'll see a yellow-looking log lying low on the ground and you must take-off in time before it. It's on the lip of the ditch. It's not the landing so much there as the take-off.

'Then there's two more thorn fences. Then there's Becher's.

'Now *there's no need to fall at Becher's*. No need at all. I watched it an' I know. If I was sitting below you on the far side I wouldn't want to see the eyes popping out of your head as you came down. Just sit back. If you lie back you'll only be upright to the ground. Don't jerk his head whatever you do. It's a long way down but he'll land steady. Just keep as still if you were a dummy, and put confidence into him.'

'What's the drop, Mi?'

'I don' know but it looks twenty. On account of the ditch at the bottom. But you clear the ditch. That's nothing to do with you. You land on uphill grass an' gallop on. Then there's a . . .

(I can't read that one! It's printed on the black. It's a plain jump anyway.) Then there's the Canal Turn . . .'

'Mi, I can't remember it all!'

'Put yer mind to it. The Canal Turn's a teaser. You got to put yer mind to it. There's a chance of horses running out there. They got a screen up to stop it but they seem to want to run out to the left. There's the canal shinin' right ahead. Perhaps that's it. They don't want to swim.

'You want to make for the middle of the jump at the Canal Turn. Don't you go skidding in to the left and saving ground. If you get on the inside as they turn an' you've just landed, God help you. Even if you can't remember anything else remember to keep to the middle at the Canal Turn. You can't go wrong. There's the Canal shinin' just in front of you. A pack of seagulls'll rise most likely as you come up. They always do.'

'Mi, I swear I can't remember any more.'

'But I gotta tell you about Valentine's.'

'I'm getting sick again. You're making me sick again.'

'You're a nice one. Wish I'd got you a double!'

'That mint stuff?'

'M'm. Gotta get all this into you. Even if I drop the rest of the jumps I gotta tell you it's twice round the Course.'

'Well I know that! Is it too early to get the mint?'

'It's not six yet. It's dark. Gosh a'mighty, look at the rain!' Mi walked to the window.

'Well, go on. But not about the jumps. Yes . . . tell me about the water jump.'

'The water jump's pink,' said Mi despondently.

'How d'you mean?'

'You got to say to yourself, "It's pink. I gotta jump all of the pink."'

'Why's it pink?'

'Everything else is grey,' said Mi, dully. 'The water's puddled on pink clay. It looks meaty. It's opposite the Grand Stand. The people'll be yelling.'

'Go on, Mi! Tell me some more!' Velvet sat up straighter seeing that her supporter was flagging.

'M'murdering you, Velvet? V'I brought you up here to kill you . . .?'

'No fear. No you aren't! You're tired. You're soppy! It's no more'n a day's hunting.'

'Oh yes it is! An' you never done a day's hunting.'

'Come on, Mi. Piebald an' me'll go round like crickets. Tell me some more.'

'I wish yer mother was here, Velvet.'

'She *is* here! She's inside me. Ain't you always telling me that if she hadn't swum the Channel I shouldn't be up here?'

'Tha's true. But you get so sick an' all. It's an awful drawback, this vomiting.'

'I'll grow out of it.'

'I'll get you some more mint when it's daylight.'

'Where's the money coming from?'

'I got that much. On'y we gotta be careful. It don' matter f'we land at the end of the race without a bean but we gotta have enough to get there.'

'How we going out?'

Mi looked at her. 'Taxi,' he said. 'That's what I bin saving up for. Chap'll do it fer three and six.'

'Gosh!' said Velvet.

'I gotta get you out there fresh . . . see?'

'Well then come on then, tell me some more.'

'Look here now, I talked to a lotta chaps. This is how it is. Them jumps in the valley you gather yer horse up, don't you?'

'Yes.'

'Well, you can't go on doing that twice roun' the National. Or if you do you gotta do it like silk. Cos when a horse gets as done as that he can't stand being gathered up not like you would at the beginning. You gotta haul him in. You remember that! You gotta haul him in s'though he . . . s'though he was a big fish that was on'y half hooked. When he gets on to the Racecourse . . .'

'At the beginning?'

'No . . . that's what they call the end. The Racecourse. It means getting on to the straight after the jumps. It's when you get off the National Course an' come galloping up on the Gold Cup Course just before the Grand Stand. They call it "coming on to the Racecourse".'

'Yes, Mi. Yes . . . well I mean?'

'What was I saying? Oh yes. When the horses get on to the second round, or a bit after (some don't do it till the second time Becher's), they begin to get their necks stickin' out so far you wouldn't know 'em. They can't jump like that. On the other hand if you pull 'em in with a jerk you throw 'em down. You want to haul. You want to take a pull an' a pull, s'gentle s'though you got 'em on a piece of silk an' it'll break. You gotta judge yourself how much you'll hustle after you've landed an' how soon before the next you'll take a little swig at the hauling.'

Quite suddenly Mi dozed. Velvet sat and looked at him and tried to remember the order of the jumps. The map had fallen out of his hand on to the floor but she did not like to disturb him to reach for it. The rain slashed and dribbled on the whitening pane. The electric light flickered once or twice as though the power stations were swimming up into daylight and meeting the morning shift. Mi woke again with a start.

'Th'Adelphi's full o' chaps,' he said at once, brightly. 'They say "Yellow Messenger's" your trouble. He's a bay. Seventeen hands. Yellow jacket, crimson sleeves. And the Yank horse too. "Bluebottle". I shouldn't bother though. Just go round s'though you was alone.'

'You bin about all night?'

'Won't hurt this one night in the year. It's nearly six. I'm going to get you some breakfast. Everybody's about already.'

'Shall I get up?'

'No, you stop there. You'll be warmer. No point taking you about till I've got to. I'm going to get some stuff somewhere to tan up your neck.'

Mi left her with the map to study and went out. Velvet looked idly at the map but she seemed to learn nothing from it. The rain and the blackness and the night had beaten everything flat in her. 'I wish Mi hadn't told me so much,' she thought. 'I like it to come to me while I'm doing it.' And she pushed the map slightly to one side and shut her mind against it. Mi came in with some coffee and slices of white bread and a square of butter.

'Mi,' she said at once, 'don't tell me a thing more. I want just to slide along till it's time thinking of nothing at all.'

'Huh!' said Mi, putting the tray on the one chair, 'think a race like this is won by luck?'

'Everyone riding today,' said Velvet, 'know more'n I do. I can't win that way.'

'What's your way, then?'

'Jus' knowin' The Piebald can do it, an' tellin' him so,' said Velvet, buttering her bread.

'Easy with that butter,' said Mi. 'Spread it thin. You've no stomach for grease. Here's the stuff for your neck. It's iodine. I borrowed it.'

'Won't it smell that blood-smell?'

'It'll wear off. We'll put a drop of water to it so it won't look so yellow. Bend your head down, let's try.'

Mi had mixed a drop or two in the tooth glass, and painted it on below the white cropped hair. 'It's that queer hair of yours is the trouble,' said Mi. 'Look like an albino.'

'What's that?'

'Soft chaps. Soft-shell chaps, like eggs.'

'Gimme the cap an' le's look.'

Mi dived into the suitcase and pulled out a black silk cap. Velvet drew it over her cropped hair and well over her eyes.

'It's not too bad,' said Mi. 'Not much hair shows. The brown of your neck's much better, but where'll I end it off?'

'Wash it round weaker an' weaker with water.'

Mi did his best.

Slowly the morning drew into wet daylight.

'Now I'm going out to the horse,' said Mi. 'I got him locked in an' I got the key. I'll pay the bill here. Don't you move till twelve.'

'All that time?'

'You'll give yourself away if you put your nose out. At twelve jus' walk down with the bag an' walk out an' pop into the taxi.'

'What taxi?'

'He'll be waiting. He don' know nothing about you but he's a chap I used to know. He'll be here at twelve sharp waiting to pick you up. Ferret-faced chap but he's all right.'

'Where'll I find you?'

'He'll bring you to where I want you, near the Course. I'll have your dinner waiting for you.'

'Don' give me anything to eat, Mi. Not jus' before like that. I'll never stand it.'

'Not a ham sandwich?' said Mi, arrested at the door.

'Oh my God!' said Velvet.

The morning drifted by. Velvet rose and became the little man. At twelve to the tick he walked sharply down the stairs carrying his suitcase. He had padded shoulders, a common suit, a dingy

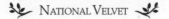

white shirt and pale blue tie, a brownish overcoat with a half belt and Mi's old Homburg hat spotted with oil.

The taxi was there, the little man nodded and stepped inside. Under his coat he had an empty heart. He was crushed by delay and the rain.

The taxi took him through the means steets for twenty minutes. It seemed impossible that so great a racecourse could lie buried in so mean a place. Suddenly there was a clearing on the right, and gates. Like the clearing and the gates of a cemetery lying in the surf of a metropolis. The taxi stopped and the little man leant out of the window. Mi walked towards him from the corner of a fence.

CHAPTER XIII

This was the North with its everlasting white railings. The stands were filling already. The Union Jack, Stars and Stripes, and Tricolour flew over the Grand Stand. The minor bookies under their stand-umbrellas had been in position since eleven. Their fantastic names were chalked on boards so that they looked like a fresh haul of fish in a market. 'Special this Day! Bream . . . Ernie Bream . . . Alfy Haddock . . . Mossie Halibut . . . Duke Cod!' They were shouting and clattering and taking turns in gangs at the Snack Bar. Everything else was more or less awaiting the glory of the day. 'Champagne Bar . . . Champagne only.' This was empty. Inside the dining-room the white tables were spread and the knowing old waiters hung like old flies swarming in doorways.

The police had marched out in a dark stream an hour before and had taken up positions round the Course. There was a constable at every jump with a folded stretcher laid beside him, its rug within its folds. Each man had a red flag and a yellow flag, with which to call his neighbour.

The Public was flowing in like a river.

The whole course was blackening on the rim like a lake that has thrown up seaweed upon its banks. It had been black since daylight, but the seaweed was deepening and deepening, the truckway was solid with life, the ten-shilling Stand at the Canal Turn was groaning, the Melling Road, which crossed the Course, from being an ivory band across the green became an ebony. Great passenger aeroplanes hummed over the stands and made their descent. A foreign king and queen arrived in Lord Sefton's box.

Tattersalls was like a thawed ice-rink. Pools had long appeared over the course. Thousands and thousands of people were wet, but not yet to the skin. And they hardly felt it.

The Changing Room for jockeys was warm and gay like a busy nursery. Jockeys' valets, with the air of slightly-derelict family butlers, had been ironing in their shirt-sleeves since seven in the morning. Two large coal fires behind nursery wire-guards were burning briskly, and over the guards hung strips of colour. Gipsy silks were all across the long tables stretched down the middle, and the valets ironed and pressed and swore and grunted and cleaned soft boots and hunted for odds and ends in their enormous suitcases, the travelling houses of their livelihood. Down one side of the room hung little saddles, touching little saddles. Below them saddlecloths, numnahs, girths. Below them on the boot boxes countless little boots. Black boots with brown tops so soft you could hardly walk in them. Boots like gloves that are drawn on to a child's ankle, and filled out with a child's toes. Boots as touching as the saddles.

Outside in the Weighing Room the hooded scales had been uncloaked and the Clerk of the Scales was already at his desk. The Declaration Counter had its pens and inks and its stacks of empty forms waiting to be filled.

In the hospital room the nurse put a few more coals, delicately with her coal pincers, on to the bright fire.

While the second race was being run Mi signed 'Michael Taylor' at the foot of his declaration card, and paused a second higher up the card. 'James Tasky' he wrote firmly. Then filled in the horse's name. He blotted the card and passed it into the box.

Then he went back to a little haunt of his.

'Now . . .' he said, half an hour later, crooking his finger in the doorway, and the little man picked up his suitcase and followed him.

'I'll take that,' said Mi huskily.

Mi hustled the little man in past the unsaddling enclosure to the holy stillness of the Weighing Room, and through the swing door into a corner of the Changing Room, pushing him down on a boot-box overshadowed by hanging garments.

'They're nak . . .' gasped the little man, sitting down.

'Tscht!' muttered Mi, standing over him.

The jockeys' valets bustled here and there, grumbled, stumbled, fell over boots. Two of their charges with hard red faces and snowy bodies were standing naked by the nursery fireguard. Mi looked grimly down at the little man.

'Keep yer eyes on yer knees,' he muttered fiercely. And knelt to hold up the white breeches he had fished out of the suitcase.

'Who's your lady-friend?' said one of the naked midgets, turning round to warm his other buttock.

'Miss Tasky. From Russia,' said Mi without a flicker.

'Speak English?' said the midget, turning again like a chicken on a spit.

'No use wasting any dope on him,' said Mi. 'Can't speak a bloody word. He's a Bolshie they've sent over. To pick the winnings!'

'You sim to be doing the lady-friend to the lady-friend alright?'

'Doin' what I'm paid for,' said Mi. 'Times are ugly down South.' I ony jus' come up.'

'Well, of all the muck-rakin' cheek,' said the other naked midget, scratching his stomach . . . 'that's that Tasky's riding that out-a-condition, pot-bellied whisky horse I saw brought in last night. Turnin' the Gran' National into a bloody circus!' and he cracked the end bone of his index finger like a pistol shot.

'Come on, Bibby, get dressed do,' begged an austere butler. 'Going to ride the National in your pink skin?'

As Bibby turned away, Tasky stood up gently, black, pink sleeves, black cap, white breeches, little black boots, brown tops. Mi pulled the saddle, saddle cloth and numnah, off the ironbracket. 'Sit down an' wait,' he said loudly as to a foreigner, pushed him back on the boot-box and stood over him.

Then, on the door opening, 'They want you for the chair,' he said.

'Thought he didn't understand English,' said a voice.

'No reason why 'e shouldn't begin,' said Mi. 'CHAIR, I said,' he yelled into Tasky's ear. 'Come on!'

Outside in the Weighing Room all was quiet and regulated. 'That's a toff,' thought Mi, seeing a tall man get off the chair. He was obviously a gentleman rider, a 'bumper'.

'Weight?' said the Clerk of the Scales.

'Ten seven, near enough,' said Mi. 'He don't speak no English, sir. Russian.'

Mi pushed the little man towards the scales. 'Sit, can't you,' he said in a hoarse whisper. 'Double up!'

Tasky sat in the chair and nursed his saddle.

'Ten six and eleven,' said the Clerk's assistant.

'Penny piece,' said the Clerk quietly, and dropped a small piece of lead into the weight flap.

'An' a half,' said the Clerk. In went another piece. The Clerk wrote carefully in his book.

'Get off,' hissed Mi. Tasky never budged.

Mi gave him a pull. 'Job, sir, this is,' he said. 'Seems more nitwit than . . .' he bustled the little man out of the room, throwing his brown overcoat round his shoulders.

'Who's that?' said someone, opening the door of the Stewards' Room.

'The Russian, sir,' said the Clerk of the Scales, looking up at the Clerk of the Course.

The heavy, streaming daylight broke on them. The worst for Mi was over, the worst for Velvet to come.

'Keep in the crowd,' said Mi. 'I got to go for the horse. Keep movin'. Don't come out into the open. Don't rush at the horse when you see me lead him out. I got to go roun' and round. Wait till you see the others walk in to the Paddock . . .'

'Paddock?'

'Rails. There. Walk straight up to near me and stand by the bushes in the middle. I'll lead him up to you. I'll jump you up.'

'Jump me up?'

'Jump you. I gotta take yer knee an' jump you. Like the horse was too high fer you to get on. I'll take yer coat and I'll lead you out an' that's all I can do for you.'

'You going now?' said Velvet, small, small in voice.

'I'm going. An' I got togs. You'll see. White leading rein an' all. Borrowed 'em off a head lad, friend o' mine.'

Mi was gone and Velvet drifted through the crowd.

But suddenly Mi was back again. 'Keep your eyes skinned an' keep AWAY from everyone who'll talk!' he hissed, and was gone again.

The crowd buzzed round the Tote, and many looked curiously at Velvet's black cap and bony childish face. She was not unlike an apprentice lad.

The horses were parading in the Paddock. There came The Piebald. Velvet stared at him in shivering appreciation. He wore borrowed clothes with a knotted yellow rope bumping on his quarters. Mi led him with a white leading rein, wide like a tape. The number . . . 4 . . . was tied on Mi's left arm. As he came into the Paddock a buzz came from the crowd and here and there laughter. Round and round went the horses, and the rain ran down Velvet's neck.

Suddenly she saw the little men go in. Wide shoulders, gay caps and little feet. She walked forward, entered the Paddock, and went straight to the bushes. There was a pause. The horses circled. Every jockey went up to his Owner. She alone had no one. She stood firm and looked around her, conscious that this was her worst moment this morning.

Then up came Mi with The Piebald. She stripped her coat off and he held it on his arm, pulled the rugs off the horse on to his shoulder, stooped to her left leg and flung her up into the saddle. Almost at once the horses moved away, Mi walking beside her to the gate.

She was quite definite, quite easy. Now it was over, the creeping like a thief, the doubts, the waiting. No one would stop her now. The worst moments had come and gone, and there could be no doubt at all that now she and The Piebald were in together for the Grand National.

'There . . . I never told you,' said Mi, low and hoarse, walking beside her. 'Don't lie up on his neck! But it's too late now . . .'

'Ssh,' said Velvet, looking straight ahead of her at something that seemed like a crane upon a raised embankment.

'I'll not "ssh"!' said Mi, his heart bursting. 'I'll say, "Think of yer ma!"'

He snipped off the leading rein by its chromium hook and The Piebald swung through the gate.

'Gawd . . . a'might . . .' said Mi, struck short. 'I never told her to ride down in front of the Stands before going to the post . . .'

But for Velvet it was only follow-my-leader. She went down easily with the other horses, turned, stood slightly in her saddle, and galloped back. Mi started running for the truckway. 'I'll never make Becher's . . . not in this crowd. Not unless there's a muck-up at the post.'

Just ahead of him, turning out from the stable-roadway, came the black motor ambulance, with the doctor sitting sideways in the back, looking at a paper. Behind the ambulance, from the same turning, crawled out a sinister, square-bottomed coffin, a knacker's cart, drawn by an enormous pigeon-chested shire-horse. Ahead of the ambulance, and blocking the way, went the horse ambulance, with its crane, drawn by two shire horses in tandem. All made their way to Becher's. Another knacker's cart was trundling along far away by Valentine's, and yet another pushed its way in Melling Road.

'Black slugs . . .' said Mi, running, panting, pushing.

*

At the post the twenty horses were swaying like the sea. Forward. . . . No good! Back again. Forward. . . . No good! Back again.

The line formed . . . and rebroke. Waves of the sea. Drawing a breath . . . breaking. Velvet fifth from the rail, between a bay and a brown. The Starter had long finished his instructions. Nothing more was said aloud, but low oaths flew, the cursing and grumbling flashed like a storm. An eye glanced at her with a look of hate. The breaking of movement was too close to movement to be borne. It was like water clinging to the tilted rim of the glass, like the sound of the dreaded explosion after the great shell has fallen. The will to surge forward overlaid by something delicate and terrible and strong, human obedience at bursting-point, but not broken. Horses' eyes gleamed openly, men's eyes set like chips of steel. Rough man, checked in violence, barely master of himself, barely master of his horse. The Piebald ominously quiet, and nothing coming from him . . . up went the tape.

The green Course poured in a river before her as she lay forward, and with the plunge of movement sat in the stream.

'Black slugs' . . . said Mi, cursing under his breath, running, dodging, suffocated with the crowd. It was the one thing he had overlooked, that the crowd was too dense ever to allow him to reach Becher's in the time. Away up above him was the truckline, his once-glorious free seat, separated from him by a fence. 'God's liver . . .' he mumbled, his throat gone cold, and stumbled into an old fool in a mackintosh. 'Are they off?' he yelled at the heavy crowd as he ran, but no one bothered with him.

He was cursed if he was heeded at all. He ran, gauging his position by the cranes on the embankment. Velvet coming over Becher's in a minute and he not there to see her. 'They're off.' All around him a sea of throats offered up the gasp.

He was opposite Becher's but could see nothing: the crowd thirty deep between him and the Course. All around fell the terrible silence of expectancy. Mi stood like a rock. If he could not see then he must use his ears, hear. Enclosed in the dense, silent, dripping pack he heard the thunder coming. It roared up on the wet turf like the single approach of a multiple-footed animal. There were stifled exclamations, grunts, thuds. Something in the air flashed and descended. The first over Becher's! A roar went up from the crowd, then silence. The things flashing in the air were indistinguishable. The tip of a cap exposed for the briefest of seconds. The race went by like an express train, and was gone. Could Velvet be alive in that?

Sweat ran off Mi's forehead and into his eyes. But it was not sweat that turned the air grey and blotted out the faces before him.

The ground on all sides seemed to be smoking. An extraordinary mist, like a low prairie fire, was formed in the air. It had dwelt heavily all day behind the Canal, but the whole of the Course had remained clear till now. And now, before you could turn to look at your neighbour, his face was gone. The mist blew in shreds, drifted, left the crowd clear again but hid the whole of the Canal Corner, fences, stand and horses.

There was a struggle going on at Becher's; a horse had fallen and was being got out with ropes. Mi's legs turned to water and he asked his neighbour gruffly 'who's fallen?' But the neighbour, straining to the tip of his toes, and glued to his glasses, was deaf as lead.

Suddenly Mi lashed round him in a frenzy. 'Who's fallen, I say? Who's hurt!'

'Steady on,' said a little man whom he had prodded in the stomach.

'Who's fallen?' said Mi desperately. 'I gotta brother in this . . .'

'It's his brother!' said the crowd all around him. 'Let him through.'

Mi was pushed and pummelled to the front and remained embedded two from the front line. The horse that had fallen was a black horse, its neck unnaturally stretched by the ropes that were hauling it from the ditch.

There was a shout and a horse, not riderless, but ridden by a tugging, cursing man, came galloping back through the curling fumes of the mist, rolled its wild eye at the wrong side of Becher's and disappeared away out of the Course. An uproar began along the fringes of the crowd and rolled back to where Mi stood. Two more horses came back out of the mist, one riderless. The shades of others could be discerned in the fog. Curses rapped out from unseen mouths.

'What's happened at the Canal Turn? What's wrong down at the Turn?'

'The whole field!' shouted a man. The crowd took it up.

'The field's out. The whole field's come back. There's no race!' It was unearthly. Something a hundred yards down there in the fog had risen up and destroyed the greatest steeplechase in the world.

Nineteen horses had streamed down to the Canal Turn, and suddenly, there across the Course, at the boundary of the fog, four horses appeared beyond Valentine's, and among them, fourth, was The Piebald.

'Yer little lovely, yer little lovely!' yelled Mi, wringing his hands and hitting his knees. 'It's her, it's him, it's me brother!'

No one took any notice. The scene immediately before them occupied all the attention. Horses that had fallen galloped by riderless, stirrups flying from their saddles, jockeys returned on foot, covered with mud, limping, holding their sides, some running slowly and miserably over the soggy course, trying to catch and sort the horses.

'It's "Yellow Messenger",' said a jockey savagely, who had just seized his horse. 'Stuck on the fence down there and kicking hell.' And he mounted.

'And wouldn't they jump over him?' called a girl shrilly.

'They didn't wanter hurt the por thing, lady,' said the jockey, grinning through his mud, and rode off.

'Whole lot piled up and refused,' said a man who came up the line. 'Get the Course clear now, quick!'

'They're coming again!' yelled Mi, watching the galloping four. 'Get the Course clear! They'll be coming!'

They were out of his vision now, stuck down under Becher's high fence as he was. Once past Becher's on the second round would he have time to extricate himself and get back to the post before they were home? He stood indecisively and a minute went by. The Course in front of him was clear. Horses and men had melted. The hush of anticipation began to fall. 'They're on the tan again,' said a single voice. Mi flashed to a decision. He could not afford the minutes to be at Becher's. He must get back for the finish and it would take him all his time. He backed and plunged and ducked, got cursed afresh. The thunder was coming again as he reached the road and turned to face the far-off Stands. This time he could see nothing at all, not even a cap in the air. 'What's leading? What's leading?'

'Big brown. Tantibus, Tantibus. Tantibus leading.'

'Where's The Piebald?'

'See that! Leonora coming up . . .'

They were deaf to his frantic questions. He could not wait, but ran. The mist was ahead of him again, driving in frills and wafting sedgily about. Could Velvet have survived Becher's twice? In any case no good wondering. He couldn't get at her to help her. If she fell he would find her more quickly at the hospital door. Better that than struggle through the crowd and be forbidden the now empty Course.

Then a yell. 'There's one down!'

'It's the Yank mare!'

The horse ambulance was trundling back with Yellow Messenger from the Canal Turn. Mi leapt for a second on to the turning hub of the wheel, and saw in a flash, across the momentarily mist-clear course, the pride of Baltimore in the mud underneath Valentine's. The Piebald was lying third. The wheel turned and he could see no more. Five fences from the finish; he would not allow himself to hope, but ran and ran. How far away

the Stands in the gaps of the mist as he pushed, gasping, through the people. Would she fall now? What had he done, bringing her up here? But would she fall now? He ran and ran.

'They're coming on to the Racecourse . . . coming on to the Racecourse . . .'

'How many?'

'Rain, rain, can't see a thing.'

'How many?'

Down sank the fog again, as a puff of wind blew and gathered it together. There was a steady roaring from the Stands, then silence, then a hubbub. No one could see the telegraph.

Mi, running, gasped, 'Who's won?'

But everyone was asking the same question. Men were running, pushing, running, just as he. He came up to the gates of Melling Road, crossed the road on the fringe of the tan, and suddenly, out of the mist The Piebald galloped riderless, lolloping unsteadily along, reins hanging, stirrups dangling. Mi burst through on to the Course, his heart wrung.

'Get back there!' shouted a policeman. 'Loose horse!'

'Hullo Old Pie there!' shouted Mi. The animal, soaked, panting, spent, staggered and slipped and drew up.

'What've you done with 'er?' said Mi, weeping, and bent down to lift the hoof back through the rein. 'You let 'er down,

Pie? What in God's sake?' He led the horse down the Course, running, his breath catching, his heart thumping, tears and rain on his face.

Two men came towards him out of the mist.

'You got him?' shouted one. 'Good fer you. Gimme!'

'You want him?' said Mi, in a stupor, giving up the rein.

'Raised an objection. Want him for the enclosure. Chap come queer.'

'Chap did? What chap?'

'This here's the winner! Where you bin all day, Percy?'

'Foggy,' said Mi. 'Very foggy. Oh my God!'

Back in the fog a voice had spoken into a telephone. It had need only to say one word. All else had been written out beforehand. And in that very second in the offices of the Associated Press in New York men had taken off the message.

'Urgent Associated New York Flash Piebald Wins.' The one word the voice had said into the fog was 'Piebald'.

Up went the red flag. The crowd buzzed. 'What is it?' 'Did he fall?'

'Must've hurt hisself jumping . . .'

'Fainted.'

'Jus' dismounted, the silly b . . .'

Dismounted before reaching the unsaddling enclosure. Objection. Up went the red flag. There was tenseness along the line of private bookies, pandemonium in the bookies' stand under the umbrellas, tight knots gathered round the opening to the Weighing Room, behind which was the Stewards' Room. Glasses were levelled from everywhere upon the board. If a white flag went up the objection was overruled. If a green it was sustained. But the red remained unwaveringly.

'Taken him round to the hospital.'

'Stretcher, was it?'

'Jus' gone through where all those people are . . .'

The doctor had got back from his tour of the Course in his ambulance. Two riders had already been brought in and the nurse had prepared them in readiness for his examination. Now the winner himself coming in on a stretcher. Busy thirty minutes ahead.

'Get him ready, Sister.'

The winner lay unconscious, wrapped in a horse blanket, his face mottled with the mud that had leapt up from flying hoofs.

'Looks sixteen,' said the doctor curiously, and knelt to turn the gas a little lower under the forceps.

'Bin boiling for twenty minutes,' said the Sister.

'Place full of steam,' said the doctor. 'Been watching . . .?' and he passed to the end cubicle.

'No,' said the Sister shortly to his back. She disliked the Grand National, and had waited behind the Stands to patch up the damage.

The constables with the stretcher placed the winner on the bed by the door, leaving him still wrapped in his blanket. They retired and closed the door. The Sister slipped a towel under the muddy head, and turning back the blanket started to undo the soaking jacket of black silk.

'Sister,' roared the doctor from another cubicle . . . 'No, stay where you are! I've got it!'

'Could you come here a minute?' said the Sister, at his side a few minutes later.

The doctor straightened his back. He had a touch of lumbago. 'I'll be back, Jem,' he said. 'You're not much hurt. Cover up. Yes?'

'Just a minute . . . over here.'

She whispered to him quietly. He slapped his rain-coated cheek and went to the bed by the door. 'Put your screens round.' She planted them. 'Constable, he said, poking his head out of the door, 'get one of the Stewards here, will you.' (The roar of the crowd came in at the door.) 'One of the Stewards! Quick's you can. Here, I'll let you in this side door. You can get through.' The crowd seethed, seizing upon every sign.

*

Mi crouched by the door without daring to ask after his child. He heard the doctor call. He saw the Steward go in. 'Anyway,' he thought, 'they've found out at once. They would. What's it matter if she's all right? She's won, the little beggar, the little beggar. Oh my God!'

The Sergeant of Police was by the Stables. 'Message from up there,' he said briefly to his Second. 'Squad to go up to the hospital door. Row round the door. Something up with the winner.'

The police marched up in a black snake. The people fell back. An ambulance came in from the Ormskirk Road and backed down the line of police. The red flag remained for a moment, then slowly the green flag mounted on the board. Objection sustained. A frightful clamour burst out in the Grand Stand.

In the Stewards' Room the glittering Manifesto looked down out of his frame and heard the low talk of this appalling desecration. A butcher's girl on a piebald horse had pounced up beside him into history.

'Got her off?' said one of the Stewards in a low voice.

'Just about. There was a bit of a rush for a second. She called out something as the stretcher was being shoved in. Called out she was all right . . . to somebody in the crowd. Good God, it's . . . I'm glad we got her off quick. The crowd's boiling with excitement.'

'How'd it get out so quick?'

'I dunno. Swell row this'll be. It'll have to be referred back to Weatherby's.' The Clerk of the Course came in. 'Crowd's bubbling like kettles out there, Lord Henry. By jove, it's the biggest ramp! How'd she pull it over?'

'Who's gone with her?'

'The doctor couldn't go. He's got two other men, one a baddish crash at Valentine's.'

'Well somebody ought to a' gone. Find out who's gone, will you?'

The Clerk of the Course disappeared.

'Tim's Chance wins, of course.'

'Yes, that's been announced. There's no question. The objection is sustained definitely here on the Course, and the rest must be referred to London. There'll be a special of the N.H.C., I should think it might be a case for legal proceedings. Well . . .' (as the door opened) 'did you find out who went with her?'

'A second doctor, Lord Henry. A young man who's here very often. Friend of Doctor Bodie's. And a constable.'

'There should have been an official. Of course there should

have been an official. What's the hospital?'

'Liverpool Central . . .'

'Isn't there a friend or relation with her?'

'Nobody.'

'Well, she called out to somebody!'

'The somebody's hidden himself all right. Well for him! She's quite alone s'far as we can make out.'

'D'she say anything?'

'Won't speak. Except that one shout she gave.'

'If my daughter'd done it,' said Lord Henry Vile, 'I'd be . . .' he paused and stroked his lip with his finger.

'Pretty upset, I should think . . .'

'I wasn't going to say that,' said Lord Henry. 'No.'

Chapter XIV

Almost as soon as the ambulance was off the ground little breezes began to blow hither and thither bearing the fact. Without the name. A girl had won the Grand National.

A girl had won the Grand National. By the look of the stretcher 'a slip of a girl'. By the memory of the crouching black and pink ant on The Piebald again 'a slip of a girl'. The news began to crack like gunpowder trailed to percussion caps. At each percussion cap an explosion. At each explosion men flung, hurled about their business.

The U.P. man on the roof of the Grand Stand went on with his telephoning (at two pounds a minute). He had laid his field glasses down now and was talking feverishly. 'Urgent bulletin,' he said violently, 'astounding rumours circulating track. Is winning jockey girl? We upchecking.' And a little later, in his shorthand Chinese, 'Stewards' decision. Quiz moved London.'

As the ambulance turned into the Ormskirk Road the news

had broken. It was flashing to London in waves of light, in waves of air. It was 'breaking' on London. At first the smaller men flashed it, unscrupulous, out for speed at all costs. The graver men hung back. Verify, verify! It *couldn't* be. The serious sporting reporters, associated for a lifetime with the Turf felt it couldn't be. Almost . . . it had better not be. Such frivolity, but God . . . what news! NEWS, sparkling, rainbow NEWS. London was disturbed, tickled, a few seconds before the graver men felt they could spring for it. Then they sprang. And the full blast swept down the lines and the airways. Like a whiff . . . the miraculous transmission of accurate, verified, imagination-shaking news. It could hardly be a scoop because before one could close the telephone box everyone knew it. But details . . . where was the girl? In a second, having delivered their blast on London, they turned like hounds after the girl. The ambulance was gone. Where? The Liverpool Central . . . Ah . . . The taxi rank was in the Ormskirk Road.

But once before the Liverpool Central had housed a Fame-Shaker. And the Resident Medical Officer was a grim fellow with yellow hair, blue eyes and set mouth. He had been through the war and he had been through that strange medical upbringing in a good Scottish hospital which gets into a man's bones and transmutes him for ever from common humanity. He was steady and wily and fine, and he could act as quick as news could flash.

And for reasons of his own connected with his attitude and their attitude towards truth and scientific thought he had a cold impatience of the press.

The murmurs surrounding Velvet came with her like raindrops on the ambulance. She had not long been wheeled into the Women's Accident Ward, and the Sister-in-Charge had hardly propped screens round her bed, before the Resident Medical Officer had mopped up the rumours, his curiously flat ears very wide awake.

'Be down from Aintree,' he thought, 'in a jiffy.'

He found, actually, that they were already drawing up at the gates.

The Resident M.O. closed the Ward doors and placed the constable who had come with the ambulance on duty.

The constable was not sure it was his right duty . . .

'Just a minute, Officer . . .' said the Resident M.O. swiftly, increasing the constable's rank and giving him a cold-water flash out of the blue eyes. 'Not more than a second while we wheel her into a private ward. Can't have the Press in round the bed. I think you'll find that's why you were asked to whip out of Aintree. Right ahead, Sister. 'Nother blanket over her . . . (*right* over her) when you get her on the trolley.'

Two white-coated men sped down the ward with a trolley.

'Over your face, girl, too, for a minute,' said the Resident M.O., leaving the constable at the door and going down the ward to meet the trolley. 'It's all right. Want to get you into another ward. Quiet.'

A nurse sprang to push the double doors back on to their catches for the trolley to pass.

A Press Association man approached the M.O.

'Let the trolley pass,' said the M.O. abruptly. 'Stand back. Operation case.'

The trolley passed swiftly out of view under the nose of bowler-hatted men who were arriving.

But the balloon of notoriety wasn't going to stay on the ground just because of the Principal M.O. The Press Bellows had now begun to blow and the balloon to lift.

Yet the little creature still lay snug like a kernel in the private ward of the Liverpool Central, with the door locked and a Sister giving her a blanket bath. Then in came tea on a tray, two meat sandwiches cut in triangles, a chocolate bun in a paper, a rice bun, a piece of plum cake and two slices of white bread and butter. Velvet snuggled down and began to wonder what next and what next and when the heavens were going to fall. And above all, where was Mi?

Mi, rubbing down the piebald horse in the stables at Aintree, was bearing the brunt of everything. He was knee-deep in the press, he was wanted in the Stewards' Room, he was wanted by everybody. Even the book-makers would have liked to get at him.

'This horse won the National, ain't it? This horse 'as got to be rubbed down. I don't know a thing 'cept that I was hired to do over the horse. Hired at the last minute. Well . . . what? Well if I'm wanted in the Stewards' Room I'll have to go. But this horse wants rubbin' and rubbin'. Who's going to do it for me?'

There were plenty of offers. There were even men who had a nodding knowledge of him.

'Why, Mi, you old tout . . . who's your lady friend? Mean to say you didn't know? What about the Changing Room? You pulled her breeches on, didn't you?'

'How was I to know? She got pants on, ha'n't she? A girl an' a boy they're that alike you gotter have the pants off to see? I on'y know she couldn't speak a word a' King's English, an' was s'flat's a pancake and as dumb's an oyster . . . Comin', Sir . . . Rub him well . . . Give his back-line a massage . . . under the saddle. Makes the blood flow . . . I'll be back in a minute. I got nothing to say to 'em. Stewards . . . My hat! . . . Comin' sir!'

In the Stewards' Room nothing could be got out of Mi. He was heavy-minded, obstinate and repetitive. Lord Henry Vile did not look as though he believed him, and finally it was decided to take his address and refer the inquest to London, at a special meeting of the National Hunt Committee. Mi gave his address as Post Restante, Lewes.

'Fishy sort of address,' said Colonel 'Ruby' Allbrow, looking at him straight.

'I can't hide, sir,' said Mi, suddenly looking as straight back. 'I'm known here to lots, an' I'm known there. The police'd lay their hands on me in a day 'f I was to monkey up.'

'And the horse?'

'Horse goes back to the owner, sir. Horse-box is coming for it tonight.'

'And not you?'

'Not me, sir.'

'And the owner's address . . . We have the owner's address, Mr Gray?'

'Yes, we have the address,' said the official. 'The owner must be behind it all, m'lord, if you'll excuse me interrupting.'

'Yes . . . that'll be looked into. Letter must be sent and so on. Who's going down to the hospital?'

A spasm crossed Mi's face. He opened his mouth but said nothing. Velvet alone in that hospital. 'S sick as a cat. But there were doctors an' all that. It'd soon be in the papers how she was.

Velvet lay in the hospital refusing her name. She and Mi had no plan beyond the winning of the Grand National. How should they? They had bitten off a piece of dream together, and like winged children accomplished it. Beyond, all was an uncharted sea. They had not had one glance at life after the winning.

Still by instinct she refused her name. The heavens were going to fall. Father was going to know, the village was going to know, Edwina was going to say sarcastic things because Teddy didn't like all the fuss. There was going to be trouble for her and Mi, though pure white glory for The Piebald. And the longer she kept her name secret the slower the trouble would be in coming. She lay and smiled wanly, and shook her clipped white head.

Indeed she wasn't pressed enormously to tell. The M.O. didn't care a rap about her name, and the Sister-in Charge of her simply washed her and fed her and choked back her curiosity because she too had had a cold-water flash from the blue eyes of the hospital's Despot. The young doctor who had brought Velvet down had disappeared, but he came back later accompanied by Dr Bodie from Aintree and the Clerk of the Course himself.

The M.O. stared at them with his curious look and told them quietly that they must not stay more than five minutes with the patient. The Sister was present at the interview. The Clerk of the Course asked formally for Velvet's name and address. Dr Bodie blustered a little when Velvet sighed and said shyly she couldn't give it. The young doctor said nothing. He was more than thrilled whichever way the situation turned. At the end of five minutes the M.O. came to say it was time.

'Shock,' said the M.O. with a grudging apology in the corridor. 'Very young.'

After they had gone the M.O. came back. 'Sorry, I must have your name for hospital purposes,' he said, and he pulled the silver pencil out of his note-book.

Velvet looked up with confidence into the ledger of that secure face, and said at once 'Velvet Brown', and spelt the address clearly for him.

'Age?' he said.

'Fourteen. Nearly fifteen.'

'There'll be a doctor up to go over you in a few minutes. Dr Bodie tells me there's nothing broken.'

'I didn't fall off,' said Velvet. 'I slid off. After the post. I couldn't feel my knees.'

'Feel any pain anywhere?'

'No thank you. I could have got up, only my legs . . .'

'All right. Right. Enjoyed your tea?'

And the M.O. went, like an iron ghost, and the door closed invisibly behind him.

At five-thirty she had a drink of bromide and chloral, and twenty minutes later the gates of the world closed down on her while the second batch of posters in London and Liverpool and all the great cities of England, France, Germany, Italy . . . fell sloppily off the printing machines, were baled up, dispatched, and, drying, fluttered at street corners and receded on the backs of newspaper cars. 'Drama of Winner of National this afternoon.' 'Unknown girl wins National.' (This paper thought the fact so first-rate that there was no need to attract by mystery.)

'Extraordinary affair at Aintree.'

'Piebald wins but disqualified. Rider found to be woman.'

Ten minutes later more posters . . .

'Girl winner in Liverpool Central Hospital.'

In the great cities of America the boys were calling 'Extra!' and the Stop Press of all the papers shone in green, red, and blue ink. From France the *Intransigeant* and the *Paris Soir* sent two men over in aeroplanes to Aintree. The Associated Press of America got an all-clear interview with the Clerk of the Course. In Shanghai the first 3.30 flash had just caught the last editions of the morning *North China Daily News*. Rome and Berlin did not trouble themselves profoundly. The thing grew and grew and grew, and turned over on itself, and heaped itself up. People walked in the streets not knowing that the air quivered with question marks. The common air, not seeing or tasting or breathing any different, was heavy with one idea, one burden, an incoming wave of query into England. This questioning air, sweeping through impediment in a silvery attack, poured round flesh, wood, and stone till it found the wireless masts and there, settling and transmuting itself into something more possible to human understanding, became the word of man.

There was a pause. The queries massed like birds and waited. 'We must know more!' cried every foreign agency and every newspaper.

'You shall know more,' soothed the deep voice of Reuter, sedate and cautious, before it ringed the world with its answer.

The reporters had been baffled at the Liverpool Central but Dr Bodie was got at. Eager, in fact, to be got at.

He could not tell the rider's name but he described this and that, and after a while, the information having been looked over and binged up here and toned down there, and written almost all in most expensive plain language (that there should be no delay anywhere in decoding), Reuter sent round the world the following message . . . '61610 Lead all stop Girl has won and lost Grand National stop Most sensational incident in Aintree history occurred today when discovered winning jockey mounted Piebald was young girl stop since women jockeys unallowed compete

National Piebald disqualified by stewards stop Girl fainted after passing post carried ambulance room on stretcher where sex discovered by doctor who states age between 14–16 years stop faint due fatigue unserious injuries stop Girl who refused reveal identity rode under Russian jockey Taskys name stop Stewards National Hunt Committee ordered fullest investigation stop For woman to complete National course regarded as one most extraordinary feats in annals British racing stop drama mystery associated this amazing affair whipped up excitement feverpitch countrywide Result race now reads . . .' (and the names of the first three horses were given).

As this message left London it flashed in a few seconds along the trunk lines that were being held open for it, through Egypt, to India, South Africa, Australia, and to Singapore and the Far East. From the arteries ran the veins. Men in Shanghai, Sydney, Capetown became disseminators almost at the same moment that they had been receivers. And in a steady spreading belt round the world ran the reply to the frantic queries.

In each country there was a Smaller Proper Machinery to receive it and its re-distribution was carried out in eddies from the main encircling belt. In each country the Smaller Proper Machinery distributed it to the newspapers, and newspapers set it up in print, printed it, issued it, sold it, and it was read by

white, brown, yellow, red and black men who exclaimed in their tongues – 'Whew!'

Heads of news agencies, heads of syndicates, heads of newspapers said in their various languages 'This is a Press Ballyhoo. Spread all out on this. This is front-page stuff.'

'We gotta be splurgy,' said a great man in New York. 'Get that dame's dope. She's swell!' And he cabled 'Ten thousand dollars for exclusive rights of personal story'. A girl in London got into a fast car and drove rapidly down to the coast.

It was the great bellows of the Glory-Machine starting to blow. But it had not nearly got its wind up yet. The pink balloon of notoriety had hardly done more than shake loose its ropes and fill out. And the little creature whose name it bore lay very slight, very sheltered, under the deep and fumey blanket.

'It's Velvet. Sure's fate it's Velvet,' said Mr Brown, standing in the street doorway. 'Come in, gentlemen!'

'Mother! Hi! Come on in here!' he called. 'Here's our Velvet gone . . . I feel hot in the stomach, gentlemen. She ain't hurt herself? (I gotta sit down.) She safe?'

Mrs Brown filled the inner doorway.

'Mother,' said Mr Brown, looking white and shaken, 'our Velvet gone an' won the Grand National. Ridden it herself . . .'

Certainly Mrs Brown's eyes changed their colour in some way. They did not gleam. They were too high in their shallows for that, but a curious light seemed to shift in them.

'She's not one for words, sir,' said Mr Brown, taking out his handkerchief and wiping his hands. '(Fingers gone all sticky. Takes me that way.) I can't take it in what she done. Where is she, then?'

'She's in the Liverpool Central Hospital . . .' began one of the reporters.

'Why?' said Mrs Brown like a pistol shot.

'Just fatigue, so we understand,' said the reporter.

'They're from the newspapers, mother,' said Mr Brown.

'She slipped off her horse, Mrs Brown,' said the reporter. 'Fainted after she had passed the winning post. No bones broken, no harm done. Is this the first you have heard of it?'

'Papers don't get here till seven,' said Mr Brown, 'On the Tilling's bus.' He looked at his watch. 'It's a quarter of now.'

'Then you have no doubt,' said another reporter, 'that the rider is also the owner, your daughter Velvet?'

'He don't even know,' said Mrs Brown suddenly. 'Don't you tell him nothing, William. I know them.'

'Why ever not?' said Mr Brown. 'She's got a bit of a down on newspaper gentlemen, sir,' said he apologetically. 'Haven't you,

mother? She had a bit of a bad time with 'em once.'

'Tell 'em what you like. You've begun,' said Mrs Brown, shutting the door. She crossed the room in majesty and went up to her room.

Mr Brown gave a lengthy interview only interrupted by the gentlemen's desire to get away and to the telephone to catch the last edition of the evening papers.

The reporters were shown the paper horses in the shell-box.

One of them thought the shell box touching, but did not say so.

'Fresh, fresh, fresh an' hot!' said another as they sped down the street.

'Old lady's bin in the news,' said another. 'Wonder how?'

'Bloody old cathedral!' said the first.

In the morning at the Liverpool Central, mother sat by Velvet's bed (mother, carrying her washing things in her old 'Art' bag).

'I've come to take you home, dearie,' she said.

Velvet, dazed with her sleep, still, and brilliantly happy, smiled through her dreams.

'Nice kettle of fish,' said Mrs Brown.

'Travelled up through the night,' said mother. 'You done well, Velvet.'

This was the summit, and Velvet felt the beating of glory.

Before coming in mother had had a talk to the Resident Medical Officer and they discovered in their wordless way that they felt alike on certain subjects. It was found that Velvet could be taken out by the laundry entrance.

'She's ser little she could go in a laundry basket,' said mother.

'No need for that,' objected the M.O. who was against exaggeration.

And Velvet (and Mrs Brown with her, for her bulk had not yet become as famous as it did a few days later) went in the laundry van, its rear backed up against the Laundry Entrance.

They reached the station in safety, for though the film of the Grand National had already been on the screens of thousands of cinema houses the night before, and the morning papers were alive with Mr Brown's interview, there were no pictures as yet (Mr Brown had not dared to ask for the one off Mrs Brown's dressing-table), and the crouching black ant flashing by on the film bore no relation to the peaky young man walking beside the big woman to a third class carriage on the 'Merseyside' as its engines got up steam.

'Better you kep' 'em on,' Mrs Brown had said in the van. 'N'anyway I never thought to bring your others. Look the proper boy!'

The carriage was full, but no one's attention was caught. Velvet behaved like the obscure child she thought herself to be.

They reached London, crossed it on the Underground, and took the local train.

A taxi stood in a dark corner of the station yard. As Velvet was pushed into its gloom by her mother she was caught by the eager hands of her sisters. 'Velvet, Velvet . . . Oh Velvet, . . . What you got on? Coo lummy, she's dressed like a boy!'

'Ssh!' said mother. 'Don't talk so . . .' The taxi started off.

'Velvet, it's glorious! All the afternoon, ever since yesterday, everybody comin' to ask. We knew it was you las' night when the newspaper men came. All the papers got pictures of us in, but it's you they're waiting to get! American girl come in a car, an' the things she asked father said it made him hot to hear her. She said she gotta get your story.'

'What story?' said Velvet.

'Don' talk ser much,' said mother. 'She don' know about all that yet.'

When the celebrated child returned home that night she was able to walk under the triumphal arch which the villagers had built with haste in the morning.

(And this arch, and this street opening, were the gateway to a village whose roofs and whose faces were the same but whose nature was changed to her. From now on she walked, fastened to that glory, whose teeth were sharp and held well, but whose wings were golden. She walked with an eagle on her back, observed by all.)

As the station taxi turned into the narrow lane of the village, shouts and dangling lights brought it to a halt. There was a rope across the street, hung with lanterns, and by its light the glossy flutter of the leafy arch could be seen. Mr Croom was at the taxi door, a bouquet of lit faces behind his shoulder, and Velvet was lifted out and walked under the arch and was carried home, rockily, on many shoulders. Mrs Brown paid off the taxi, and strode with her face glum. She was reminded of Calais.

In the living-room at home there was not room for everybody, and the villagers hung in the doorway and shuffled in a tail in the street. The bottle of port came out but there was not much in it, and Mr Brown sent Mally out for more. It was not long before Mrs Brown bore Velvet, like a child of paper, to her bedroom. 'You'll lay there,' she said, 'an' I'll bring you your supper.'

Greatest wonder, it was Edwina who brought her a hot-water bottle, who stayed to talk in marvelling whispers, and listened with Velvet to the clamour down below. Mother brought the tray

up, cold salt beef and chopped beetroot and a cup of cocoa. Velvet nibbled gently, changed feet on her hot water-bottle, watched the dark sky through the undrawn curtains.

'No one's to come up,' said Mrs Brown. And Velvet finished her supper and lay and waited for Mally and Merry, who came when the visitors had melted.

Mi turned up, having mysteriously come by a later train for nothing. Velvet slipped on her clothes again.

'You got up?' said Mrs Brown as Velvet walked into the living-room.

'It's dark now. Pitch,' said Velvet, 'I mus' just go up the field an' fetch him in.' She turned and took her shell-box of paper horses off the sideboard.

'They seen that, Velvet.'

'Who did?'

'The newspaper men,' said Mr Brown. But Velvet did not seem to understand.

Mrs Brown expanded her breast in an unusual and vigorous sigh.

'She won't pass no one now, though the whole village's bin hanging round the horse from what I hear. Better let her go. She won't pass no one ser late. Heigho . . . I bin a darn donkey once in my life an' it seems I bin it twice.'

Velvet, dressed in her own clothes, went up the road between the ditches with Mally. The cats' eyes gleamed and shifted and went out. Nettles and cats' eyes and stars and stillness and not a soul about. The Piebald was flashing his colours under stars by the gate. The other horses hearing her step cantered down the slope whinnying. They greeted her with little jealous screams and lashings.

'D'you know what you've done?' said Velvet to The Piebald, but he shook his head suddenly as though a night gnat was on it.

'Wasa matter, Pie ole darling? Hasn' he gone in at the haunches terrible, Mally? Just in one day.'

'. . . An' what a day!' said Mally.

Velvet, her cheek on the top of the gate, Sir Pericles' breath blew her hair. 'The worse was I got my mouth open an' couldn't shut it because the wind dried it. What was *your* worse, Pie ole darling?'

Velvet turned solemnly to Mally. 'He'll be in every book, Mally. He'll be the horse of this year, that won it this year. Though they disqualify us they'll never dare to drop him out altogether. He won't be on the Aintree Roll of Honour . . .'

'What's that?'

'A brown board with gold letters. But he'll be in the books the writers write. The first piebald horse that ever won the National.

By what I've heard about it they'll try to buy him, but I'll never sell him. SELL you, Piebald!'

'The poor others!' said Mally. 'Do they mind?'

'No, no . . . Pericles! Little sweetie . . . Mrs James! You're squealing, you jealous old woman. She's tried to kick George, Mally. Get away . . . there . . .'

'George deserves all he gets,' said Mally. 'He pokes his nose in everywhere and it's food he wants, not love. He and Mrs James thought you'd come with a bucket.'

'Come on, Piebald,' called Velvet, searching for the old halter they kept behind the wall. But The Piebald was cropping the cool night grass away with a layer of dark air between them, as though horses that had won the Grand National were turned out to grass in the early spring every night. Unceremonious and incredibly enduring, he moved away.

'Come on,' said Mally, 'I should leave him. It's warm. He won't hurt. Mother said not to let you stay long. You're dead tired.'

'I gotta see Donald before I sleep,' said Velvet.

'Donald?'

'I thought about him the night I was going to ride. In that hotel bedroom. I was sick as anything . . .'

'Oh, poor Velvet! An' all alone!'

'No, Mi kep' comin' in an' out. I thought about if I was killed an' never saw Donald again. On'y for a flash, but I thought it.'

'Funny thing to think. Why Donald?'

'It was funny. But I thought it anyway,' said Velvet doggedly. 'I mus' jus' see him when I go in.'

They entered the house.

'Velvet wants to see Donald,' said Mally, somewhat aggrieved.

'I wanter kiss him in his bed,' said Velvet.

'She's overstrung,' said Mrs Brown. 'Go on up, he's dead asleep.'

Donald lay flung out in an abandoned and charming attitude. His eye-lashes were tender, bronze and shadowy; his hair a touch damp. The strangeness of his youth and exposed face, his battle for power by day and his abdication by night was something that Velvet had hardly expected. A gateway drew open within her and the misery and wild alarm of life rushed in.

'Velvet's crying over Donald!' said Mally aghast, running down to the living-room.

'Carry her to her bed, father,' said Mrs Brown calmly. 'It's to be expected.'

CHAPTER XV

Next morning the Browns rose as usual. Edwina came down to take in the milk and the greeting of the milkman was a little long because it contained moderate congratulations. The milkman was a steady fellow.

From then on, however, nothing else was as usual. The crowd began to collect up on the Green in knots about nine, and by ten it was definitely clotted and pooling in the street. Mally, with her twitching nose, went out towards it early and scented radiations. The crowd, which was small and scattered at the time, definitely stirred as the front door opened, and something in the white faces and black eyes all looking one way made Mally shut the door again.

'I believe it's about Velvet,' she said with a gasp into the scullery. 'Ther's people outside.'

'People?' said Mrs Brown. 'Someone want her?'

'Just people,' said Mally. 'Standing about.'

Mrs Brown went to look. She pulled the front blinds down over the cinerarias. So on a sunny morning at the end of March Velvet started her first day of glory as though someone had died in the house.

The crowd grew denser during the morning and none of the Browns put a nose out of doors. Mrs Brown set the four girls at little jobs in their bedrooms and told them to keep the yard end by the canary cages. The crowd made a great deal of noise in the street as it drifted about, and the house seemed very small.

'Are you sure it is only about Velvet?' said Meredith. 'It isn't a revolution?'

Mr Brown finally decided that this wouldn't do and he must go down to his shop. He went out the back way and was not definitely recognized, except by the local man on the Worthing *Witness and Echo*. This man walked beside him and asked him questions as he went towards his shop. Mr Brown was not at all unwilling. 'She was always a one for horses,' he said, and gave a lot of details.

'I kin do without me shopping,' said Mrs Brown in the gloom at home. 'There's enough of that cold salt beef.'

'Jolly!' said Edwina. 'Winning the Grand National an' living with the blinds down an' eating cold salt beef. I don't know that Velvet's done us much of a turn.'

The first gloomy morning of fame went by, blinds down, salt beef, and everyone immured in the house. In the one local paper which they took there was a lot about Velvet, but no one thought of sending out for all the other papers.

'The ink don't print up Velvet's face too good,' said Mrs Brown with distaste. It was only what she expected.

The picture was called 'The Gate-Crasher at the Grand National'.

'Dam' silly title,' said Mally. 'She didn't knock a thing.'

Velvet was suffering from reaction and sat about limp. She did not bother about the newspaper except to glance at her picture.

'I'd like to go out an' look at The Pie.'

'You don't no one leave this house,' said Mrs Brown. They yawned and moped and grumbled.

'We'll have to go to an hotel if this goes on,' said Edwina, who had once been to an hotel.

'That's what we'll do,' said Mrs Brown surprisingly, 'if it don't blow over in a day or two. It's not but what I'm not proud of you, Velvet. But what's the good of you standing up for them gaping loonies to look at. They can't get no more out of you than they have done. You done your best up at Aintree and that ought to be enough. But what gets me is this gaping an' gaping an' handshaking an' behaving unfriendly an' curious as though you were a savage they'd caught on the beach.'

'Did they do it to you, mother, too? When you swum it?' Velvet jerked her head to the sea.

'They'd no modesty,' said Mrs Brown shortly, and said no more.

'Mother'd like to go out with a broom,' said Meredith, after Mrs Brown had left the room, 'an' sweep 'em away.'

'Mother's a one,' said Mally, pulling a chair up for her feet.

But the middle-day post consoled Edwina and gave them all something to do. The door bell had been rung incessantly by the representatives of newspapers, but Mrs Brown had the big bar-arm down and stuffed a duster in the bell. She knew the postman's knock, however, and he had had the sense to go round to the back.

There was an enormous box of chocolates for Velvet from an unknown admirer, and almost at the same moment a florist's man appeared groaning under a silver wicker basket loaded with pots of ferns and pink azaleas, and draped from head to foot in pink ribbon. This was from two of the Aldermen on the Worthing Corporation.

But in the post itself there was something incredible. Among seven letters for Velvet, six were love letters, and again among them two were proposals of marriage. Edwina and Mally read them aloud with yelps of delight.

But the seventh, addressed to Miss V. Brown in a clerkly hand, was a different affair. It was written on paper like cardboard, its heading was neat and in fine scrollwork, and it explained to her that the Stewards at Aintree, not being satisfied with explanations given on 23 March, the matter was referred to the Stewards of the National Hunt Committee, and the inquiry into the running of The Piebald by an unqualified rider would be held at 15, Cavendish Square on the following Tuesday, at which meeting Miss V. Brown, Owner, was requested to appear.

'Trouble's got to come,' said Mr Brown, when he had heard the letter too. He had by degrees, and through the day, night, and morning, become a father who walked on air. 'Trouble's got to come, Velvet, but nothing can take away what you done, my girl.'

In the early afternoon the crowds grew denser.

'Brown family totally surrounded,' read the headlines in the London papers. 'Extra police drafted in.' This brought more crowds. Worthing made hurried arrangements for a special bus-line, that people might see the crowds and become part of them.

Mrs Brown closed the door upon reporters. And closed her lips. And closed her eyes and thought. To her the house seemed threatened. Edwina, Mally, Meredith . . . even the canaries seemed threatened. And Velvet most of all. The warmth, the cosiness, the privacy of life were blown with draught. Her house had a side taken out of it and she could not close it four-square.

How long would it take to live it down? It was like a gale. It was like staying indoors in a gale. She let the spaniels into the living-room, as one calls in a yard animal in a dangerous hurricane.

'I gotta get some air,' said Velvet feverishly at three o'clock, and stepped out of the back door to the orchard.

'Good day, Miss Velvet,' said a slim lady instantly.

'Good day, Miss,' said Velvet.

'I just wanted to ask you,' said the lady –

'I've got a car here,' said the lady. 'Let's sit in it.'

Velvet hesitated. It was not in her to refuse. She crossed to the lane, looking back at the cactus window.

The lady opened the door of the car and Velvet got in.

'Now,' said the lady, settling down with Velvet beside her, 'you're a great girl. Why you're not as much as fourteen!'

'Fourteen,' said Velvet shyly.

'Got any boy friends?'

'Oh . . . Mi. Mi Taylor.'

'Who's he?'

'Dad's help. Father's help. In the slaughter-house.'

Velvet was without defences. Her innocent and murmured sentences were like poppy seeds in a corn field. The field went scarlet and smelt narcotic and bloomed. But mercifully this was in America, and Velvet never knew what was written and said.

They had not got far (but far enough) with the interview when Mrs Brown intervened. She called from the back doorway and Velvet, breathing relief, sprang from the car and went to her. The lady followed. 'One moment . . .' she said, crossing the road too.

'No!' said Mrs Brown sharply, and sent Velvet in behind her bulk.

'Excuse me,' began the lady, 'it's for the American Press.'

'In England we got rights,' said Mrs Brown, and shut the door in her face.

A big Daimler pushed its way up the street at three-thirty. Out of it got a little man with a big head, and a garden of rich fur on his coat collar. He had a talk with Mr Brown, whom by luck he saw going in at the street door. He sat in the living-room for half-an-hour and as he rose to go he was heard to say that he would send his Daimler for both of them.

'Both who?' said Mrs Brown, coming in when he had gone.

'Gentleman from the pictures,' said father. 'An actor. Well, an actor-manager. Come from Elstree in Essex. Come all the way to ask if Velvet could go an' pose for them.'

'She going?'

'Says he's sending fer her tomorrow.'

'Well,' said Mrs Brown, coming further into the room, 'had she ought?'

Mr Brown looked at her uneasily. 'Hear that, Velvet?' he said to Velvet, who was sticking pictures of The Piebald into an album. 'What do you feel about it yourself?'

'Think it might be fun,' said Velvet carelessly.

'There y'are,' said Mr Brown irritably. 'An' I don' see any harm. He wants the horse too. He's sending down a horse-box . . .'

'Wants the horse?' said Velvet looking up.

'Says he's made for a film, that horse.'

'Can't have the horse,' said Velvet swiftly, and went on pasting.

'What's that?'

'Piebald on the films!' said Velvet with a light firmness that had never been there before. 'He seems to forget.'

'What's he forget?'

'That *that's* the horse that won the National.'

'That's why he wants him, Velvet,' said father with unaccustomed patience.

'*I'll* go,' said Velvet, getting up. 'It won't be half bad for us all to go and see me doing things on the curtain an' the band playing and us sitting looking. But The Piebald! He doesn't know, he wouldn't know. He's out there in that field steady and safe. He believes in me. I wouldn't let him in for a thing that he couldn't understand. He's not like a human. He doesn't know how to be funny, and he shan't learn!' And the tears of her unwonted defiance streamed down her face.

'Well!' said Mr Brown.

'An' what's more,' sobbed Velvet, 'an' what's more . . .'

'Well?' said Mr Brown.

'I've read about horses . . . horses that has won . . . an' they write about them n-nobly's though they were statues. How can you write about a horse nobly if it goes on the films!'

'But what'll they be writing about your horse more'n they have done?'

'Not in the papers,' said Velvet, now fairly howling, 'not in the p-papers. That's nothing. Mother–mother–mother l-lights the fire with that! In books! Big books. Roll-of-Honour-books where they put down the winners an' call them the Immortal Manifesto.'

'The Immortal What?' said Mr Brown.

'Manifesto. N' how can they call him the Immortal Piebald if he goes on the . . .'

'More like call you the Immortal Velvet!' growled Mr Brown, thoroughly taken aback.

'Me! That's nothing. I'm nothing. If you could see what he did for me. He burst himself for me. N' when I asked him he burst himself more. N' when I asked him again he – he – doubled it. He tried near to death, he did. I'd sooner have that horse happy than go to heaven!'

'Behave yourself, Velvet!' said Mrs Brown sharply. 'Get upstairs. Merry's in an awful mess. She's upset the canary cage, water an' sand n' all on your bed. Get on up and help her.'

As the door shut – 'That child's got something that you don't value, William! That child's more mine than all the rest.'

'I valued you all right once, didn't I, Araminty?'

'You did, William. Or maybe was it the pop an' squeak roun' me?'

'Now Araminty,' said Mr Brown rising, 'don't you go an' cut queer with me over this. I'm bound to say I don't know whether I'm on my head or my heels sometimes. It's like having a gunfire of bouquets thrown on you all at once n'you hardly know where it's coming from. It's like them sweepstakes that we all read break up the home, but we won't let all this to-do break up this home, will we?'

'You always was a nice chap,' said Mrs Brown. 'On'y I'm so buried under me fat I feel half ashamed to tell you so. Love don't seem dainty on a fat woman. Nothin's going to break up this home not even if you lose yer head, but it'll make it easier if you keep it. On'y leave that child to me. She's got more to come.

You think the Grand National's the end of all things, but a child that can do that can do more when she's grown. On'y keep her level, keep her going quiet. We'll live this down presently an' you'll see.'

After this, the longest speech Mrs Brown had made for years, she went out into the yard to look for Donald.

She found, as she had hardly expected, that Donald was talking to a reporter.

There had been a pause. The reporter had not before tackled a mind which answered when it chose, on what lines it chose, or not at all.

Donald's interest in him was flickering, subterranean, critical. He was as usual torn by the suspicion that there might be something better to do.

'But she's a nice girl, your sister?' said the reporter desperately.

'She wasn't a nice girl larse . . . July,' said Donald. 'She didn' pull the plug after she'd sat down. Mother said she wasn't nice.'

'Oh well!' said the reporter almost gaily. 'That's nothing! I've got a Gertrude that does that. She gets smacked for it.'

'Older'n me?'

'Much older than you.'

'I like pulling the plug but I'm not allowed to.'

The reporter's note-book remained blank.

'Yes but . . . all that's no good to me.'

'Velvet tried to pull it,' went on Donald. 'She broke it. It wouldn't pull. Father said it was a trashy plug.'

'Tell me something more about her.'

'She doesn't wash her neck sometimes.'

'Tell me something different,' said the reporter. 'When your sister, Velvet, was a little girl . . .'

'I wasn't here,' said Donald quickly.

'No, of course,' said the reporter. 'You were . . .'

'I wasn't a star either,' said Donald, 'I was somewhere. Doing things. Where do you smack your Gertrude?'

'Tell me, like a nice little chap . . .' (contempt surged over Donald and his lashes half veiled his eyes) 'what sort of things does your sister play with?'

'My sister, Velvet?'

'Your sister Velvet.'

Donald considered. The reporter waited.

'See where I cut my ankle?' said Donald, holding up his leg. 'I arsed fer the iodine myself.'

'Yes,' said the reporter dully, 'it looks a bad cut.'

Donald, like Jacob, could do a thousand things at once. He could hear, feel, see, gauge, forecast, decide, act. He was a twinkling surface, giving off and taking in. He was an incredible

telephone exchange run by motes and atoms and impulsions. He had heard Velvet crying, he knew it was nearly dinner time, he knew there was a broccoli stump blocking the water gutter, he knew at last that this fellow was as empty as a bladder, and his mind went white towards him and turned red and blue and yellow towards everything else.

'Velvet's bin crying,' he remarked, practically to himself.

'Why's that?' said the reporter keenly.

'I gotta go,' said Donald, seeing his mother coming, and walked away.

CHAPTER XVI

Velvet Brown, at a tender age and of a tender sex, won the Grand National. The mind of the public was at once stormed, irradiated and convulsed with a new surprise, fresh, keen, voracious. The fact crashed in the papers like a set of bells. The Mind of the public swung like bells too, pealing, pealing. As newspaper edition after edition came out the peals were set going in waves one after the other. The Mind could only swing and swing and ask to be pushed again. And the pushers flocked to push. The bell-ringers pealed and hauled. The music of news broke and poured over the land. Portions of the Mind began almost at once to rebel. There are people who prefer Wonder to arc through the sky, fall with its own curve, and cease on its fall. But the professional bell-pealers and wonder-mongers were not going to allow much of that. Bells must be handled again as their sound dies; wonder must be propped up and carry on in a straight line through the sky;

the gaping Mind which had come alive like a young chicken must be stuffed with details and choked with news.

The enormous and delicate and intricate machinery which hangs on the fringe of news was set going. Men hammered tin because piebald horses must prance on the heads of tie-pins, women painted little mugs and teacups in Staffordshire, Velvet galloped across nearly a mile of white cardboard, stamped out in diamond-shapes and bent to hold a pound of chocolate creams. It was for the second impossible to be more notorious.

For a time Velvet and the sisters wandered in Arcady. They became princesses in Eden. People gave them sweets, adored their horses, took their photographs. What was so piquant in the papers was that in a row of beauties 'it was the plain one that did it'. This was somehow full of salt.

Only when the portraits of the paper horses, surreptitiously lent by Mr Brown, appeared below a picture of the shell-box in a Sunday paper did Velvet say slowly, 'Who gave them that?'

'What?'

'My shell-box.'

But this blew over, and the shell-box was safe again on the sideboard, and Velvet hardly remembered that she had felt little scratches on her youth.

'Coo lummy . . .' began Edwina one day.

'You will please . . .' said Mr Brown, 'remember that you are now in the public eye.'

'It's Velvet's public eye,' said Edwina rather rudely. She was getting out of hand. But except for Edwina's rudeness, and that was always latent in the poor, upgrowing, beautiful child, and except for Mrs Brown's not unusual silence, and for little plumes of unhelpful vanity in Mr Brown, there was no real deterioration in the Brown household.

Mally and Meredith adored the fuss and the sweets and the visits from newspapers, and the marvel of the cinemas, and took delight in spotting 'Velvet Novelties'; that piebald horse which now definitely galloped on the head of a tie-pin at Woolworth's, and postcards with Velvet crouching in a black shirt tearing past a winning post.

'Let's collect them!' said Mally. And they began to make a collection.

When Velvet saw her face for the first time on the cinema she felt a little strange. It was an enlargement face, done thin on the canvas in black and white. It seemed like her. She could not say it wasn't.

'I look like that,' she thought. And took it for granted that she did.

The same face, transplanted on to postcards, became almost

a code-sign. She could not have said what she felt but it was queer. However, she shook it off. 'If you want something for your collection,' said Edwina one day, 'there's a brown silk in the window at Tinkler's called "Velvet Brown".'

'Tinkler's?'

'In Worthing.'

'Is it expensive? Could we get a yard?'

'Ask them to give you a sample bit with the label pinned to it.'

'Will they?'

'Get Velvet to ask them.'

'Oh yes, of course.'

That was one of Velvet's very little burdens. The sisters always pushed her forward to ask for anything they wanted. Nobody refused Velvet anything. She became aware of this and grew delicate and obstinate.

When she went out she felt an insistent desire on the part of other people to get in touch with her. And once in touch it was quite literal – they touched her. They shook or held her hand, since the hand is not private but only the body.

They came with a rush, with eagerness, as though they could get virtue, as though they could draw meat and drink. And when the 'touching' was over and the child's hand had been shaken they hovered a second with baffled hunger, and murmuring 'It was fine', retired. It crossed Velvet's mind occasionally to think they wanted something more of her.

Mally kept the 'collection' with energy. It was in a box in the bedroom and was beginning to look like a ragbag. There was a powder-puff called 'The Velvet', in gold letters on printed voile, and a mechanical piebald horse that wound up and hopped across the floor. There was a cartoon in one of the evening papers of Velvet coming over Becher's sitting between the wings of Pegasus, and all the other horses looking scared. It was called 'The Unseen Adversary'. There were marvellous love letters from strangers, and boys at school, and workmen. One of the best began 'Divine Equestrian' – but they all got very crumpled up and difficult to find.

There may be wonder in money, but dear God there is money in wonder. And nothing is so cheap as a newspaper, where, when true news is truly breaking it starts up under the feet like a hare on the downs, and prince and poor man come in on the equal and swing along for their pennies while the news runs. And now the news was running hot and strong and pouring from it as it ran the true authentic scent. No basket hare this, let out and egged on to trot tamely by its keeper, and while Velvet lasted there was no need to bring carted news to the Meet.

While the day approached for the sitting of the National Hunt Committee, the whole world was made to believe it was waiting for details.

'Coo lummy . . .' said Velvet, late on Monday night. And Mr Brown found this excusable.

'Can't eat you,' said Mrs Brown, and glanced at Mi. It was Mi they could eat, she felt.

'We'll get away an' up to London early,' said Mi. 'We don' want to be messed up with hand-shaking tomorrow.'

CHAPTER XVII

In an upper room in 15, Cavendish Square, round a Board Table, the Board had assembled. It was a distinguished company, mainly of robust and kindly men. They had as their spokesman Messrs Weatherby's lawyer, Mr Simkin, and as their Chairman, Lord Tunmarsh. The others were Colonel 'Ruby' Allbrow, a man with an extraordinarily scarlet forehead, which turned his name into a better joke than it already was, Mits Schreiber, who had ridden in the National three times, Lord Henry Vile, Mr Little (a descendant of Captain Joseph Lockhart Little), and Mr Thomas, who was no descendant of 'Mr Thomas' (since the famous bearer rode under a pseudonym) but liked to think he was, Mr Seckham, Mr Coleman, Sir Harry Hall, and others. The Clerk, Cotton, was in attendance.

'Sickening, this Velvet uproar,' said Mr Little, as they met.

'I've read none of it,' said the Chairman, taking his seat, 'or as little as I could help. I'm in a position to judge the case on its merits. I only read *The Times*.'

'What about the evening papers?'

'The evening papers,' said Lord Tunmarsh, 'are for the servants' hall. Is the girl here?'

'She's downstairs, waiting.'

'Very well, Mr Simkin. Will you tell us our position? Is it a case for prosecution? Is it a case coming under our own laws, how we stand in fact?'

Mr Simkin delivered a small oration on the laws of impersonation, standing as a black silhouette against the windows facing on Cavendish Square. He sat down. 'It's beyond my imagination,' he finished – 'that is why I find it so difficult to give you, gentlemen, a crisp ruling – it's beyond my imagination to suppose that a female should have done such a thing. Should have so deceived US.'

'But a female *has* done it, you ass!' (muttered Mits Schreiber). 'Very much done it.'

Simkin rose and went to a row of yellow calf volumes on the shelf.

He took down one. Over clapped the pages, flying under his dusty thumb. His long upper lip closed over his teeth.

'Attempting to defraud,' he muttered. He looked sharply over

his shoulder. 'It's understood that we judge the case entirely –'
There was an irritable and suspicious note in his voice.

The Chairman looked up sharply. 'You're not referring to the
newspaper hurly-burly, I hope, are you, Mr Simkin?'

'No, well, I hardly imagined, Mr Chairman, no. And this
is a case of – (if I'm not mistaken) of fraud. I have it here.
"Attempting to obtain money under" . . . "Obtaining money
under" . . . no, she hasn't "obtained". Attempting to obtain.
That's it. Attempting to obtain. It's very clear.' He looked up.
'We can prosecute.'

'Legal, is it?'

Lord Tunmarsh looked uncomfortable. 'Let's see the girl first.
She's waiting?'

'Downstairs.'

'Let's see her,' said Colonel 'Ruby' Allbrow. 'Have her up.
After all it was a good show. A first class show she put up. What's
her age?'

'Her age,' broke in Mr Simkin, looking at the Chairman, 'is said
to be fourteen. This I should say was a romantic understatement
on the part of the Press. Might I say, Mr Chairman, before the . . .
young woman . . . comes into the room that I think that it would
be a pity if any note of admiration be acknowledged during the
interview. If indeed any is felt.'

The Chairman nodded. 'I think, Mr Simkin, you can leave that to me. No admiration can be felt for what is practically a criminal proceeding. Involving forgery very probably. We'll have to look into that question of the faked Clearance.'

Mits Schreiber addressed the Chairman.

'But if she's fourteen, can we prosecute a child of fourteen? Who put her up to do it?'

'Apparently nobody.'

'Impossible! Are we prepared as to what . . .'

'Have her up,' said the Chairman. 'We shall know better when we see her. I'm not prepared, any more than Mr Simkin is, to take it from her that she is fourteen. We have been loaded with more or less inaccurate (I daresay) descriptions of this young woman morning after morning. I need hardly say that – Not that we've any of us read 'em all, but –'

'Every bally word, Mr Chairman!' broke in Mits Schreiber. 'I'm a Velvet fan.'

Lord Tunmarsh did not smile.

'Well keep it to yourself, Mits. This is a meeting of the National Hunt Committee, and for myself I feel that we have been extremely offended by a piece of vulgarity. Mr Simkin feels the same on behalf of Messrs Weatherby. Please ask her to come up.'

'Call her up, Cotton.'

Velvet was shown up to the Committee Room of the National Hunt Committee.

The dusty stairs were dark. The door opened. The room was light.

All the men sitting round the table rose. Lord Tunmarsh drew a chair out for her. Velvet sank, sat on the edge, folded her hands. Fourteen men saw a feather-weight plain child in a red jersey, dark blue wool skirt, blue wool coat with brass buttons and childish brown shoes with stub toes. They drew a breath.

'Good afternoon,' said Lord Tunmarsh at last. 'You are Miss Velvet Brown?'

'Yes,' Velvet nodded gently. (Oh God, don't let me be sick . . .)

'I really . . .' said Lord Tunmarsh, after a pause, but stopped himself.

'Well, was it you all right riding that Piebald? It was you, wasn't it, Miss Brown?' broke in Colonel 'Ruby' Allbrow on the silence.

'Me.'

'What put it into your head, girl, to do a frivolous thing like that?'

Velvet slowly spread out her thin hands and counted the fan of muscles. She breathed something about the horse.

'What's that?'

'I knew the horse could do it,' she said again.

'But why *you* riding? What d'you want to ride him *yourself*? Why not get a professional?'

'He . . .'

'Yes?' said Lord Tunmarsh, leaning a little towards her.

'He goes very well for me.'

There was a pause.

Like an explosion, 'He DID do that!' from a red-faced gentleman in checks.

'I think we shall have,' said Lord Tunmarsh, 'to ask Mr Simkin to explain to her . . . just what . . . what we feel about the matter.'

Mr Simkin rose with alacrity. Rustled his papers. Blew out and drew down his upper lip.

Velvet looked up at him with her docile look. The fine bone round her white temple was blue with shadow, her newly-cropped pale hair hung close and uneven round her ears, she raised her head, and watched him with mild, intelligent eyes. Her lips parted slowly over the gold band and white teeth. Lord Tunmarsh whispered to his neighbour 'hard to believe' and the neighbour whispered and shook his head.

Mr Simkin read his clause from the yellow volume, under the

heading, 'Attempting to obtain money under false pretences'.

'You being a female,' said Mr Simkin . . . 'and not an accredited male rider . . . come under this heading. It was a . . . for the time being . . . successful deception. Upon . . . ah . . . US. Upon Messrs Weatherby (and the Committee of the National Hunt). It was done to obtain a prize of . . .'

'No, no, it wasn't!' said Velvet.

'Eh . . . what . . . why not? You stood to get the prize?'

'Yes, sir. Yes, I did. But it wasn't done for that reason. It was done because . . .'

'And why was it done? We should like to know that?'

'Because,' said Velvet, looking out of the window into the chimney pots of Cavendish Square, 'the horse jumps lovely and I wanted him to be famous. I didn't think of the money when I planned it all.'

'Ah, and now we come to that!' said Mr Simkin. 'You say you planned it all. That, Miss Brown, is hard to believe. You are, I understand, a child. You have obtained a false-certificate from my . . . er . . . people. From US. From Messrs Weatherby. You posted an Esthonian Clearance to us and in exchange we forwarded to you the usual Licence. It was a monstrous imposture. How was it done?'

Velvet looked at him, her eyes full of light.

'There was so much to be done,' she said at length.

'You mean that I am choosing only one of the grave impostures which you and your friends have . . . er . . . practised. It is precisely the name of those friends which we wish to have laid before us. This is . . . Miss Brown . . . a very SERIOUS OFFENCE. A grave deceit has been practised not only . . . upon US . . . but upon the Public. The money of the Public is in our trusteeship. We guarantee to the Public that this great and famous race . . . into which you have entered so lightly, so frivolously, so mockingly, is a race which is run in such a way that they can put their money on it . . . er . . . safely.'

'"Safely's" a bit strong, Simkin,' said Lord Tunmarsh.

'"Safely," m'lord,' said Simkin with obstinate pride. 'Weatherby's pride themselves that they make racing safe up to the limits of the usual chances.'

Lord Tunmarsh bit a piece of nail off his thumb. Mits Schreiber laughed.

'How old are you?' said Lord Tunmarsh suddenly.

'Fourteen, sir. Fifteen next month.' This no longer seemed doubtful. Mr Simkin resumed.

'Who has helped you in this?' he said startlingly to Velvet.

'We want the names of your friends!'

'Mother knew. At the end,' said Velvet.

'Your mother knew. That is important. Your mother is Mrs Brown.'

'My mother was Araminty Potter. She swam the Channel once.'

'Her mother was Araminty Potter!' said Sir Harry Hall, whistling. 'Swam the Channel breast-stroke twenty years ago. She downstairs?'

'No, sir.'

'Your father's a . . .'

'Butcher, sir. A slaughterer-butcher.'

'He knew?'

'No, he didn't know. Only afterwards. When I got my fall.'

'So Araminty Potter married a butcher and got you?' said Sir Harry Hall. 'And you've gone and swindled the almighty Weatherby's and won the Grand National . . .'

'Sir Harry,' intervened Mr Simkin, 'I don't think this conduces to her understanding of the situation. Doesn't help. Doesn't help at all. If your father didn't know, Miss Brown (supposing this to be exact), and only your mother knew, then we must look for *other supporters*. I should like to begin with the Esthonian Clearance? How was that got? And who procured it?'

Velvet looked at them, halting. Gazed at them. The light filled her face and she seemed to rest and wait. It was not a question of deciding. She and Mi had decided already. Both had known that they would have to pay for The Piebald's fame. In Mi's case he was paying for Velvet's.

'Mi's downstairs,' she said at length. 'Mi will tell you. We knew he would have to.'

'And Mi is . . .?' said Mr Simkin, still standing against the windows in silhouette.

'Mi is Mi Taylor. He helps my father in the slaughter-house,' and even to her child's ears it seemed a rummy description of the glory of Mi.

'This Mi Taylor . . .' said Mr Simkin, and stooped to whisper to his neighbour. The neighbour sent a paper round to the Chairman. Lord Tunmarsh nodded.

'Will you wait downstairs, Miss Brown?' he said. 'We should like to speak to Mr Taylor.'

Velvet disappeared and Mi was before them. His cap in his hand, his hair already rising from the damp comb he had run through it on the stairs (having spat on the comb).

'Mi Taylor,' he said, nodding.

'Mi . . .?' said Mr Simkin, writing.

'Michael,' corrected Mi.

'And you are Mr Brown's assistant in the business?'

'I landed up there,' said Mi, 'to do anything. Clean the slaughter-house, buy sheep, help their ma and so on. The boy's a handful.'

'A boy?'

'Just a small one. No account yet.'

'Well now, Taylor,' said Mr Simkin clearing his throat, 'I don't need to tell you that a frivolous and monstrous outrage has been committed. An impertinence and also I imagine a legally-punishable fraud.'

'Yes, sir.'

'This fraud has ostensibly been committed by a child, the young lady we have just seen, Miss Velvet Brown. Obviously she could neither have planned it nor carried it through. Without help. Without the direction of another mind. What part did you play in all this, Taylor? We have got to know and we are going to know and I warn you to make no trouble over speaking the truth.' Mr Simkin sat down abruptly and gave the table a pencil tap. Everyone looked at Mi.

'I knew a boy,' said Mi very simply, and he paused and sucked the hollow beside his tooth. 'This boy knew a boy. . . . It was at Lewes races. Well it was at Brighton races first and then I saw the other boy at Lewes races . . .'

'Their names?' said Mr Simkin, writing.

'No,' said Mi. 'I ain't going to give you their names. You kin judge fer yourself when I've done. There was a whole trail o' boys. All talkin'. You know what they are at these races. Ain't got nothing to do. Lean up against each other an' jabber. More an' more kept coming in. No good to give you their names, I don't know 'em all. But the upshot was there was someone knew a fellow coming over that had a Clearance from Esthonia. Going to ride a horse that come by air and dropped dead at Croydon. Then he hadn't any horse, see? So I met him. 'Long of these fellows I'm telling you about. They didn't do anything but jabber, so it's no good giving you the names. All they did was to say they knew a fellow had a Clearance and didn't want his Clearance. I oiled up the fellow an' got his Clearance. Didn't want it so I got it. He didn't think any more about it. He's a half-Russian boy's bin riding out there for some Count. He's gone back now. Never thought no more about it. Then I just posted in the Clearance and got a Licence. See?'

'And this boy from Esthonia? Where is he now? He is, I suppose, the boy whose name is on the Licence? Tasky?'

'That's him. Where's he now? He's in Russia, s'far as I know. He got orders to cut off the hoof o' the dead horse an' take it back to the Count. Fer an inkstand, I daresay. They make them into stands. Told me he was going straight to Esthonia, and then on to Russia where the Count's got a winter job as a sort of a riding master with the Bolsheviks. Tasky and he, they go together most winters, so he said.'

'Not much chance,' whispered the Chairman to Colonel Allbrow, 'of getting at Tasky. ('Less he ever comes again.) Looks to me as though the only culprit's here, in the room.'

'So it seems to me, Taylor,' said Mr Simkin, 'that the whole of this monstrous affair has been engineered by you and by you alone, if we are to believe you?'

Mi chuckled. Or the shade of a chuckle brushed him. He flicked it away and answered, 'No.'

'No, sir,' he said. 'There's Velvet. Velvet thought out the thing. It come to her. It come to her like the horse did, out of the sky.'

'How did the horse come to her?' asked Captain Little, leaning forward.

'Why she got it fer a shilling in a raffle in the village! There were yards about it in the *Express*!' said Mits.

Mr Simkin frowned.

'Is that so, Taylor?' he said sharply.

'Yes, sir. You can go down to the village an' see. Anybody'd tell you. The horse belonged to Farmer Ede an' it made a filthy nuisance of itself, getting over walls and tearing down the village street. Nearly killed a child and nearly had a pushcart over twice. Ede couldn't do anything with it. He stuck it up for a raffle at the village fair in the summer. Didn't do badly: got nine pounds six shillings. Velvet took a ticket and won it. Then things went on an' on and she got moony about the horse, religious. She's a queer child. An' one day . . . when I see it jump a five-foot wall by itself an' make away . . . I said . . . just kind of careless . . . just said . . .' (Mi waved his hand) '"Make a Grand National jumper, that would!" Then Velvet never said anything but she never let up on that. She just went on.'

'It seems not possible . . .' said Lord Tunmarsh. 'I never heard such a tale!'

'It's no tale,' said Mi earnestly. 'It's just Velvet. I know what's in her blood because my old father . . .' he paused.

'Your father?' said Mr Simkin drily. He did not like the eager, little-boys' interest the Committee was taking in the tale.

'My father was old Dan Taylor,' said Mi, 'an' he was a Channel trainer. He trained Araminty (Velvet's mother) to swim the Channel. *An'* she swum it. Against the tide in a terrible dirty morning in a storm . . .'

'I remember!' said Sir Harry Hall. 'It was a bigger thing than anything that's bin done since. It was done breast stroke. It seemed incredible.'

'Well then, that's her mother. It's in her blood. If you'd see her mother now you'd never believe it. Great old woman she is, all muscled up an' tight. An' silent. An' plucky's fire still. The father, he's not added nothing. It's the mare that's done it. An' Velvet, fer all she's such a sickly bit, she's like her. She'll sit on a horse like a shadow and breathe her soul into it. An' her hands. . . . She's got little hands like piano wires. I never seen such a creature on a horse.'

'What are you by trade, Taylor? A professional rider?'

'I can't ride,' said Mi slowly.

Sensation in the room.

'You can't ride, Taylor?' said the Chairman, after a pause.

'Never bin on a horse,' said Mi, and it seemed to come home to him. He looked out of the window at the chimney-pots.

'What's your history, then?'

'I couldn't swim,' said Mi. 'An' my old man carried on terrible. I went inland. I couldn't bear the sea. I wouldn't stick the sea down there at the coast now if it wasn't for Velvet. I went up North and I did this an' that. Got in with this lot an' got in with that lot. I was all round the race-courses and the livery stables. Doesn't take me much to live. I walked from here an' there an' landed up at Lewes at the races an' did a job fer Mr Brown. Velvet's father. He asked me to help fer a day with some sheep in the slaughter-house and then I saw that Mrs Brown was my old man's Araminty. So I stayed.'

'Well, gentlemen,' said Mr Simkin, looking more sour than ever, 'We've heard the history of how it was done, and on the face of it, and *for the time being*, it seems as though this deception *might* have been carried through in this way and by this one man. I say 'might'. We shall have to verify. It remains now of course to decide on our course of action. The man can be proceeded against legally, I should suppose, for attempting to obtain money under false pretences. There is no doubt in my mind that had this fall of the rider's not taken place and had the prize money of £7,560 (not to speak of a Cup worth two hundred pounds) been awarded, as it would have been if no objection had been lodged, then this man Taylor stood to gain, either the whole sum (the child being obviously under his influence) or in the case of the family being in the plan then no doubt the money would have been divided. It is not there . . .'

'Here!' said Mi. 'What are you getting at!'

'. . . it is not therefore . . .'

'I'm no thief!' said Mi. 'The money'd a bin Velvet's. She's the Owner, isn't she? I did no more'n believe in her an' talk to her an' get her the Clearance. She's the little wonder 'at's done it all. It would a bin her money an' I'd a' seen that she kep' it. Her mother knew about it. She's no soft chicken. As for the money . . . Why, we were so busy pulling it off we hadn't begun to think about what Velvet would do with the money. It was the horse she was thinking of. 'Putting the horse in history' she called it. She'd got that out of somewhere an' she kept thinking it and saying it too, sometimes. She'd think it at her dinner, and at her tea. You could see her, with her eyes shining and her stomach heaving too, pretty often. She's got a terrible stomach, and when she gets excited she's an awful vomiter. *Me* the money. What's the use of seven thousand pounds to me?'

'Seven thousand pounds, Taylor, is always useful.'

'I shouldn't know what to do with it? What'd I do? I don't want to live any better'n I live. It suits me. I don' want to be cluttered up. I wouldn't know the first thing what to do with seven thousand pounds. It would give me the itch. Maybe I'd bury it.'

'The whole story,' intervened Lord Tunmarsh, 'is so strange that I think we should like to discuss it alone. Will you wait downstairs, Taylor? There seems to be a commotion outside, Allbrow.' The Chairman turned towards the window. 'Is it a fire?'

Mr Simkin looked outside into the Square.

'Crowds of people,' he said. 'Thick on the pavement.'

The door was knocked upon and hurriedly opened. A clerk

came swiftly in and looked enquiringly at Mr Simkin. Mr Simkin pointed to the Chairman. The clerk whispered.

'Good God!' said Lord Tunmarsh. 'Open the window, Simkin.'

Mr Simkin struggled with the dusty catch. Mr Seckham helped him and the ancient window flew up. A roar flooded in on the air. The Committee listened.

'They want the child,' said the Chairman. 'Taylor, go down and look after her. Bolt the doors, Simkin! Get down and see everything's shut. What's your back way out?'

'The bar's down across the street door, m'lord,' said the clerk. 'But they're all up over the window sills. They seem to think Miss Brown is getting . . .'

'Getting what?'

'Two men, m'lord, shouted through the doorway as I was shutting it, "You tick her off an' we'll cut your livers out!" m'lord.'

'"Ticking her off", they think! Well, so we are. Come on, young Mits! You get her out the back way!'

'The crowd's gone round there like water flowing, m'lord.'

'I suppose there's a roof exit?' said the Chairman, looking at the ceiling. 'These old massive roofs . . . Where's your fire exit? Here she is?'

'I brought her up,' said Mi. 'Such a din and faces at the

windows. You better up here, an't you, Velvet?'

'What do they want?' said Velvet, looking white.

'To save you from us,' said the Chairman. 'It looks to me as though you're going to get a Lindbergh-Amy Johnson week. I suggest we adjourn the Committee and that Captain Schreiber takes the victim out over the roof. Here y'are, Mits! Take my card as Chairman.'

'The police are coming,' said Mr Simkin, looking down. 'Mounted police.'

'Oh, let me look!' said Velvet.

She hung out of the window and the crowd caught sight of her. A roar went up.

'Now you've done it!' said the Chairman.

It took the police an hour to disperse the crowd. Meanwhile Mits Schreiber, Velvet, Mi and a clerk crossed the roofs of Cavendish Square and descended by J. Denvers' 'Cotton House'. They knocked at the glass window of the fire escape and were let in by a typist.

'Fire down the Square?' said the typist.

'Yes, we're from it,' said Mits briefly. 'Is this the way down?'

They went down into the street by the iron staircase and were met by the Manager of the Cotton Works at the bottom.

'Card,' said Mits Schreiber. 'Thank you very much. Thank that girl of yours for letting us through.'

'Fire, m'lord?' said the Manager.

'Kind of fire,' said Mits. 'There's a taxi. Come on while the crowd's busy down there.'

They left the clerk behind and bundled into a taxi. Velvet and Mits sat together and Mi on the strap seat.

'Where d'you want to go?' said Mits to Mi.

'Victoria Station, sir,' said Mi. 'But I'd like to take her to the pictures first.'

'I shouldn't,' said Mits Schreiber. 'Not today. You'll be mobbed. They're still running the film of the National. But you'll be mobbed if you put your nose inside. The place is simply feverish today.'

'Where to?' said the taxi-man.

'Victoria Station,' said Mits, 'and drop me off at Brook Street.' The taxi started. 'I've got to get to Scotland tonight.'

'What'll you all do to us?' said Velvet timidly.

'Drop the whole thing, of course,' said Mits absently. 'But you won't get your money or your cup, you know.'

'That bay'll get it,' said Velvet. 'He was a good bay.'

'I'm not sure you won't be officially warned off, too. No Newmarket Plate for you now.'

'Oh . . . THAT . . .' said Velvet.

'Yes, I forgot. It's not much after winning the Grand National. What are you going to do now?'

'Oh, jes' go home,' said Velvet. 'I expect I'll go out an' have a look at the horse tonight.'

'Look here . . .' said Mits Schreiber earnestly. 'We're getting to Brook Street. I've bin all over the world with horses an' I want to say this. You try to keep life just the same for you from now on. The public's been after you, but they're flogged tired, and they'll drop it soon. There'll be a tale about our flight tomorrow in the Press, and that clerk Cotton'll go an' give away what he dare. You've been having a queer kind of hot air puffing round you. You've bin blown up like a pink pig in the air fit to burst, and maybe now they'll let you die away with a squeak like a pink pig does. Don't let me find you one day with a hard face an' a dirty bit of cigarette and nerves all gone to blazes, looking for this hot air again! It's bad stuff. Mi – what's yer name, look after her! Here I am. Stop man, stop! Blast he's over-shot the house. I bin in some funny crowds an' I know! That child's bin written across the sky like somebody's pills. You see she gets over it! Goodbye both of you. Off you go. Victoria Station, Brighton line.'

'Oh, isn't he nice!' said Velvet. 'So they're going to let us off! Aren't they sweet, Mi? I say, Mi, have you got money for the taxi?'

'No, I haven't,' said Mi. 'I got the tickets an' a shilling. I knew I hadn't.'

'It's two and nine,' said Velvet, leaning forward. 'Here's the station, too.'

The taxi drew up and Mi opened the door and got out. As Velvet stood in the door there was a soft fluttering noise, like veiled pistols being shot into blankets. Velvet was snapped and snapped again from every angle. The black hoods of the cameras were turned on her in a set circle. She saw hooded men kneeling, squatting, standing. Mi clutched Velvet by the arm and swung her towards the taxi-man. 'I'm short,' he said. 'Ain't got it, Percy. Give you a shilling an' . . .'

'It's all right. I can lend it to you,' said a nice-looking boy in a blue suit.

('Gentleman!' thought Mi.)

'Here y'are, taxi,' said the boy. 'Look here, Miss Brown, I've got a car here. I'll drive you . . . both . . . down to Brighton. Drive you home, see? Sports Bentley.'

'You the Press?' said Mi shortly.

'You come in my car and see,' said the boy. 'I won't publish a thing you don't . . .'

'Come on, Velvet,' said Mi. 'Run for it!'

It was too late. They couldn't run in a heavy sea. The crowd pressed in from behind to see what was happening. 'What's a matter? Accident? No, that girl that won the National. They're photographing her. Where? What? National Velvet!'

'National Velvet!' shouted the crowd as Mi and Velvet pressed slowly forward.

'Won't you let me pass!' said Velvet in a small voice. She had her foot trodden on. Several shook her hands. Left hand, right hand. She lost her purse.

'No fun about this,' muttered Mi. 'This is awful.'

'My purse has dropped. Now I've no ticket,' she called to Mi.

'Leave it. Don't stoop down. You'll be trodden on,' said Mi, getting his arm round her.

They surged past the fruit shop and the telephone boxes and a door opened in the great ticket office and a man swept them inside. Velvet dropped on to a chair, panting.

Half an hour later the police got them into their train. An hour later the red Buicks were tearing up the Embankment from Carmelite Street . . . 'National Velvet at Victoria Station.'

'National Velvet had up before the Hunt Committee.'

'Great Crowds in Cavendish Square. Fight with Lord Tunmarsh over the roofs.' (This was an error, owing to the card.)

The fever about her raged until the findings of the National Hunt

Committee came out in the evening papers. *They had decided to drop the whole thing.*

Again the news machinery was set in motion. Cleared lines gulped that which sped along them. But by the morning the story was dead. The public had been overwhipped. It could stand no more. Dead news like dead love has no phoenix in its ashes.

'Velvet Brown,' said the man in New York, whipping out his orders down the tubes. 'Cut her out. Gone limp. That Jane rates a couple of sticks.'

Chrysanthemums, roses in winter, glacéd sweets, love letters, interviews, satin pillow-dolls, – the house had flowed with gifts. Edwina, Mally and Merry had eaten themselves sick, but Velvet, who did not care for flowers, could not stomach many sweets, did not read the love letters, never played with dolls, remained with her real desires sharp and intact, the ascending spirit with which she was threaded unquenched by surfeit.

While the glory had sedged and seethed about her she had been aware that as she moved so had the public rippled. That she had been like a boat that made a wake, that waves on either side had clapped and sparkled.

But no one had learnt anything about her. No one had formed the slightest picture of her, and she had gathered an impression of isolation as she moved, was touched, hemmed in. Her thin face on the sheet of the cinema was not more strange than her portrait had been in the minds of those who had surrounded her. Her name, which had blazed in the sky, now hung there in a quiet corner with the letters unlit. The arch at the opening of the street first withered, then blew down. The village took her back. If people called her 'National Velvet' it was in fun and affection, and like a dig in the ribs. It meant 'What next, you little blighter! Get on with your growing.'

Mrs Brown found an old trunk for the chocolate boxes and the flower ribbons and Mally's collection. It was April. The gymkhana summer was all before them.

Thus Velvet was not fifteen when the thing left her and passed on, the alienating substance, the glory-wine. She was like a child who is offered wine too young and does not really drink. She put her lips to the goblet while thinking of other things. She got off. She glanced the most acute and heady danger and got off. The Press blew, the public stared, hands flew out like a million little fishes after bread. Velvet had shone, a wonder, a glory, a miracle child.

And now, finished with that puzzling mixture of insane intimacy and isolation which is notoriety, Velvet was able to get on quietly to her next adventures. For obviously she was a person to whom things happened, since in a year she had become an heiress, got a horse for a shilling, and won the Grand National.

HERITAGE CLASSICS TO CHERISH FOREVER

EGMONT PRESS: ETHICAL PUBLISHING

Egmont Press is about turning writers into successful authors and children into passionate readers – producing books that enrich and entertain. As a responsible children's publisher, we go even further, considering the world in which our consumers are growing up.

Safety First
Naturally, all of our books meet legal safety requirements. But we go further than this; every book with play value is tested to the highest standards – if it fails, it's back to the drawing-board.

Made Fairly
We are working to ensure that the workers involved in our supply chain – the people that make our books – are treated with fairness and respect.

Responsible Forestry
We are committed to ensuring all our papers come from environmentally and socially responsible forest sources.

**For more information, please visit our website at
www.egmont.co.uk/ethical**

Egmont is passionate about helping to preserve the world's remaining ancient forests. We only use paper from legal and sustainable forest sources, so we know where every single tree comes from that goes into every paper that makes up every book.

This book is made from paper certified by the Forest Stewardship Council (FSC), an organisation dedicated to promoting responsible management of forest resources. For more information on the FSC, please visit **www.fsc.org**. To learn more about Egmont's sustainable paper policy, please visit **www.egmont.co.uk/ethical**.